To Anne a...

Enjoy the ...

C000047698

Sam Galliford

SKYFIRE

Limited Special Edition. No. 15 of 25 Paperbacks

Sam Galliford

Sam Galliford is a scientist who has authored over two hundred research papers, reviewed articles and conferenced presentations in biochemistry and chemical pathology. It was when a colleague described one of his scientific offerings as "fiction", he thought, "What a good idea!" *Skyfire* is his first novel.

Sam Galliford

SKYFIRE

AUSTIN MACAULEY PUBLISHERS™

LONDON · CAMBRIDGE · NEW YORK · SHARJAH

A CIP catalogue record for this title is available from the British Library.

ISBN 9781528913959 (Paperback)
ISBN 9781528960687 (ePub e-book)

www.austinmacauley.com

First Published (2019)
Austin Macauley Publishers Ltd
25 Canada Square
Canary Wharf
London
E14 5LQ

Many thanks to Jane Weightman, friend and critic, for her artwork on the cover.

Chapter 1

The old lady was dreaming.

"Gwen, Gwen, wake up!"

It was Alice's voice.

"Come and see the fire in the sky."

She was being shaken but it was all warm and snug under the bedding.

"You must come quickly or it will be all gone."

"Come, my little bairn."

That was Mother's voice.

She stayed boneless as the blanket was wrapped around her and she felt herself lifted. She gave a short cry as the cold air licked at her feet and she pulled them back into the warmth as Mother's hand pressed against the back of her head.

"Hush, my bairn. There's no need to fret. Just you come and see the great big fire in the sky. It's all over the place."

She was bundled downstairs to the front door where the cold east wind washed her face and the night air rushed up her nostrils waking her completely.

"Look, look our Gwen. Look," called Alice.

She rubbed her half-asleep eyes and looked down at Alice shivering on the doorstep. She only had on her nightgown and her teeth were chattering in the cold, but she was excited and jigging around on her bare feet and ignoring the chill that cut through the hills from across the North Sea.

"Up there, Gwen, up in the sky," she pointed. "See? It's a great big skyfire."

A crackling sound drew her attention upwards and she saw the huge fire hanging above them, roaring against the blackness of the night. It filled half the sky, blotting out the stars and sending a rain of sparks spitting and flying away from it in all directions. She stared at it wide-eyed.

"Fire," she echoed in her baby tones.

"That's right, my pet. It's a great big skyfire." There was fear in Mother's voice. "They're rotten ones, my bairn. Rotten devils. They've come over to see what damage they could do to the Works. But they'll not get it. Our lads will see to that. They'll not come over here to get you, my little bairn."

Mother jiggled her comfortingly while a thunder rolled down on top of them. She gave a start as a vast puff of luminous smoke blew out, obliterating more sky and highlighting the twisting display blazing from end to end. Alice squealed and Mother's arms tightened instinctively around them both.

"It's coming down, Mam," shrieked Alice. "It's coming down."

More cracking and tearing fell down on them and the massive silver thing folded near its front end where a huge black cross had been ripped apart. Sparks spewed out of it to scatter and fall and finally disappear down behind the silhouetted chimneys and roofs of the Pit and Iron Works on the opposite side of the valley. They reminded her of the glowing pieces of taper that fell into the hearth when her dad stood by the fire and lit his pipe.

"That's it, my bairn. They've got the beggars. They'll come here no more."

Mother's words ground out through her fear-tensed jaws. The roaring beast was dying. Its front end had broken loose and was falling but its tail continued to flame, rising higher and higher under its own heat and breaking up as it did so. And as it rose, six stars flew out of its belly like bright beads on a string. She watched them and, young as she was, she counted them. Six five-pointed stars that seemed to wave to her as they fell. They burned and flailed and called to her with a noise that sounded like the siren when there was an accident at the Pit, only further away. Uncertainly, she waved back to them before a shudder ran through her and she let out a cry and reached out her hand to try and catch one of them, but they slipped through her fingers until they too became lost

8

behind the black and jagged shapes of the roofs of the Ironworks.

A small cry started out of the old lady as she woke.

"Goodness me," she gasped, feeling her heart pounding in her chest.

She blinked a few times and sniffed at the moisture that had collected in her eyes. Her cocker spaniel was whimpering anxiously at her feet, swishing her tail stump on the deep carpet and tapping at her mistress with an enquiring paw.

"Yes, I'm quite all right, Rani," she reassured the dog. "There is no need to worry. It was just a dream."

She reached for her handkerchief and checked her surroundings. The only noises in her house were the steady tickings of her clocks. The tray with its cold cup from her afternoon tea was on the table in front of her but nothing seemed out of place.

"It was nothing, Rani," she repeated. "It was only an old memory of something that happened a long time ago, when I was a child."

Her heartbeat began returning to its more normal stroke.

"Even so," she continued, "it was a strange dream to be having, a very strange dream indeed. I wonder what it means?"

It had unsettled her more than she thought was reasonable.

Chapter 2

"I suppose it was Janet Brinsley's bloody awful murder."

Gerard mumbled the words, only half intending his elderly aunt to hear them. But they rang as clear as a bell to Aunt Gwendoline and jolted her as she prepared to bid him goodbye. It was not how their afternoon had started.

"She smashed it, Aunt Gwendoline, smashed it beyond repair," he had begun.

"So you keep telling me," she replied. "But I'm still not sure what you expect me to do with this intelligence."

Gerard smiled. It was exactly the sort of reply he needed in his present mood and only Aunt Gwendoline could have delivered it to him. He looked at her sitting elegant and erect in the chair opposite him. He reminded himself she was actually his great-aunt, his grandmother's sister, born in the time of the War to end all Wars, so he should not be surprised that their regular Wednesday afternoons with dainty sandwiches, fussy cakes and Lapsang Souchong tea, always left him feeling that it only needed the gloved butler and for him to be in something other than jeans to complete the transformation back three-quarters of a century.

"So, tell me more about my sister Alice's vase," she invited him, refreshing his cup.

"I'm very upset about it," he answered.

"I won't tell her if you don't," she chuckled.

Gerard grinned and relaxed at the joke. Great-aunt Alice had died several years earlier.

"It was a special piece to me, especially as it was given to me by Aunt Alice, but I have to admit I didn't know much about it. Its style was English, probably late eighteen hundreds, and it was chunky enough to be made for export. Mother insisted on describing it as Ming."

Aunt Gwendoline's chuckle burst out into a laugh. "Forgive me for saying so but your mother would have difficulty distinguishing Ming china from the sort of plastic ware one can buy in supermarkets these days," she declared. "But you are mostly right. It was Chatterwood, early Australian colonial porcelain made at the Chatterwood factory in Victoria around the late eighteen sixties. It was nothing special. It came from my parents' home where it stood on the mantelpiece above the fireplace and held the paper tapers our dad used to light his pipe."

She stopped in mid-speech, puzzled as to why that particular memory should come so suddenly into her mind. She brought forward the recollections of pieces of charred taper, some with the dying glow still in them, falling into the hearth as her father stoked his pipe. And superimposed on them came the image of sparks falling from the blazing skyfire in her dream.

"I didn't know Chatterwood had a factory in Australia," Gerard interrupted her thoughts.

"It's not a terribly well-known piece of our history," she continued half distracted. "One of the sons of the English Chatterwoods decided to kick over the traces and go to Australia for the gold rushes. No doubt the poor fellow couldn't help himself and he ended up in the colony of Victoria in the mid-1860s. He didn't find any gold but he did stumble upon a very fine deposit of clay whereupon his family background mercifully reasserted itself. He set up a factory near Ballarat and began to make some better quality china, which he proceeded to sell to all those who had found gold and who lived in large and ostentatious houses in Melbourne which they liked to decorate in the European style. He was enormously successful, even managing to export some of his china back to England, which is how your vase came to be here. He was generously philanthropic and was made a baronet by Queen Victoria. But I cannot think that any of this gives us the reason why your lady friend, what is her name?"

"Susan," he replied.

"Why Susan decided to demolish your vase," she completed.

She suppressed her annoyance with herself. She knew the girl's name, of course. It was just that she always had difficulty recalling it. Somehow, she had never been able to put 'Gerard' and 'Susan' together in the same sentence and feel it harmonious. But it was not really her business and if Susan was her grand-nephew's choice, then so be it.

Chapter 3

Gerard had become lost in the caress of his great-aunt's voice and her question shook him back into attentiveness. He had sunk, as he always did, into the calm embrace of her sitting room, becoming one with the mellowed browns and golds of its magnificent old furniture all kept in such fine polish so as to show off the glory of each beautiful piece. Aunt Gwendoline's whole house was a treasure trove from an earlier time, an eclectic collection of furniture and ornaments with each piece firmly in its place and standing proudly against a background of Persian rugs, brocaded velvet and a faint scent of lavender. Somehow, his seemingly ageless aunt had managed to drag forward into the turbulent present the manners and habits of a more genteel and rational past, and in her sitting room especially, she had created an atoll of calm, a harbour in which he had often found shelter when his life was in turmoil. For some reason he felt he needed that harbour now.

"I don't know why Sue smashed my vase," he replied. "All I know is that I feel very unsettled about it. When Sue and I…" he hesitated.

"When you and Susan moved in together," Aunt Gwendoline completed for him. "Do you really suppose yours is the first generation to consider such possibilities? I can assure you that in my day far more than that was forbidden, which, of course, made such possibilities much more exciting. But that is one of the misfortunes you younger folk will have to live with. Please continue."

Gerard laughed. "When Sue and I set up house together," he grinned, not conceding the point completely, "we bought an old pedestal in a junk shop and with much ceremony placed Aunt Alice's vase on top of it. We stood it in our hallway where it could be seen by all our guests and visitors. It became a symbol of our relationship. We became known as the couple with the vase."

"Wasn't that a rather precarious place to put it?" Aunt Gwendoline asked. "And as regards it being a symbol of your relationship, that sounds something of a superstitious exaggeration if you don't mind my saying so."

She was still puzzling over why she should feel there was a connection between the skyfire in her dream and her sister Alice's vase being broken. It had to be more than just the memory of the sparks falling from her father's pipe-lighters.

"I don't agree," he countered. "We both felt that way about it. As long as Aunt Alice's vase was on its pedestal then everything else would continue to go well. It must have been important to us or else we would never have spent so much time guarding it. In the end, we lost count of the times it was nearly toppled over. Its glaze had become so cracked and fractured and it had been broken and repaired so many times it was a wonder it still held together. Yet in the beginning…"

He stopped and sat staring down into his teacup, and Aunt Gwendoline let a full minute elapse before interrupting his thoughts.

"Forgive me, Gerard, but is it your vase we are talking about or your relationship with Susan?" she enquired gently.

He did not reply immediately, and when he did it was not to answer her directly.

"She smashed it, Aunt Gwendoline. She took one of my golf clubs, lined up Aunt Alice's vase, and with one swinging stroke smashed it into so many pieces it can never be repaired ever again. And then she walked out."

"So you say," she replied. "But it sounds as though trying to preserve it any longer was beyond all stamina and reason."

Gerard looked at his aunt sitting solitary and regal in her elegant grey, with her fine furniture all around her and her spaniel companion at her feet, and always with her aspidistra in its decorated pot on the table behind her. She was right, of course. He and Susan had come to the end of their relationship. It was simply difficult for him to admit it.

"Some more tea?" she asked again.

"No, thank you," he answered, coming out of his reverie. "I really must be going. I have to get back to the university and mark some assignments for my students."

"In that case you must promise to come round again next week and tell me more," she announced.

"More about what?" he asked as he pulled on his coat.

"About your vase," she replied. "You have given me no indication of what it was that precipitated your lady friend into taking such destructive action with it. I am sure my late sister Alice would like to know and so should I."

"Of course I will," he smiled back to her.

She was strangely insistent. He shrugged and attempted to be dismissive.

"And I suppose," he half mumbled, "that the precipitating event which eventually led to Sue smashing our family heirloom was Janet Brinsley's bloody awful murder."

Aunt Gwendoline rocked back on her heels as the blazing image of the skyfire exploded in front of her, positioning itself shimmering and transparent in the space between her and her grand-nephew. It cracked and broke and crashed to earth, spewing out six fiery, five-pointed stars as it did so, each star flailing and waving and making a noise like the siren when there was an accident at Felderby Pit. Without thinking she reached out her hand to try and catch one, but then she realised where she was and the image faded. She withdrew her hand.

Rani whimpered anxiously around her feet as she gave Gerard a parting wave and watched him as he latched the garden gate behind him. She closed her front door and leaned against its solid timbers.

"Oh, dear," she gasped. "Oh my goodness, oh dear. This is not good. There is something dreadfully amiss, something wrong and our Gerard is in the middle of it. This is not good at all."

She took a deep breath to settle her heartbeat from its jolting and stood unsteadily upright while Rani looked up at her with questioning eyes.

"I think we should have another cup of tea," she decided. "Something stronger, something with a bit more stiffening in it. Some Assam tea I think, and a nice piece of biscuit for a good and patient dog. We cannot possibly let anything happen to our Gerard, can we, Rani? Oh dear, no. Come along and we'll see what we can find."

Chapter 4

"I don't know, Rani," Aunt Gwendoline sighed, leaning back in her chair and stirring a fresh cup of tea. "It is a very strange dream I am having and I'm not sure that it was something I should even be able to remember. I really was too young at the time it happened."

She cross-checked her thoughts while Rani snuffled up the last few crumbs of biscuit from the carpet.

"I was born nine months to the day our dad volunteered to join Lord Kitchener's army at the outbreak of the First World War, so I would not have been two years old when the Zeppelin flew over Low Felderby, coming all the way across the North Sea to toss out a few small bombs and see if it could do some damage to Felderby Pit and Iron Works. Our sister Alice would have been able to remember it because she was two years older than me. But I should definitely have been too young to recall anything from that time."

She sipped her tea and stirred her memories.

"I can remember our Alice telling me that our dad's clothes were returned by post in a brown paper parcel some weeks after he enlisted. They were all covered in mud because the army didn't have enough uniforms for its new recruits at the outbreak of the War, so they had to do their training in their ordinary clothes. Mother cleaned them and pressed them and put them away in his drawer, and I remember her pulling them out on several occasions over the following four years and brushing them down and crying and praying over them in her simple faith, and then packing them away again for the day of his return. I remember all that, but I am not sure I should remember the Zeppelin."

She gave an involuntary shudder and grasped her shawl closely around her.

"Poor, poor men," she muttered, and braced herself to face the memory.

It was not only the image of the stricken Zeppelin that had persisted with her over the years. It was also the memory of the six, five-pointed stars that fell from it as it died.

"I know there were six stars, Rani, because young as I was, I counted them."

Her child's eyes had seen six five-pointed stars, flailing and waving to her and making a noise like the distant accident siren at Felderby Pit as they came down. It was only with the passing of years that she came to see those incandescent, falling shapes not as stars but as men on fire, casualties of war, the crew of the Zeppelin unable to escape, and the sound she heard was them shrieking out their agony as they plummeted blazing to merciful oblivion several hundreds of feet below.

"Poor, poor men," she repeated. "But why should I be dreaming about them now, at the same time that our Gerard's lady friend broke our sister Alice's vase?"

"You're a good girl, our Gwen. Look after the family for me. Keep them together."

"You were a spoiled and selfish cat, Mother," she fired back at the aspidistra sitting in its ornamental pot. "Why could you not have asked one of the others, our Alice or our Lizzie? Why me?"

Because in the end, there was only her, Gwen, the middle of the three sisters, to keep an eye on them all. Older sister Alice had married Will, a tinker who came with his horse and cart selling pots and pans and other goods useful to the working folk of Low Felderby. He had worked hard and done well and had eventually sold his cart and bought a shop, and it was the tragedy of his and Alice's lives that they had died childless. Then there was younger sister Lizzie, as dizzy and as scatterbrained as anyone could imagine, born one year after their dad came home from the War. She had married Jack, a foundryman from Felderby Iron Works, and it was the defective heart she had been born with that gave out a few short months later in the final push for the birth of their daughter, Gerard's mother.

"And now our Gerard is all there is of our once productive line, isn't he, Mother?" Aunt Gwendoline sighed. "A single child. Still, he is 'a good 'un' as our dad would have said, certainly the best our family has produced though how on earth he ever came out of sister Lizzie's line, heaven only knows. A more dottily irresponsible individual you could never wish to meet, all of which traits she managed to pass on to her daughter who cannot distinguish Ming china from fairground pot. Fortunately, our Gerard seems to have escaped that bit of his mother's and grandmother's inheritance, doesn't he?"

The aspidistra did not move but Rani agreed with a vigorous swishing of her tail stump.

Somebody had to take care of the family and so in her knowing way Mother had chosen her, Gwen. And with that thought, her dream of the skyfire recreated itself in her mind, together with the panic and tears she felt as she had reached out her hand to catch one, any one, of the tragic stars falling from it.

She listened to the tickings of her clocks and followed her thoughts, fighting the conclusion they were dragging her to.

"Our Gerard seems to have got himself into some sort of fix, hasn't he, Rani?" she summarised. "And we are going to have to catch his star before it drops to earth."

She shook herself and tried to focus on the fear that was silently approaching.

"It seems likely that whatever fix he has got himself into has something to do with Janet Brinsley's bloody awful murder. It is not like our Gerard to use bad language and so we know he means it literally. So, how do you suppose he has got himself involved in a murder that was both bloody and awful? And what has my late sister Alice's vase got to do with it? It is all a very puzzling."

She let her mind wander to see what other threads it could gather. Her head nodded forward, and Rani settled her chin on her paws at her mistress' feet to watch and wait.

Chapter 5

"You mentioned something about Janet Brinsley being murdered," prompted Aunt Gwendoline as soon as Gerard had settled into his usual chair the following Wednesday.

Her dreaming of the skyfire has not given her much rest in the meantime.

"Was she a friend of yours from the university?" she asked.

The tea was Earl Grey, the sandwiches were smoked salmon and tomato and the cakes were chocolate buns. She had specially selected the chocolate buns. Her grand-nephew was notorious for being a most enthusiastic chocoholic.

"Janet Brinsley?" he answered, trying to sound casual. "Yes, she was a friend, although it was her husband Mark who was the pal from the university."

He had been upset that his parting comment on his previous visit had driven past his guard as he said goodbye to his aunt. She was an old lady, refined and genteel, who prepared a civilized tea on Wednesday afternoons in the shelter of her sitting room. She was from another time, a gentler age and she had a right to live out the last of her years unexposed to the turmoil of the present day. He should never have mentioned anything as violent as Janet Brinsley's murder.

"I only ask," Aunt Gwendoline persisted, "because you mentioned something about her murder having some bearing on why your lady friend..."

As so often occurred, she hesitated over the name. Although it was a simple name to remember, she always had difficulty recalling it.

"…why Susan broke your vase," she finally managed. "It seems rather an oblique association if you don't mind my saying so."

"Just a vague association," he agreed. "The Brinsleys were good friends of ours. Sue and Janet got on well, went shopping and did all the usual girly things together, and Mark and I had some very useful professional collaborations going."

"None of which provides us with a particularly strong motive to start breaking the family china," she countered. She saw him shrug. "My dear Gerard, I really do not understand why you persist in thinking of me as nothing more than a frail old woman. I have lived through two world wars, the Great Depression, several years of food rationing and such social upheavals as your generation could only know through the benign medium of history books. Now, I really do want to know why your Susan broke my late sister Alice's vase."

He looked into her blue and determined eyes and knew he was not going to be allowed to avoid giving a full account of what happened.

"Then I suppose I had better tell you," he conceded. "I would hate to think that you were not sleeping well at night because of something I said."

He deflected her warning look with a grin and settled back into his chair.

"Not surprisingly," he began, "I was the connection between us all. I first met Mark when I came back from that archaeological dig I was involved with in Thailand. It was a fascinating dig site, going back over five thousand years with human habitation throughout. You don't get many archaeological records like that. Anyway, at around two and a half thousand BC, we came across some pots which had some black, sticky stuff inside so I brought them home with the idea that someone in the chemistry department might be able to tell me what it was. That was how I met Mark, or Dr Brinsley to give him his official title. The university had recently appointed him as a senior lecturer and by repute he was an absolute wizard of an organic chemist. He was immensely popular with the students, had a very dynamic approach to his research and was all in all a very approachable and well-liked individual."

"Was he able to identify your sticky material for you?" queried Aunt Gwendoline.

"Yes, it was honey. Honey from four and a half thousand years ago."

"And from Thailand too," she added. "Quite fascinating. But please tell me more about Dr Brinsley."

She saw him hesitate then look down at his hands. The enthusiasm that always flooded his face when he talked about his beloved archaeology drained from him, and his words crept out as if testing themselves against the stillness of the air that had gathered about them before agreeing to give up their sound.

"The only words I keep coming back to are 'bloody' and 'awful'," he choked. "I cannot imagine what it must have been like for Mark to walk into his home and find his wife dead like that. They had only been married three years. They were so happy."

"It did sound rather terrible in the newspapers," Aunt Gwendoline agreed.

"That wasn't the half of it," he continued. "The first two police officers to arrive walked into Mark and Janet's bedroom and walked straight out again and threw up. The female officer told me it had taken them both a full hour to recover before they could talk to their colleagues on the murder investigation team. They were just two uniformed officers who happened to be closest in their patrol car when Mark's call came through. He, poor fellow, was in complete shock when they got there, unable to speak or move, crouched against the wall on the floor in the hallway, gripping the telephone, staring at nothing and pointing silently in the direction of the bedroom. He had been the one to find her, the first one to see her and see what had been done to her."

Aunt Gwendoline could see her grand-nephew was struggling with his words, but he needed no more prompting.

"Janet had been raped," he stated. "Several times and brutally. There was blood everywhere. Her naked body was still half in the dressing gown she had put on when she got out of the bath and the fresh clothes she had laid out to dress in were all crumpled up in the mess. She was spread-eagled on the bed and her body had been mutilated, cut horribly in numerous places. Her ribs had been slashed at and there were vicious gashes down both her legs. Some of her teeth had been broken and the post mortem showed she had also been part suffocated and strangled as well. It was horrible, beyond description. None of us could imagine the madness she must have had to endure before she finally died. I still cannot even begin to think about it." He forced in a deep breath and felt the sob of it kick in his lungs.

"I suppose we can only be grateful that even the lowest of the gutter tabloid press chose not to publish all the details," Aunt Gwendoline commented.

"But even that is not the whole story," he sighed. "I only know what I do because I sat with Mark at home while he talked, and I have been able gradually to piece together the bits of the story from what he told me and what the police said. They have been wonderful, the police, so easy in their questioning of Mark and Sue and me, not that Sue and I could tell them anything other than some background on Mark and Janet. They were such a loving couple, so full of life and enthusiasm for the future. He had just got his promotion, they had just bought their new house and they were talking about starting a family."

He paused and looked up from his hands. "I'm sorry, Aunt Gwendoline. I didn't mean to unload all this on you but it has been perhaps more terrible than I thought."

"You must talk to someone," she reassured him. "I am only concerned in so far as it is affecting you. Continue when you are ready. You say the police spoke to you and…" Again she hesitated. "… Susan," she completed.

He ordered his thoughts, dimly heard the striking of the hour by the grandfather clock in the hallway, and took another deep breath.

"They questioned us only briefly," he resumed. "Sue and I took care of Mark immediately after Janet's murder. He was in a terrible state and not fit to look after himself, and there didn't seem to be anyone else around to help. He was in complete shock and Janet's parents had enough to deal with on their own once they had been told. And Mark's own parents are in Canada where his father has bad arthritis so cannot travel easily. So, after the doctor gave him a hefty shot of sedatives we tucked him up in our spare room and left him to come round in his own time. It was my idea really and I would have to say that Sue did not like it. Janet's murder had scared the daylights out of her and she quickly developed the idea that the killer might come back for Mark or, by association, one of us. I told her it was nonsense but that was how she felt. I understand it is different for a woman so I can sympathise, but Mark is a friend and he needed help. Even now I can't understand Sue's attitude entirely, but from the start she did not like Mark staying with us."

"Is that when she broke your vase?"

"Oh, no. That was later," he replied, puzzled by the question. "Aunt Alice's vase was still safely on its pedestal at that time."

He refocussed his thoughts. "Mark seemed to bounce back very quickly and after only a few days with us he announced he was going home, so Sue and I did not have to put up with him for very long. The police had quickly ruled him out as a wife beater and murderer. They had finished their forensic work at his house and, since he seemed calm enough, there was no reason to stop him going back. In fact, it seemed like a good idea to let him go and start putting his life back together again. He still had his wife's murder to deal with but he had the support of all of us in that, including the police. I have to say that I cannot imagine a more determined bunch of officers. They were adamant they were going to get whoever had killed Janet and from the way they talked when they spoke to us we could only believe them. Janet's murder seemed to strike something very deep in all of them and that would have given Mark some encouragement in what were for him very dark days."

"So, he went home and your vase remained intact," concluded Aunt Gwendoline.

"Yes," Gerard finished simply.

He sighed with the release of some of the fatigue that had been bottled up inside him since the time of Janet's death. Aunt Gwendoline joined him in a muted sigh of her own and as the silence extended it was clear he was not going to say anything more for the moment. It did not surprise her. She could wait. She got out of her chair and walked over to the aspidistra, standing pensively in front of it while brushing the surfaces of a couple of its leaves with her thumb and forefinger.

"Would you like some more tea?" she finally asked, turning back to him.

"No, thank you," he replied. "As always I have to be getting back to the university. I am trying to organise another dig, this time in Vietnam, with the Anthropology Department at Hanoi University. I have a good number of letters to write to get the process moving."

"Vietnam?" she queried. "I didn't know the Vietnamese were interested in archaeology, but then I would have to confess I know very little about them as a people."

Gerard smiled warmly to his great-aunt. "It is because of the French," he explained as he shrugged himself into his coat. "When Napoleon Bonaparte went to Egypt, his archaeologists followed his army and deciphered the hieroglyphics on the tombs of the Pharaohs. It became a habit. Wherever the French army went after that their archaeologists followed, and wherever they dug they gave the locals a taste for doing the same. That is why today there is a big interest in archaeology in what was French Indochina, or what is today southern Thailand, Laos, Kampuchea and Vietnam."

"Interesting," commented Aunt Gwendoline, "although still not a reason for your lady friend breaking your Chatterwood vase."

"And as regard Sue's shattering of Aunt Alice's vase," he replied, "that did not happen until after Mark Brinsley sobered up."

"Goodness me. Do you mean to say that your vase and Dr Brinsley got smashed together, if I may use the modern idiom?"

"See you next week," he called as he gave her a wave and stepped off smartly up the street.

Chapter 6

"Away, our lass. Away to the dugouts. Go with the other women and bairns. Sharp now and we'll be getting along."

Granddad's tall figure was silhouetted in the open doorway against the fearsome furnace of the skyfire hanging threateningly above them in the darkness.

"Aye, Dad, we'll be there directly."

The candlelight in the hallway caught the lines in Mother's face, and her voice was cut with fear.

"Alice, go get some clothes on or you'll catch your death. Sharp now, put on your coat and shoes and bring our bairn's coat down too."

Alice raced upstairs to obey.

"You stay with me our bairn," Mother cooed. "You just stay with me."

She buried herself in Mother's neck and enjoyed the comfort of the instinctive jigging.

"Alice, Alice!" shouted Mother.

"Coming, our mam."

A thudding of feet down the stairs brought a panting Alice into view.

"All here then?" Granddad bellowed above the roar of the skyfire and the popping of guns from near the Works. "Right then, we'll be away. Keep close and mind your footing."

He led off swinging a lantern for them all to follow.

The night was clear and cold but the skyfire shone down enough light for them to see their way. Mother's chest was creaking with each breath as the low path by the railway line became the high path past the allotments, and on up the hillside to where the men of Low Felderby had hollowed out some dugouts for them to shelter in.

"Keep up, our Alice. Don't get behind. Keep up," Mother panted.

Mother was only little, not like great tall Granddad in his high hat. Over Mother's shoulder there was a line of dark shadows bobbing and stumbling all of a jumble behind them in the dark. Another lantern shepherded them along from the rear.

"Alice! Alice!"

Alice had tripped in the dark and fallen full length in the mud.

"Away now," called the woman behind. "Don't you worry about your Alice. I've got her. You look after your Gwen."

The horizon swung around and back again as Mother turned in a bob of gratitude to the unseen neighbour then stumbled onwards once more.

Inside her blanket her breath puffed out into the night to condense near her cheek. She burrowed deeper into Mother and from her bastion of safety looked up at the monster that roared above them. It was all orange flame and silver with a big black cross and numbers on its underside, and it rose majestically like a breaching whale into the sky, carried upwards by the uncontrolled inferno of its own burning. Its nose rose higher, seemingly trying to escape the guns that popped around it from the ground. Then it howled in agony as flame erupted from its body a third of the way back from its head. Its nose dipped, and bright against the blackness of the sky its exposed skeleton cracked under the strain of its gaping wounds. It broke, and glowing shards showered from it to the ground like the pieces of charred taper that fell into the hearth when her dad lit his pipe. And five stars ejected themselves from the furnace that was the beast's belly. Five five-pointed stars that waved and shrieked as they descended, calling out like the accident siren from Felderby Pit. Frantically she dragged a hand out of her blanket to try and catch one of them, to stop it falling, but before she could do so the black edge of the dugout roof cut across her view and lantern light splashed on the dirt walls that surrounded her.

She called out to the burning stars, reaching out her hand again to them through the diminishing opening of the cave, but it was no use. Mother staggered and sank to a panting rest and she was put down on something wet and hard. She yelled.

"Sorry, my pet. It's just a sandbag." Mother picked her up and began jigging her again.

"It's all right our Gwen," reassured Alice, covered in mud but beside her once more. "It's all gone. It can't get us in here."

Aunt Gwendoline opened her eyes to the fading evening light. A last sunbeam was falling across the rosewood casing of her antique bracket clock standing on the gleaming mahogany of her Sheraton secretaire. It was more than an hour since Gerard had left. She listened to the quiet pulse of the clock, and the bureaucratic beat of her Edwardian station clock, and the commanding tread of her Victorian oak-cased grandfather clock standing sentry in the hall, and to the petulant ticking of her ecclesiastical clock trying to assert its precedence over all things in the earthly domain. All seemed in order. Rani sat up at her feet in trembling welcome to her return to the world of wakefulness and supper.

Chapter 7

"So were you able to organise your Vietnamese friends for your next archaeological adventure?" asked Aunt Gwendoline.

It had been a long week and her worry about him had not diminished.

"Most certainly," replied Gerard. "They are more than enthusiastic. They are straining at the leash to start digging and we do not have all the funding in place yet, but hopefully we will get there."

She poured his tea, Darjeeling because she wanted him relaxed, and offered him a honey-roast ham and tomato sandwich.

"I am pleased to hear that the Vietnamese enjoy their history," she continued. "But are you sure your proposed dig is not being pursued in a somewhat remote and dangerous part of the world?"

She could not deny to herself that Southeast Asian pre-history was probably very interesting, but with flaming Zeppelins falling out of the sky and family vases being smashed it was now more than ever that she wished her grand-nephew had focussed his chosen career closer to home. She was sure there was no end of respectable Celtic and Roman ruins that still needed investigating.

"There is no need to worry, Aunt Gwendoline," he beamed back to her. "The world is a pretty tame place these days compared with what it was, and Indochina is not as remote as you might think."

"Maybe not," she replied. "But I am aware of reports in the newspapers of people coming to grief in that part of the world in what are generally referred to as encounters with warlords and bandits."

"I shan't be going anywhere near any warlords or bandits," he grinned.

"Possibly not," she persisted. "But I did also read of a police chief in Laos who committed suicide while leading a patrol in search of such characters. The report went on to describe how this talented officer had managed to shoot himself in the back five times with a machine gun in order to achieve his end, and that does not give me much confidence in the local forces of law and order where you are going. You will be careful, won't you?"

Gerard could not help himself but laugh, but his great-aunt held him with her unblinking eyes and he could see in them the depth of her concern. For her part, she blamed her sister Lizzie and her notions of what constituted parental responsibility that she passed on to her daughter, Gerard's mother. She should never have allowed him to pursue his preference for archaeology in such wild and jungly places as Indochina.

"Now, your Chatterwood vase," she resumed, re-joining the conversation. "You have yet to tell me how it got broken, and you did say something about Dr Brinsley requiring sobering up beforehand. So how did that happen?"

"I'm not sure what I have already told you," he waved casually, "but I will fill in a few more details for you if you wish."

He saw her gaze become less penetrating, and her eyes softened as she relaxed back in her chair.

"I was working late in my office when I first heard about Janet's murder. I gather the police called the university trying to find someone who knew Mark and somebody gave them my name as a close friend. They called my home and Sue called me. It was just after ten when I got home, just as the police doctor was telling Sue that Mark was in no fit state to look after himself. I said we would take care of him. Somebody had to and, damn it, Mark is a friend, a good friend. I don't see that I could have done anything else. So after the police left, I undressed him and put him to bed.

"Sue was not happy about my saying he could stay. We had very few details of what had happened at that point but Sue already seemed to be reacting to something a lot deeper than I could see. We tried to talk about it but the shock of it all began to hit us and, as it was very late, we went to bed. I was dead beat and ready for sleep straight away but Sue was awake at every little noise throughout the night. Eventually I had to sit on my temper, with her constantly waking me with her tossing and turning, so we were both grey-eyed and dozy over breakfast next morning.

"Mark, as far as we could tell, slept soundly all night. It was probably the sedatives he had been given but we never heard a peep out of him. He was only just waking when I took him in some tea at around nine o'clock. He did not look good but at least he had slept. I told him I would call the university and tell them about what had happened and he seemed to accept it very calmly.

"'Thanks,' was all he said.

"I telephoned the dean and the head of the chemistry department and brought them up to date with what news I had, and I also called my own department to say I would not be in either. I was just too tired and I had the feeling that Sue would need some looking after as well.

"I couldn't fathom Sue. She was edgy, nervous, ready to jump at small noises, and for the first time since I had known her, she lit a cigarette. It puzzled me, seeing her sitting at the breakfast table smoking as if she had always done so. I was not aware that she had ever smoked. I don't smoke and she had not done so since we had known each other. But she sat flicking the ash into the saucer of her teacup as if it was regular behaviour for her, so familiar and easy to do. I didn't comment, largely because I knew I was in no fit state to engage in a discussion that would probably end up at cross purposes, but it did puzzle me that you could live with somebody and think you know them but at the same time not know bits of them at all. It was very odd. I suggested that she too should take the day off work, and she nodded her agreement and lit another cigarette while I made the telephone call for her. All in all, it was a rather silent day.

"The next few days were stressful. Mark was quiet about the place but he gradually came round as the shock and the sedatives wore off. A detective sergeant and a constable came around to interview Sue and me, more to exclude Mark being the abusive husband and perpetrator of the crime than anything else, and we were able to assure them that it was not in Mark's nature to be violent in any way. He was the sort of fellow who would carry a moth gently out of the house and release it in the garden rather than see it swatted indoors. I have never heard him raise his voice in anger at anybody, even under the extreme provocation of some of his more obstreperous students. I have never seen an angry expression cross his face. He is calmness itself and he only lived for his chemistry and his wife who he adored. And she adored him in return. It was impossible to imagine a violent word passing between them, much less a blow or an attack sufficient to kill her. But the questions upset Sue.

"'Get him out of here. I want him out of here as soon as possible,' she hissed at me on several occasions.

"I couldn't believe her. Janet and Mark had been our friends, possibly our best friends since we had first met them. It seemed almost inhuman of her to turn on Mark at the very time when he most needed our support.

"'You don't really know what he's like,' she insisted.

"It was astonishing how within the space of forty-eight hours we developed the habit of whispering our speech at each other, keeping the volume low so that Mark should not hear us and breaking off in mid-sentence if he suddenly appeared.

"'How do you know he is not a threat to us, to you, to me. You don't ever really get to know people all that well and he could have a history of violence that we never found out about. People can be very clever at hiding it, you know.'

"'For goodness' sake, Sue. Did Janet ever give you any hint that he might be violent?'

"'No, but then she might have kept it quiet out of a misplaced sense of loyalty to her marriage. Women are built

33

to be extremely loyal to their marriages you know, even under the most violent of circumstances.'

"'Ease up, Sue. You have no evidence that Mark is anything other than a gentle man who has just received one of the nastiest shocks it is possible to get in life. His dearly loved wife has been murdered in a particularly nasty manner, for God's sake. I'm sure that if he had been violent, then Janet would have said something to you about it. Damn it, you and she spent enough time together. I'm sure you would have picked up on something, woman to woman, if there had been any doubts about Mark's personality.'

"It was odd, strange. I couldn't understand how she could change so dramatically towards him. In his presence, she remained smiling and calm and joined in the general chat at breakfast and dinnertime. But there was an undercurrent in her that left her a lot less bubbly than she had been in the past. I put it down to the sudden shock of what had happened and some instinctive fear that women feel when faced with violence of such an order, and the stress of knowing that somewhere out there in the neighbourhood is some animal who can do such a thing and who would be capable of doing it again. I just hoped it would all blow over when the police eventually caught whoever did it."

Gerard stopped and looked up at his great-aunt. She was still looking straight at him, sitting relaxed but upright, watching him calmly with her hands folded elegantly in her lap in the manner of an Edwardian lady in confident command of an empire.

"I don't seem to have been doing much talking about poor Mark, do I?" he sighed. "I seem to have spent most of the time talking about Sue and me and how we reacted to Janet's death."

"I had noticed," Aunt Gwendoline replied. "But it doesn't matter. It is all part of the same story and it will eventually lead to why she broke your vase. But you might finish the story for me. You said that Dr Brinsley did recover from his immediate grief and return home."

Chapter 8

Gerard refocussed. "It was no more than five nights Mark stayed with us," he resumed. "He was never any trouble. I don't doubt that he lay awake most of those nights with the turmoil and grief going round and round in his mind, but there was never a sound from his room. On the contrary, it was Sue who paced the floor, taking herself out to the kitchen to have another cigarette at various times during the night. As the days passed, ashtrays began appearing all over the house and were left half full of smoked butts, something which I admit I found offensive, but I let it slide.

"Of the two of them Mark seemed to take the shock of his wife's death much more calmly, presenting himself cleanly showered and shaved at breakfast each morning. All in all, he did a very good job of not being a nuisance. He went into his department briefly on about day three and brought back some papers but it was too difficult for him to concentrate on them. He might have sensed Sue's reaction to him, although I would hate to think he felt he was not welcome. But her attitude was difficult to avoid."

"Did you try and talk to her about what was disturbing her?" asked Aunt Gwendoline.

"Yes, but again it was difficult. She said something about being afraid but would not be specific. I asked the police to send a female officer around to talk with her. One came, and she was very calm and understanding. But Sue remained wary of her and would not talk to her so after a while she left, leaving her card with a direct contact number for support if needed. Finally, the police told Mark that they had finished with his house and he could go home when he was ready. They told me quietly they had organised a visit by a team of cleaners to clear up the blood and other mess left behind by the crime so that Mark would not have to walk into it all over again. And so he left.

"Then a strange thing happened. After I had seen Mark into a taxi and waved him on his way, I walked into the spare room where he had been staying. Sue was there and I said to her 'there you are, he's gone.' Bad joke, I suppose, or bad timing, but I was completely thrown by the look she gave me. I couldn't read it, much less understand it. In most ways it was just a stare, but there was something else in it. It certainly wasn't relief and I couldn't help feeling it was fear, but a fear all the more frightening because she was unable to explain it. I suddenly noticed she had pulled some of her clothes out of the wardrobe and had put them on the bed.

"'It's been a tough few days,' I added. 'But we have our own space back to ourselves again so hopefully we can begin to relax.'

"She didn't reply and I just left her to whatever she was doing. It never occurred to me that she might be wanting to leave. She had no reason to go. We were living so well together. But in retrospect, I suppose that is how I should have seen it. I still don't understand it but for the next few weeks we dropped into a sort of silent, uncommunicative existence."

"And at the moment Dr Brinsley left you your vase was still intact?" Aunt Gwendoline asked.

The question momentarily irritated him, but he smothered his annoyance and smiled. "Yes, it was," he confirmed.

Chapter 9

"Aunt Gwendoline, would you excuse me?" he asked. "We have been talking for some time and the Darjeeling has more than worked its way through me. Would you mind if I visited your bathroom?"

"Of course not, dear boy. You know where it is."

She listened while his footsteps went up the stairs and waited until she could hear them no more, then she rose from her chair and went over to the aspidistra in its decorated pot. She looked at it firmly and fussed with its leaves for a few moments.

"Our Gerard has got himself into some sort of scrape and it is one that could be very bad for him. That much is obvious."

The plant did not respond so she spoke to it directly.

"If you are going to play one of your little games, then there is not much I can do about it, is there, Mother? But you are going to have to be a bit clearer if I am going to do anything to help him. We cannot let anything happen to our Gerard. He is all we have left."

The aspidistra still gave no stir and she sighed at it in exasperation.

"I did notice that the first time I dreamed about the Zeppelin in flames over Low Felderby there were six stars falling from it as it crashed to earth, just as it happened all those years ago," she continued. "And the second time I dreamed about it only five stars fell from it. One star was missing and that was after our Gerard had told us about the murder of Dr Brinsley's poor wife."

She continued staring at the plant and roughly tested its soil for moisture.

"There is no need for you to look so pleased with yourself, Mother," she admonished it. "I also noticed that when I first dreamed of the wounded Zeppelin we were on the doorstep of our home, and the second time I dreamed about it we were on our way to the dugouts in the hillside above the village. I suppose that means we are at least going in the right direction, towards a place of safety even if not of comfort."

She recalled the feeling of the wet sandbag against her back. The line of thought was becoming distressing.

"We are going in the right direction and one of the original stars, the one that is no longer there, was for Janet Brinsley," she summarised. "Is that it?"

The plant remained unmoved and only Rani looked up at her mistress and shook her tail stump in encouragement.

"You will have to give me more help, Mother. You have left me with a worryingly large number of stars to account for and if one of those burning, falling, flailing stars belongs to Gerard…"

She let the thought hang unspoken.

"I am going to have to catch his star. I cannot let it fall."

Not a single leaf moved.

"And what has Miss Susan breaking our Alice's vase got to do with it?" she demanded before finally turning away in annoyance.

She picked up the tea tray and carried it out to her kitchen.

"I thought we might have some fresh tea," she called over her shoulder to her grand-nephew's footsteps descending the stairs. "Not Darjeeling this time. If I have any more, I will likely fall asleep. I think we will change to Assam, light enough for the afternoon but strong enough to keep me alert while you tell me the rest of your story. And yes, Rani, I am sure we can find something for a good dog too."

Chapter 10

"So, Dr Brinsley went home and you and Susan returned to your daily routine," Aunt Gwendoline summarised after they had settled back into their chairs.

"More or less," Gerard answered hesitantly.

Sometimes he did not know how far to express his feelings to his great-aunt. She had always been an old lady to him, a "spinster of the parish", a phrase he had one day laughingly read out from an old newspaper cutting she had shown him. "In my day, that is what we were called," she had informed him firmly. "There was no shame in it." He had accepted the reprimand but it left him not knowing how to explain to her the disappointment of being met by a turned face when familiar womanly hips were pulled forward in an embrace that had always before ended in a full and passionate kiss. He could not see how she could understand the confusion of being refused the compliant breasts after formerly welcome hands had encircled the tempting waist from behind, or the frustration of being denied the close and naked skin in the dark hours when the passions are at their peak.

"Sue did become less tense after Mark left," he compromised. "I cannot say things went entirely back to normal but there were a few times when I thought we managed to regain something of our former closeness."

Aunt Gwendoline watched him and stirred her tea.

"Outwardly, Mark was quite calm and rational and able to deal with life," he continued, sitting back in his chair and consciously dismissing any thoughts of returning to his desk at the university for the rest of the afternoon. "But he was distracted and more fragile than he seemed. The press and television people did not help. From the day of Janet's murder, they parked themselves outside his house and pushed microphones and cameras at him at every opportunity. 'How do you feel about what happened, Dr Brinsley? Do you miss your wife, Dr Brinsley? Is there anything you would like to say to the person who murdered your wife, Dr Brinsley?' I saw him recoil from them and look over to me for help. I did what I could. They pestered his neighbours, his friends, the staff at the local supermarket where he shopped, and even the postman and the garbage men who collected his rubbish. 'What sort of man would you say Dr Brinsley is?' 'Did he and his wife ever have any arguments?' 'Does he like animals?' The questions were so inane and they seemed only to want to find out bad things about him."

Aunt Gwendoline sat more upright in her chair. Her movement was not enough for Gerard to notice but she felt as though she had been prodded between her shoulder blades by a finger, much as she had been as a child when Mother, sitting behind her, thought she was not paying enough attention in chapel.

"There are some sections of the press that have a reputation for disrespectful behaviour," she commented to cover her discomfort.

Rani sat up and looked at her quizzically.

"'Disrespectful' is an understatement," Gerard snorted. "They are animals as far as I am concerned, far worse than any I have ever encountered even in the wildest jungles of Southeast Asia. Not surprisingly, Mark wasn't up to facing them, so it was not long after he returned to his own home that he called and asked if he could come back to stay with us again. Of course, I said 'yes' and he sneaked round under cover of darkness. Sue reacted immediately."

"It must have been very difficult for her," Aunt Gwendoline agreed. "The situation was, in her mind, dangerous and she was helpless to do anything about it."

"I think 'dangerous' is overstating it," he countered. "And in any case, we didn't create the circumstances. They just happened. Mark needed help and I don't see that we could have done anything else. He is a friend, a very good friend. He was going through hell and all the press wanted to do was tear him apart. I suppose you could say that it was unwise of me to step in as I did because next morning we found the press pack camped outside our house too, so I asked the police to give us some protection and they sent round regular patrols to shoo them away. It helped, of course, but I don't regret giving Mark some shelter from their relentless hounding. It made me want to have nothing to do with press people ever again, but even so I didn't consider the situation dangerous."

Aunt Gwendoline sighed inwardly. *"You're a good girl, our Gwen. Look after the family for me. Keep them together."* It was a big responsibility. She glanced across to the aspidistra and shifted in her chair to avoid the finger poking into her back again. Suddenly, she was aware that she could remember Gerard's ladyfriend's name without effort.

Chapter 11

"What happened next?" she asked.

"Much to our relief the intense attention from the press cooled off after a few days, although they still hung around," Gerard resumed. "They finally realised they could get no more from hounding Mark, Sue and me than they could from the daily police briefings.

"The police put together a highly experienced team of detectives and forensic specialists, and it has to be said that their investigation into Janet's murder galloped along. In addition, the detective sergeant leading the investigations, Sergeant Chak, went out of his way to give us such extra information as he could, which was hugely reassuring for all three of us. In a short while, he became quite a friend. He made a point of telling Sue in particular how the investigations were going, that they were going well, that there was no reason for her not to feel safe, and that an arrest could be expected very soon.

"Mark also had separate, almost daily, updates from the police. He was putting a huge emotional investment into their enquiries, which was not surprising. He noted every detail as it emerged and analysed it over and over again, discussing with me how such-and-such a piece of information might fit in with a particular scenario in Janet's life, where she might have been, who she might have met and so on. It was partly the scientist in him but it was also his way of dealing with her killing, distracting himself with the details and trying to fit them into a picture. He became quite obsessive about it."

Aunt Gwendoline felt her heart kick in her and begin beating with a faster stroke. She noticed that she had jolted some of her tea out of its cup and into the saucer in her hands. Rani gave an anxious whimper.

"I went with Mark to Janet's inquest," Gerard continued, not noticing. "That was a bad day. Mark found more bits and pieces in the details of the coroner's proceedings to fit into his picture of events and he noted them all down very carefully in his notebook. But suddenly he froze, stopped taking notes and sat back ashen. There was one detail he had not known, not even suspected, and it was dropped almost as an aside by the pathologist into the list of the autopsy's findings. Hearing it in the quiet, professional tones of the medical expert only added to its impact, and I wasn't sure that I had heard it correctly until I looked over and saw Mark's reaction. In the middle of the description of the horrific wounds and beatings inflicted on Janet before she died, and in the summary of the ultimate cause of her death, the pathologist announced that she had been six weeks pregnant.

"Mark told me later that he didn't know she was with child until then. Janet had not said anything to him. But it explained so much of what she had been up to just before her murderer broke in on her. It explained the sweet-scented bath she had just stepped out of and the fine clothes she had laid out ready to put on. It explained the new perfume she had bought and the special dinner she had prepared for them both, and all the other evidence of the special effort she was making to greet him when he got home from the university. She had kept it a surprise until she was certain, but the night she was murdered was the night she was going to tell him that their first child, of the family they had both longed for and wanted so much, was finally on the way. I suppose it was reasonable for the police to assume that Mark knew his wife was pregnant, so nobody thought to tell him. But he didn't know, not until he heard it in the pathologist's report at his murdered wife's inquest. It shocked us all, and it only served to emphasise the horror of everything that had been done to Janet before she died. But it hit Mark hardest of all, and it inevitably became another banner word for the headlines in the tabloid press the next day. Aunt Gwendoline, are you feeling all right?"

The crackling roar of the death throes of the Zeppelin were pounding in her ears, and the heat of its dying made her feel stuffy and uncomfortable. She attempted to dismiss the question with a wave of her hand but feared she might drop her teacup if she tried. Her heart stormed in her chest and the sound in her ears roared more intensely into life, throwing out a final wave of heat and flame, and then it disappeared and was gone. All was quiet again except for the ticking of her clocks and an anxious whining from Rani looking up at her with obvious concern. The cool comfort of the sitting room returned as did her more regular heartbeat, and Aunt Gwendoline slowly put her teacup down. She dropped a hand to reassure her distressed companion.

"Yes, I'm quite all right, my dear boy," she answered. "It's just a twinge of old age. Please go on."

Chapter 12

Gerard was not convinced. He looked at his dearest aunt intently, searching her face for any covert sign of distress.

"I have been prattling on for quite a while now and I wouldn't be surprised if you were tired of hearing the sound of my voice. There is more to tell, of course, but none of it is urgent. Would you like us to take a break?" he asked.

Aunt Gwendoline did not move. She was not able to. There was the pressure of a hand on her left shoulder, holding her in her chair and forbidding her to do anything other than to sit still and listen. Rani was looking up at her, shivering and giving an intermittent flick of her tail stump.

"Not just yet," she smiled gently to him. "I was thinking of us having a break sometime. Indeed, I have some lamb chops in the refrigerator which I was going to cook for tea with some garden peas I purchased at the market yesterday. I was rather hoping you would join me."

She shrugged her shoulder and the hand loosened its grip. A small cushion fell from the back of her chair on to the floor beside her.

"That would be good," Gerard nodded, smiling an immediate acceptance. "That is if you are sure you have enough for both of us and are up to doing the cooking."

"I have and I am," she answered. "So if we carry on for a short while longer, we at least know we have some sustenance to look forward to. Now, you say the press were horrible, but I do seem to recall them reporting that someone was eventually arrested for Janet Brinsley's murder. Is that not so?"

"Yes, it is," he replied, still cautiously watching his great-aunt for any sign of unease. "Two men, Billy and George Crater, were charged with the crime. It was quite astonishing, but only about four weeks after Janet was murdered there was a great trumpeting of a breakthrough in the case and the highest-ranking police officers paraded themselves before the cameras and microphones of the television news channels to announce the effectiveness of modern criminal investigation techniques under their command. Film was shown repeatedly of vanloads of armed police in black flak jackets and helmets, storming through the iron gates of a heavily fortified country mansion reportedly bought with the proceeds of crime and racketeering. And the finale was footage of the two Crater brothers being bundled into the back of an armoured police van with blankets over their heads.

"It was all very spectacular and came as a huge surprise to Mark. The first we all knew of the Crater brother's arrests was the announcement on the morning radio news. Mark was very excited about it but as the day wore on his mood changed. I began to sense that he felt almost hurt by the police not telling him about their suspicions beforehand. We had been told repeatedly that an arrest was expected but we had no idea it would happen so quickly. I suppose it is understandable that the police should withhold some information from the public before the final strike is made, if only to stop word getting out to the intended targets of their inquiries. But the thought that they were keeping him very closely informed about what was going on had kept Mark buoyed up during those early days after Janet's death. Now, he suddenly felt let down by them, that they were not telling him everything and that he could no longer trust them or rely on them quite as much as he thought. It was nonsense, of course. Sergeant Chak and his crew are a superb bunch of officers and they remained very supportive. But Mark was not himself and I can only believe that such thoughts would never have entered his head had he been thinking straight."

"Are you saying he changed?" asked Aunt Gwendoline.

"Maybe, temporarily," he replied. "I talked to Sue about it, and she said that she felt there was something different about him. She did not necessarily share my confidence that he would eventually settle back into being the Mark we had both known and liked before the whole ghastly business had blown up. But, yes, for the moment, he was different.

"I must admit that I too had been mildly annoyed by the announcements. A bunch of very senior police officers who we had never heard of before were hogging the limelight in the press and on the television news. Sergeant Chak and his team were simply brushed aside. I talked to Mark about it later that evening. The police hierarchy obviously regarded the Crater brothers as very significant criminal catch, and it was clear from the way they conducted themselves in front of the cameras that there were good measures of glory and recognition lying around and that they were going to scoop them up. Mark saw it too. 'OBEs,' he snorted. 'Standing for Other Beggars' Efforts'. It was not like him to be so cynical, but I had to agree with him that was how it looked. All the people who had done the actual work of tracking down Janet's killers, who had put in the hours and the legwork to get the result, were sidelined. In retrospect, I have wondered whether Mark sensed that something in the criminal justice system went wrong at that moment. It might sound stupid, Aunt Gwendoline, and I do realise that I could just be imagining a pattern in a lot of unrelated coincidences, but that is how it looks to me even now. Because, as you know, the prosecution of Billy and George Crater did go wrong, and I have to wonder whether it was at that moment that something in the search for justice for Janet began to go wrong and that Mark first began to lose his way."

He stopped and gripped his brow with his hand. He closed his eyes and took in a long, deep breath. His mind had become inexplicably blank.

Aunt Gwendoline let the silence extend while a searching beam from the late afternoon sun swept across the chequered inlays of her astragal glazed corner cupboard, and moved on to create a red and gold blaze on the mahogany of her Sheraton secretaire. It was not until it had inched its way across to the aspidistra that Gerard opened his eyes and looked up at her again.

"My dear boy," she smiled gently to him. "I feel it is perhaps now time for our break. Your story is most intriguing, but I fear I would not have the stamina to hear the end of it without some sustenance. Shall we go and prepare dinner?"

Incapable of other thought, he nodded his reply.

"Could you bring out the tea tray and begin shelling the peas for me?" she asked, rising from her chair with considerably less stiffness than she felt. "I shall set about the lamb chops, and if you would like a sherry feel free to pour one for yourself as well. It is over there on the small table. Come along, Rani, I imagine it is also time for a good dog's supper. Yes, I am sure it is." She headed for the kitchen.

Chapter 13

Gerard sighed and shrugged some life back into himself. He felt surprisingly fatigued. He had not been fully aware of the emotional load he had been carrying ever since he had first heard the news of Janet Brinsley's murder, although he had guessed at it and perhaps it had been more than he thought. He sighed again and hauled himself out of his chair.

He poured sherry into each of the two stemmed glasses standing beside the Victorian diamond point engraved decanter on the table his great-aunt had indicated, and with that small activity his thoughts began to move again. He looked around the room.

"This is Staffordshire porcelain," Aunt Gwendoline had said to him one day as she handed him a small statuette from inside her velvet lined Edwardian display cabinet. "There was quite a fashion for portrait pieces in late Victorian times. This one is of a well-known actor of his day in the role of Richard the Third." He looked around the room some more and spotted one of his favourite pieces, a pale green saucer dish which his great-aunt had always handled with great affection. "It is in a style called 'famille verte', from the Kang Hsi period in China," she had informed him. "It is quite different from our English porcelain and it caught my eye when I saw it in the sale room." She had then looked at him very directly. "One thing I have always found to be true. The best of any age, and of any culture, always go well together. It is something you might like to remember."

He had been only young when she had said that to him and he had never forgotten it. He freely acknowledged that it was Aunt Gwendoline and her sitting room that had started him on his career in archaeology. She had always shared with him so freely her love and enjoyment of her collected things.

Every piece she had ever shown him had only ever been described with an affection that spoke only of the pleasure to be had in its beauty and the skills of its creator, never in its monetary value.

Yet monetary value was there, and he was well into his adult years before he began to wonder how his great-aunt's sitting room had come about. Her father, his great-grandfather, had been a miner like his father before him, a poorly schooled man who hacked the iron ore out of the Cleveland Hills to feed the blast furnaces of Felderby Iron Works and turn wheels of nineteenth century industry. He was not a man of money or learning. The local village girl he married, his great-grandmother, also had precious little by way of goods or schooling. She was a woman of her day, a good provider of food and warmth for her family as they lived in their rented two-up-two-down, back-to-back terrace house in the company village of Low Felderby. The times through which they lived had not been generous so an education beyond the legal minimum for their three daughters was a luxury they could not afford, and necessity demanded that as soon as the girls left school they should take up jobs in domestic service which was all they were qualified for. So, Gerard could only shake his head and wonder where the knowledge and the money had come from to set Aunt Gwendoline on her path to acquiring such a sitting room full of treasures.

And like his archaeological digs, there was always something new there for him to discover, like the small table in front of him bearing the sherry glasses. He had not seen it before, with its burred walnut veneer and its finely executed marquetry centre panel. This harbour of a room which had so many times offered him shelter and secure anchorage only appeared static. It did change with time. The only constant seemed to be the aspidistra with its shiny leaves sitting in its ornamental pot in the corner. It alone was forever present and only it never seemed to grow any bigger or alter in any way. Unthinkingly, and without knowing why, he grinned at it and winked as he turned to carry the two glasses of sherry out to the kitchen.

"There you are," Aunt Gwendoline greeted him. "I was beginning to think you had got lost. I have the grill on and a pan of water for the peas, so if you would like to shell them, I will just clear these tea things away. Your health."

She took one of the sherry glasses and raised it while he did likewise with the other.

Chapter 14

They talked about all manner of distracting things over dinner, the ancient city of York and the Romans and the Vikings who settled there, the discovery of gunpowder by the Chinese, the relative merits of the waters of Bath and Harrogate and possibly Lourdes for curing arthritis, and the fine quality of the pottery produced by the women potters of southern Thailand millennia before the names of Wedgwood, Spode, Worcester or Meissen came into being.

"Or Chatterwood," added Aunt Gwendoline as they settled back into the sitting room with a tray of green tea.

"Yes," agreed Gerard. "Or Chatterwood, like Aunt Alice's vase which is now broken."

He had appreciated the interlude brought about by the meal but it was time to return to the events of Janet Brinsley's murder and he wanted to tell his story through to its end. He could not explain why he could recall so clearly all the details of the events, of his break-up with Sue and why the emotional turmoil he still felt seemed out of all proportion to the way their relationship ended. Perhaps Sue had been more important to him that he realised. On the other hand, she did smash his family vase, which led to him pestering his dearest old aunt with the story of how Mark Brinsley coped with his wife's death. But his thoughts were calmer as he settled into his chair, and he felt the sitting room wrap its peace around him while the insanities raging in the world outside were consigned to impotence beyond its walls.

"With great fanfare Billy and George Crater were arrested for Janet's murder," he recounted. "Like most of the law-abiding public, neither Mark nor Sue nor I had ever heard of the Crater gangland family until their names were blasted out in the news after they were arrested. We had the impression that most of the press were also ignorant about them and had to go scuttling through their archives for information in short order. But the Crater family was well known to the police which is why Billy's and George's arrests came only four weeks after Janet's killing.

"Background stories started to emerge. Apparently, the Craters are a dynasty of gangsters sired by an immigrant grandfather of unpronounceable surname who anglicised it to Crater. He staked out a criminal territory in his adopted country and that territory was subsequently expanded into a minor empire by his son, the present head of the clan. He, the son, in turn has three sons, Frank, Billy and George, and between them they are said to control all drugs, people trafficking, gambling, night clubs, prostitution, racketeering and anything else with an illegal edge to it in the east end of the city. Assuming that at least half of it is true then we can only conclude that the Craters are a very nasty bunch of characters."

Aunt Gwendoline sipped her tea and listened. The twin circles of light thrown out by two small table lamps were sufficient for her to see every expression in her grand-nephew's face and only the sound of his voice and the ticking of her clocks disturbed the quietness of the room.

"I am surmising an awful lot," he continued, "but I gather that the police had been trying to build up a case against the Crater family for a long time. According to Sergeant Chak, the Craters had proved very clever at staying out of any line of evidence that might lead directly to them, just like the gangsters in crime fiction. Whenever the police got on to something likely to incriminate them they always managed to escape prosecution using all the devices that could be bought by their vast, criminal wealth. They employed the best, extra-smart legal teams, witnesses and evidence disappeared at unfortunate moments during police investigations, alternative witnesses were found to provide them with unassailable alibis, and the widows of victims and former associates suddenly found themselves with a house and a healthy bank balance and life style in another, sunnier country from which they could not be extradited. It all sounds unbelievable but from what Sergeant Chak told me it is all true. Then suddenly, out of the blue and quite out of pattern, Billy and George Crater murder Janet Brinsley. The police could not believe their luck. At last, they had a case against the Craters that could not be sunk.

"The arrest of Billy and George Crater had a big impact on Mark. Here were the faces of the two men who had so sadistically abused his Janet and then killed her and their unborn child. It gave him something to focus on, something for his scientific mind to analyse and try and understand, and I suppose it helped him. I can only imagine that the spectre of revenge, justice, an eye for an eye and all those sort of thoughts was suddenly delivered to him, even though he is not in his deeper parts a vengeful person. He was noticeably recharged, up on his toes, intense in a way I had never seen him before.

"Sue and I continued to look after him. He came around for dinner on a number of evenings, more often than not if I really want to add them up, and he usually ended up staying the night. Sue was tense and cautious in his company and always more relaxed after he left, but she did a good job of hiding her feelings and of putting up with him. I know I was spending a lot of time with him and maybe Sue felt I was neglecting her, although I don't believe I was. Mark's problems were huge and I don't think that offering him the odd meal and bed for the night was unreasonable. He still had a lot to deal with. But even though I could see he wasn't himself I can honestly say there was nothing about him that gave either of us any inkling of what was to come. That surprised us both."

He paused and shook his head, as if still disbelieving the story himself. Aunt Gwendoline waited but no reaction came from her surroundings. Rani lay quietly watchful at her feet with her chin on her crossed paws, and the aspidistra remained unmoved in its pot.

"It was inevitable that the arrest of the Crater brothers sparked renewed press and media interest in the three of us all over again," Gerard continued. "Again, they became a nuisance with their microphones and cameras and their relentless pursuit of us whenever we stepped outside the house. It made life very difficult. Sue in particular found it a strain, especially when Mark stayed with us. I worried about her, so much so that at the height of the renewed press frenzy I suggested she might like to go and stay with her brother until all the attention blew over. She had a married brother on the other side of town near her work, so it would not have been an impossible arrangement for her."

"And how did she take your suggestion?" Aunt Gwendoline asked.

"Her reaction was extraordinary. She looked at me with an expression I could only at first describe as horror. It then quickly faded into disbelief that I should even make the suggestion, and then she rejected the idea furiously. She became tearful and acted hurt, but also shocked as if she was frightened. I tried to reassure her that I only wanted to take the pressure off her but I didn't get the feeling she heard me. She seemed totally confused, as if she was afraid of staying but at the same time afraid of leaving. I couldn't work out what she was thinking."

Aunt Gwendoline once again felt the prod of finger in the middle of her back. "But she stayed?" she asked.

"Yes," he replied. "She stayed, at least for the time being."

Aunt Gwendoline shifted in her chair to relieve the pressure between her shoulder blades. "Afraid of staying, yet afraid of leaving," she repeated quietly. She knew the feeling. She had learned it the night Mother had carried her to stumble in the dark along the workmen's path to the dugouts above Low Felderby. Home was solid, warm and familiar. Outside there was the Zeppelin blazing in the night sky. More certain safety might indeed reside within the dugouts on the hillside but to reach them required a walk in the dark along a path under the threat of whatever the skyfire might drop on them. To stay or to leave? That night everyone in Low Felderby faced the question, and in the end they had all left. But Susan had not left. When offered the more certain safety of leaving she had stayed.

Aunt Gwendoline reached out into her surroundings with every sense she had but found nothing to tell her what it was that had held Susan back. She left her thoughts to puddle themselves in the back of her mind while she returned her attention to her grand-nephew.

Chapter 15

Gerard had paused in his story to give his emotions a brief rest. He sighed and looked up at his great-aunt, smiled, and then continued as if there had been no break.

"Billy and George Crater were refused bail at the preliminary hearing," he resumed. "A trial date was set for four months later. Sergeant Chak and his team remained very confident they would be convicted. He told us the police had collected a substantial body of evidence and that it was all very solid. It was almost entirely forensic, so short of a mass assassination of all the expert witnesses and a burning down of all the laboratories that did the analyses, it was unassailable. For once there were no witnesses to be intimidated, bought off or made to disappear. There was no question that Billy and George Crater were the two who had murdered Janet Brinsley and this time there was no way out for them. They were going to face the judgement and retribution of a justifiably shocked and angry society.

"We were very relieved. Then, as he was leaving us, he turned to us and said, 'I'll probably not be seeing you again.'

"We were stunned. 'Why not?' we asked.

"'A new set of officers will be carrying the investigations forward from now on.'

"As he began to explain what he meant, we all felt that he was trying to appear more confident than he really was.

"'The Craters are a big crime family,' he told us, 'and keeping tabs on them and all that they are up to is beyond the resources of a local murder squad like ours. So, the pursuit of Janet Brinsley's murder case has been handed over to the Major Crime Division to finish off. I want you to have every confidence in them, as much as you have had in us. We have done all the work anyway so there is not much for them left to complete. I'm sure you'll get along with them fine and that they will get the result you want. So good luck, and keep your chins up.' He shook hands with us and left."

Rani stood up, not to stretch or yawn but to stand immediately on the alert, looking at something in the distance, ready to point or defend as the circumstance demanded. Aunt Gwendoline could see nothing herself. She leaned forward to put her cold teacup on the low table and gave Rani a pat of acknowledgement.

"What happened next?" she asked.

"Everything went back to normal," Gerard replied. "The new police team had two meetings with Mark in the days that followed and asked him some vague questions about how he had found Janet. Then, in his words, 'they dismissed him'. They didn't bother with Sue and me. We all had the feeling of anti-climax.

"Mark went back to his chemistry laboratory and his lecturing. He was not very focussed and there were occasions when he drifted off into nowhere while talking with one of his students or a colleague. But everyone was forgiving. He kept in touch with his parents in Canada and with Janet's parents too. He came round to dinner with us on a few evenings while we all waited for the big day in court, and on those occasions he was sociable enough, although quiet. Sue remained tense in his company, but she covered it well and I doubt that he noticed it. Sue and I became a bit closer, something like we had been before Janet's murder, although not quite. At least we felt we could once again go about our daily lives without being under the threat of murderous harm. But all three of us were in a hiatus where we could only wait for the trial to begin. Sue worked, and I began drafting my report on my Thailand dig, but by and large we just drifted."

"And your Chatterwood vase remained safe on its pedestal in your hallway?" asked Aunt Gwendoline.

Gerard felt a flash of annoyance run through him. He had forgotten about Aunt Alice's vase. It was irrelevant, but he looked at his elderly aunt and collapsed his impatience. She was an old lady, living out the last of her days in gentleness and quietude, and like all old people her horizons were narrowing down to the closely familiar.

"Yes, Aunt Alice's vase was not in any danger at this point," he answered her gently. "But I would have to say that a sense of doubt about what was happening had closed in around the three of us. I certainly felt it, although Mark was the first to voice it. 'Something's wrong,' he said, and we could only agree. Ever since Sergeant Chak had said goodbye to us, we had felt uneasy. The team of officers who knew by heart every detail of Janet's murder, whose instincts had been present at every interview with every person questioned since Mark's first telephone call, had been replaced by a new group who knew nothing about what had happened except what was written in the files. We were certain that Janet's killers would be brought to justice while the investigations were in the hands of the men and women who had been eating, sleeping and breathing the case from the start. But suddenly they were not there. Maybe it was sensible to hand everything over to officers who were more skilled in the pursuit of organised crime. And maybe those who made the decision did look at the case and conclude that the surest way to convict the Crater brothers was to bring the full resources of the Major Crime Division against them. Or maybe, as Mark said, the Craters were such a big crime family, and the police had been after them for such a long time, that the desire for success and the political and promotional rewards that went with such a victory stirred the ambitions and muddied the visions of those whose job it was to run things from the top. I suppose we will never know, but I do know we were not comfortable."

Aunt Gwendoline tuned in to her own instincts. Rani had relaxed and, for the moment, in the dugout of her sitting room, there was safety and reassurance against the terror in the night outside just as there had been in the hillside above Low Felderby all those years before. But outside the skyfire was still burning and five, fiery, five-pointed stars were still falling to their deaths. The comfort and warmth left her and the coldness of a wet sandbag pressed itself against her back.

"And if I remember correctly, you were right to feel uneasy about the new arrangements, isn't that so?" she commented.

"Yes, in hindsight, we were absolutely right," he confirmed.

Chapter 16

"The four months to the trial were very difficult for Mark," Gerard continued. "I used to see him walking out across the university campus at various times during the day and, if it was around lunchtime, I would join him and we would sit out in the sun and eat our sandwiches, feed the ducks and listen to the cacophony of the students as they raced around the 'ant heap' as we call the university during term time. We didn't talk about anything much and many times we didn't talk at all. We had some work we were doing together. An archaeologist pal of mine from Shanghai had been impressed by Mark's analysis of the Thailand honey and had sent over some fabric that had been wrapped around a mummified body from around 50 BC, found in some old salt mines on the Silk Road. Mark was analysing the dyestuffs in it. But overall there was nothing we could do but wait.

"We were aware that there was a lot of pressure to get a move on with the prosecution of Billy and George Crater. Janet's murder and its aftermath had been widely reported so there was a lot of public interest in the result, and 'law and order' is one of the government's present catchphrases. The Minister Responsible was getting asked questions in parliament and he in turn was demanding answers from the police and the Crown Prosecution Service. They too were anxious to score a big hit against one of the country's bigger crime families so matters trundled along at quite a fast pace.

"Mark sat on his patience very well and seemed mostly able to keep his feelings under control. He never discussed the details of Janet's sufferings in the presence of Sue or any other woman and, as far as I know, he might only have ever talked about them with me. He was not by nature a vengeful person, but when we talked, he usually drifted into the topic of what had been done to Janet before she died. He had all the details. His scientist's mind had insisted on having them and the police, the first team engaged in the criminal chase, had given them to him accepting that he needed them to help him come to terms with what had happened. So, he had no doubts about the Craters' guilt. He knew it was Billy Crater, the psychopath, who had actually killed Janet, and he knew that both Billy and George had each had her more than once before she died. He knew when they had tied her up with her own stockings, and broke her teeth on the bottle of brandy they had pushed into her mouth to wash down the drugs they had forced her to swallow. He knew the size of every bruise on her body and the length of every cut they made on her and the sequence in which it was made, and he knew how long they had kept her alive while they had their fun with her and how long it had taken her to die after they had finished. He knew all that, and all he wanted was for our system of law and justice to deliver the only verdict that was possible on the two men who had done it all to her. Life imprisonment with no possibility of parole for as long as they lived. It was, from any perspective, the only fair and reasonable verdict that could possibly be reached."

"But it was not to be, was it?" recalled Aunt Gwendoline.

"No, it was not," he confirmed.

She felt the sitting room fill with a solid silence in which even the ticking of her clocks became muted. The pressure across her shoulders pressed down hard upon her. She made a great effort to take a deep breath and clear her head, and momentarily she feared she was going to pass out.

"Aunt Gwendoline?" asked Gerard, suddenly startled. "Are you sure you are all right? It's very late. Are you certain you want me to continue?"

The moment passed and the deafness left her ears. "You had better tell me what happened next," she whispered into the quietness.

He looked at her carefully and at the anxious Rani quivering at her feet and looking up at her. He needed to complete his story but he was suddenly more conscious of his ancient aunt's frailty.

"If you are sure you are all right," he offered.

"I am," she answered more firmly. "And I'm sure if my old bones can take it then so can yours."

Her tone did not leave him any room to doubt her. "Very well," he resumed watchfully.

"The first day of the trial arrived and started off quietly enough. Mark and I got to the court early, but the television and press were already out in force and there was much thrusting of microphones and cameras into our faces as we struggled to get through them. We fought our way inside the court building and found our way through to the public gallery. There was some nudging and pointing in our direction by the other members of the public as we took our seats. Mark took it all in his stride, although he was pale and tense and had probably not slept well the night before."

"Susan did not go with you?" Aunt Gwendoline asked.

"No. She didn't want to have anything to do with the trial. Any time I mentioned it we both quickly ended up looking for an exit from the conversation. Whatever it was that was frightening her was still there and I was no nearer to finding out what it was. I do remember her kissing me goodbye that morning as she left for work. She had a look of concern, even anxiety, on her face. Her eyes were moist as she looked unblinking at me for a few seconds and brushed down my lapel. Then she said 'goodbye' and 'do look after yourself', before quickly leaning up and giving me a kiss before turning around and going. It took me completely by surprise. I had not had a kiss like that from her in a long time. It was a very soft, moist kiss. There was love in it I am sure, but also unhappiness and a whole lot of other emotions I couldn't unravel. I couldn't get it out of my mind that it felt like a kiss goodbye, and not just goodbye to go to work. I did wonder at odd times throughout that day whether she would be at home when I got back and I am pleased to say she was. But that kiss did puzzle me."

"And your vase also was still intact when you got home?"

"Yes, Aunt Gwendoline," he replied patiently. "It was still intact."

She nodded her acceptance of the information and once again felt the pressure of a hand on her left shoulder holding her in her chair. She tried to shake it off, but its grip held firm.

"I'm still here, Mother," she gritted out silently through her clenched teeth.

Gerard noticed nothing.

Chapter 17

"I know we should have faith in our system of justice, but to see the great lumbering beast in action does stretch one's credulity," Gerard sighed. "Mark and I sat patiently as a herd of barristers rustled in with much smiling and handshaking and passing of sheets of paper between them. It was all very theatrical and we felt we were watching a play. They divided into two groups, the Prosecution forming up on the right. There were three of them led by an almost stereotypical QC, about as wide as he was short, and two assistants who busily set about emptying a supermarket trolley full of documents on to the table in front of him. They tried to appear impressive but from the start they looked a pathetically small force to muster against the tribe of silks and barristers who seated themselves on the left for the Defence. Each of the Crater brothers had his own QC and each QC had at least three assistants, each bearing their own trolley of weighty books and bound and tagged folders which they proceeded to lay out on the groaning tables on their side of the court. They were quite an army. The court officers had to bring in extra chairs to seat them all."

"Not a good start," commented Aunt Gwendoline.

"Not encouraging and it didn't get any better," Gerard confirmed. "No sooner had they all settled after their lengthy fussing than it was all upstanding to welcome the Judge, and by the time he had given his preliminary address about the case to be tried followed by another little speech about the jury selection process, it was time for lunch, which the Judge decreed should take two and a quarter hours. It was impossible to feel there was any sense of urgency to get on with the business in hand."

He took a deep breath to control the frustration that came back to him by recalling the events.

"After lunch the Judge moved to begin selection of the jury. Immediately one of the defence barristers was on his feet with some point of order or something. The prosecution barrister responded with some filibuster while one of his assistants rapidly flicked the pages of one of the legal books they had carted into court with them, and a defence barrister countered with a reference to something in one of the books on the Judge's desk. At that point the Judge decided that further discussion was needed in his room out the back so out they all trooped. We twiddled our thumbs for about three quarters of an hour, then no sooner had they all returned to the court than a different defence barrister raised another objection, at which point the whole business of the Judge and barristers trooping in and trooping out for a quiet chat began all over again. This continued for the rest of the day, interrupted, of course, only by a break for afternoon tea. It took another day before the jury was in place."

"It does sound tedious," Aunt Gwendoline agreed.

"It was more than that. The pace at which things happen in court is glacial. I'm sure that if the rest of us conducted our everyday life in the same pedantic manner we would still be debating the relative merits of reeds versus rushes in the roofing of our mud huts. It was so frustrating, especially when you know the answer and all you want to do is get to the decision and get on with the rest of your life. I was only relieved that Mark was able to hold himself together while all the nonsense was going on. But finally the jury was in place, except that it was now a quarter to four in the afternoon of the second day so the Judge offered the Prosecution the opportunity of delaying the start of the case until next morning. And that offer was, of course, accepted."

Gerard took another deep breath to calm the anger he still felt at the pace of the proceedings.

"Mark never gave any outward show of impatience," he continued. "I saw him look over at Billy and George Crater in the dock and study them on a few occasions. Neither showed any remorse or any feelings whatsoever, only a sort of supercilious boredom and indifference to what was going on. I saw them look back at Mark once or twice and then at someone over our heads. I turned around to see who it might be and immediately had to swallow hard. It was Frank Crater, their elder brother.

"For no particular reason, when Mark and I arrived in the court on the first day we seated ourselves at one end of the front row in the public gallery. Being humans and creatures of habit we made for the same seats every day without particularly thinking about it. It seems that Frank Crater made a point of waiting out of sight for us to arrive before quietly taking his place, one seat in from the opposite end of the back row. He was there whenever I looked, although he never returned my glance. The end seat was taken by I don't know what you would call him, a friend, a minder, a bodyguard. The press and gawping members of the public filled in the seats in between. I suppose I should not have been surprised to see him there, but it was not the most comfortable of situations. I worried in case he and Mark should accidentally meet on their way into or out of the court, but by the time we stood up to leave at the end of each session he was gone so they never did meet and I don't know what I would have done about it if they had."

Aunt Gwendoline pressed her hand to her forehead. The hand on her left shoulder was becoming unbearably heavy. She was tired and she needed to go to bed. It was very late and her age would not let her cope with the night hours as she used to. If only the hand would let her go.

Chapter 18

"Day four of the trial arrived," Gerard continued. "Unknown to us, it was to be the last. By ten o'clock we were all in our places in the public gallery, ready finally to hear the opening shots in the case for the Prosecution. We were all called to stand while the Judge ambled in. He sat, we sat, he adjusted his spectacles and blew his nose, shuffled some papers and then he invited the Prosecution to begin. Incredibly, even before the prosecution barrister was able to get to his feet, Billy Crater's man was standing up and interjecting. 'May it please Your Honour…' he blasted out, and then followed up with something very fast in that mixture of Latin and legalese that lawyers employ in order to remain incomprehensible to anyone familiar only with plain English. The prosecution barrister looked stunned and started gasping like a freshly landed fish. 'Your Honour, I object…' he attempted, but he was drowned out by Billy's man talking very quickly and loudly over him. And then everything deteriorated into the closest thing to a pub shouting match I should ever imagine is permitted in a court of law. We in the public gallery could only look on open mouthed.

"The Judge had great difficulty restoring order and eventually did so by sending a stern look in the direction of the Defence and raising a determined hand to silence a possible interruption by the Prosecution. 'Do I take it…' he finally asked Billy's QC into the interlude he had created. He then enunciated something in legal Swahili which was again beyond comprehension by us in the public gallery and Billy's man immediately agreed. 'Your Honour I object…' the prosecution barrister attempted again, but once more the Judge raised his hand. 'You may well object,' he acknowledged, 'but this is an interesting line of argument which is going to need the most careful and detailed consideration. Members of the jury, you will retire while I listen to the arguments. I will ask the ushers to clear the court. Return the prisoners to their cells.'

"I know I groaned inwardly. 'Here we go again,' I thought, and I assume Mark felt the same. The prosecution barrister was not happy. He had clearly been caught flat-footed. In the public gallery, it was apparent that only Frank Crater and his minder had any idea of what was going on. They sat immobile and emotionless while the rest of us gaped at each other in bewilderment until the ushers arrived to guide us out.

"Mark and I waited outside the court, then after an hour of nothing happening we wandered out into the sunshine. We had a coffee followed by something to eat. There was no recall to the court after lunch and the sneaking suspicion that something had gone seriously wrong started to grow in us as the afternoon passed. At half past four it was clear that nothing more was going to happen that day, so we pushed our way without comment through the press corps and left the television presenters to fabricate their flapping speculations for the evening news bulletins all on their own.

"We found out the next day the magnitude of the Prosecution's defeat. When we arrived in the court, the place was a mess. It looked like a classroom from which the wild and uncontrolled class had dashed out at the end of school without putting anything away. There were books and papers everywhere. Teetering piles of legal tomes covered the barristers' tables and the Judge's bench, all open at various pages and sliding off each other on to the floor in all directions, and a forest of folders covered every other available surface. The court was a shambles.

"At ten o'clock the Judge arrived. We stood, he entered, he sat, we sat and then, after clearing his throat, he turned to the jury.

"'Members of the Jury,' he began. 'The prosecution and defence counsels and I have been engaged in some very detailed and technical legal arguments over the past day. I do not intend to describe them to you. Indeed, I would not expect you to understand them if I did. Nor is it important that you should do so. But after considering all the compelling arguments from both sides I have decided that in the particular cases that you were called to decide upon, namely the Crown versus William Crater and George Crater, the defendants have no case to answer. That is how I now rule. You are therefore discharged from your duties and the defendants are free to go.'

"He tried to add something about his ruling not being interpreted as prejudicial to the defendants or something similar, but his words were drowned out by the roar and pandemonium that erupted from the public gallery. He did not try to control it. Those of us who were still paying attention were called to rise, the Judge retired from the court and mayhem and disbelief were left to reign. In the dock Billy and George Crater punched the air and did a little dance of victory while their barristers sat back smugly in their chairs with their legs stretched out in front of them. The prosecution barrister slammed a few books down on his table before giving his defence counterparts a begrudging handshake. 'Interesting point of law,' I heard him mutter to them.

"Mark stood rigidly on his feet looking ashen, facing them all in stunned incomprehension. The case was over and not a single item of evidence had been presented. 'No case to answer' was the verdict. None of Janet's suffering, none of her pain, none of her terror, nothing of the hours of agony and degradation she had been forced to endure, was ever going to be presented in a court of law for the world to see and adjudicate upon. And the two criminals who had done it all to her were going to walk away free without even the shadow of a question mark hanging over them. It was too much for anyone to accept."

Chapter 19

Silence settled into Aunt Gwendoline's sitting room and filled it to its darkest corners where the light of the two table lamps would not reach. Out of the blanketing darkness she heard the striking of her oak-cased clock in the hallway, its voice reminding her of what she already knew, that it was late and that she was very, very tired. The pressure on her left shoulder which had held her in her chair while her grand-nephew had been telling his tale lifted and she was free to move again.

"My dear Gerard," she sighed. "I had not realised how late it has become. I am most desperately tired and you, dear boy, must be the same. It has been a fascinating story and I am sure there is more to come, but I do feel we have done all we can do for today."

Gerard came out of his thoughts and also smiled tiredly. He became suddenly aware of exactly how dark it was outside.

"It is late and I'm afraid I have kept you up much beyond your usual bed time," he agreed. "It has been a great help for me to talk about Mark and Janet and what happened around the time of the trial, but once I got going I'm afraid I just bored ahead. I hope it hasn't been too much for you, me talking on like that."

"That is what great-aunts are for," she consoled him. "But I will now bid you good night and send you on your way. I must give Rani her supper and take myself to my bed." She bent down and caressed the dog's soft ears. "You have been a very patient dog, haven't you? Yes, you have. And exceptionally good dogs should get a nice supper before they go to bed, shouldn't they?"

"Can I help with the clearing up?" Gerard asked half-heartedly.

"I'll see to it in the morning," she smiled to him. "But now have a safe journey home, and promise me that you will come again soon and complete your story for me. There is a lot you haven't told me. I am still no nearer to knowing why your lady friend Susan broke my late sister Alice's vase in the precipitate manner she did. And then there are also the three falling stars which I must sort out."

"Three falling stars?" he queried.

She stopped and looked at him, her smile wavering momentarily into puzzlement.

"Three stars? Did I say that? Goodness me, I must be more tired than I thought. It's just an old lady's mind wandering because of the late hour," she dismissed. "Now you really must go. And don't forget, you have promised to come again to finish your story for me."

"Yes, Aunt Gwendoline, I will. And thanks again." He wanted to give her a bear-hug out of love and gratitude for her, but he satisfied himself with a gentle embrace.

She closed the front door after him, secured it for the night and then stood a moment looking at her oak-cased clock. Just six feet tall it called out the quarter hours and stood an unsleeping sentry in her front hallway. It had been her dad's clock, the one he had given Mother on their wedding day, and it was not difficult for her to see within its dial the face of the man who had brought it home so proudly to his bride.

"You were a dashing blade," she murmured to it. "No wonder Mother fell for you. You scrubbed up very handsome, with the sweet smell of pipe tobacco in your waistcoat replacing the sour dampness of the mine in your working clothes."

Mother had been forever proud of the clock too. She had kept it spotlessly polished and dusted while he tickled its workings with a feather of light oil and wound it every eight days for all of their lives together. That was except for the four years of the Great War when he was away and Mother had kept it wound and tickled all on her own. It was still polished and dusted after he died, although it stood silent until she, Gwen, had rescued it and wound it once more and gave it back

72

its voice and a home at the end of Mother's life. She looked up at it through her tiredness.

"You were a good man all your life, our dad, in spite of all that life, and at times Mother too, dished out to you. For all her odd ways, she always loved you and was never less than proud of you. But I'm sure you knew that. And our Gerard is a good 'un too. There's a lot of you in him, our dad. He's not short of fight if he needs it, but he is in trouble. Help me bring him home, our dad. Help me catch his star."

She walked slowly back into her sitting room, deeply pensive.

"Why did I say that about three stars?" she asked herself. "Why did I say there were three stars falling when at last count there were five?"

She looked hard at the aspidistra sitting in its decorated pot.

"What is it you are trying to tell me, Mother? I think you rather enjoy making things difficult for me, don't you?" She got no answer. She switched off the two table lights and closed the door on the darkness, and left the room to watch over the spent tea tray with its dirty cups and cold teapot until morning.

"Come along, Rani," she called. "We will get you your supper and then we can go to bed. It has been an exhausting day and I am so very, very tired."

Chapter 20

Her sleep was not to be undisturbed. The burning Zeppelin kept forcing its way into her dreams. Sometimes she was on the doorstep of their home in Low Felderby, being jiggled in Mother's arms and looking up at the great blazing beast with sister Alice dancing around her in bare feet and teeth chattering because of the cold.

"Skyfire, skyfire," piped Alice.

"Alice, go and put some clothes on. You'll catch your death."

The maternal command was ignored and together they watched the silver skin of the monster blister in the inferno of its burning, and the great black crosses that marked it crackled and twisted into shards of glowing taper that dropped from it all over the valley until its skeleton roared and broke.

"It's coming down, our mam. It's coming down!"

Five five-pointed stars fell from it, flailing and waving and making a noise like the accident siren from Felderby Pit.

At other times she was being jostled on Mother's shoulder, being carried past the three black ponds at the top of Low Felderby on the high path alongside the allotments, hearing the creaking in Mother's chest and the sobbing in her throat as she splashed desperately forward in the river of fear that buffeted them all in the darkness, desperate to gain the safety of the dugouts in the hillside ahead.

"They're rotten devils my little bairn, rotten devils. Alice, Alice where are you? Keep hold now. Hold on tight or I'll tell your dad." And then more quietly the prayer, *"when he comes*

home. Please, God, let him come home. Look after the family for me our Gwen. Keep them together. Please, God, let him come home."

She buried her face deeper into Mother's shoulder and held hard around her neck, sensing the fear that was around her but not knowing what it was.

And at yet other times she was nowhere except flying midway between the land and the sky, looking down on the glows from the furnaces of Felderby Iron Works and on the darkened two and a half rows of works terraces that were the homes of the men who mined the ores that fed them. On the back of her head she could feel the heat from the Zeppelin blazing above them while her feet froze in the east wind that whipped in from the sea. Turning around she felt the fire warm her face as she looked up at it, burning and snapping like the pine cones that were thrown in with the coal to stretch it and give an extra cheeriness to the flames in the fireplace at home. And like the flying sparks from the pine cones and the pieces of burnt taper that fell into the hearth when our dad lit his pipe, there were always stars falling, falling, falling from the skyfire.

"They're rotten devils, they are. Rotten, rotten."

"But they are men, our mam. Men."

Five of them falling to their death like the sixth that had already fallen and was gone, and she reached out her child's hand to catch one that was left and save it and ease its hurt on its way down to its death. But it slipped through her fingers.

"Hush, my bairn. Don't cry, don't fret. We're nearly there."

Mother didn't understand. They were not stars, they were men, and she reached out again and again as they continued falling towards the dark shapes of the Iron Works buildings on the horizon across the valley. Then as she watched the three leading stars separated from their companions and began to flare more brightly in the night sky. They blazed so fiercely she could almost feel the extra heat of them.

"They're rotten devils, my bairn. Rotten to the core, and they deserve no better. We're nearly there. Not far to go now."

She hesitated to put her hand out to them. They were so bright she knew they would burn her if she caught one. They were too hot. But she pushed back her fear and forced her hand out again towards them. She had to save one. She almost reached them but again Mother stumbled in her striding and her hand was pulled away.

An explosion of gas broke the back of the Zeppelin and she flinched as debris was sent scattering across the valley. Momentarily dazzled, she lost sight of the three brightest stars against the fire and flames of the dying skyfire, and when she found them again it was to see them falling, fanned to incandescence and disappearing in a final flash of extinction. Burnt out to nothing they continued their fall to earth unseen against the blackness of the sky. She let out a cry. A watery cheer went up from the struggling adults pushing their way forward to the shelter of the dugouts. As the roof closed over her she looked up. The three stars were gone, but there were still two others still falling. They dropped more slowly and they were not so bright, but they were still burning and five-pointed and shrieking like the siren at Felderby Pit when there was an accident.

Chapter 21

She woke with a start, her hand grasping at the darkness that surrounded her.

"Oh, my goodness," she gasped.

She struggled to gather sufficient thoughts to find the switch on her bedside light. The muted glow that half lit the bedside space illuminated Rani, standing looking up at her and trembling uncertainly, whimpering with anxiety.

"Yes, I'm all right, Rani," she panted. "Just give me a moment and I will be all right."

She collapsed back on her mountain of pillows and let her hand drop to be comforted by the dog.

She stroked the silk of her companion's ears as her strength regathered itself, her heartbeat gradually regained it synchrony with the ticking of her oak-cased clock and the tightness in her chest eased with her more regular breathing.

"Oh, my goodness me," she eventually sighed. "Now I wonder what all that was about. It really does not do an old woman like me much good to have her heart pounding away like that in her sleep, does it, Rani? I really will have to be more careful. I only had one small lamb chop for dinner with a few fresh peas, and only one glass of sherry beforehand."

But in spite of her words, she knew the source of her dreams and the knowledge did not improve her temper.

"Come along, Rani," she said at last, pushing back the tangled bedclothes and reaching for her dressing gown. "I know it is one o'clock in the morning but I really do feel I need a cup of tea. I need something to settle me down after all the fuss and bother that has gone on. A cup of Jasmine tea should be just right, and I am quite sure we will be able to find a small morsel of something for a very understanding dog who has eaten all her greens today and is not likely to get fat. Come along, and let's see what we can find."

She made only the slightest pause at the closed door to her sitting room as she passed it, glaring through it with impatience before moving on to the kitchen. In no time at all the tea was made and she was sitting at her kitchen table savouring its steam, and starting the process of forcing her thoughts back into order.

"There were six stars to start with," she began. "And then there were five, and now the five have divided themselves into three and two. And the three have become particularly bright and have burnt themselves out in a violent burst of flame and disappeared into nothingness before they can reach the ground. Now what do you suppose can we make of all that?"

She sipped the tea and broke another piece of biscuit for Rani.

"If the first star that was lost was for Janet Brinsley," she mused, "then that would leave us with five stars which is correct. We will accept a single star for Janet Brinsley even though she was six weeks pregnant at the time she was murdered."

She felt that was right. To Mother and most other women of her time pregnancy was a threat to life and family. It was to be feared. And Mother had particular reason not to count an unborn child among her stars, but that was another story.

"So, we are left with five stars," she confirmed.

She was still annoyed at being woken in such a state at so early an hour but she stamped on her anger and refocussed her thoughts.

"So now, three of the remaining five stars are burning out before their time. That has to be correct because I said as much to our Gerard as he was leaving this evening, and that was before I dreamed it. So why did I say that? Who are the three stars for, and why are they burning out so suddenly?"

She slapped the table top in desperation.

"Mother!" she cried out, "I cannot save them all. I am an old woman with very little influence in life. I do not have the resources or the strength to catch them all. I can only do what

I can for our Gerard. You cannot ask me to look after the others as well."

She dropped her head into her hands and trembled. It was mostly tiredness but in the middle of it there was also the ice blade of fear digging deeply into her heart. She fought her conclusion, but in the end could not get past it.

"There is only one trio in our Gerard's story, isn't there, Mother? The threesome of Gerard, his lady friend Susan and his friend Mark Brinsley. Is that what you are trying to tell me? Are they our three stars that are going to burn out before their time?"

She left her head resting in her hands and closed her eyes.

"I don't know that I can make any other sense of it. I do hope, I really do, that it is just an old woman's mind playing tricks on her in her old age and none of it means anything at all. I do hope so. Because if it does mean anything then I can only worry that our dear Gerard is in the middle of something considerably more dangerous than digging up pottery in bandit country in the jungles of Southeast Asia. Please let it be nothing more than my mind wandering and being silly in my old age."

She lifted her head and sighed. The aspidistra remained obstinately unhelpful. She could not convince herself that her dreams were benign, and Rani had sensed something too and was sitting at her feet looking up at her and swishing her tail stump in encouragement and agreement. She let her thoughts speak their conclusion.

"When we left our Gerard's story earlier this evening, the two criminals, Billy and George Crater, were alive and well and had just got away with a most terrible murder. That would account for the last two stars, wouldn't it? And the fact that their stars too are falling would at least indicate they will eventually get their comeuppance, which is something to be grateful for, although perhaps not for some time. But in the meantime, our Gerard, Miss Susan and Mark Brinsley are in trouble, although how Miss Susan smashing our sister Alice's vase is going to help I really don't understand."

That said, her thoughts were exhausted.

"Time for bed again," she smiled down at Rani. "However, we do know who is responsible for disturbing our sleep, don't we? And that we can do something about."

She strode to the door of her sitting room as determinedly as her years would allow, threw it open and switched on the light. She glared at the aspidistra but said nothing. She walked directly to the tray of dirty china left over from her after-dinner tea with Gerard, marched it out to the kitchen and washed it all up.

"There," she announced defiantly as she returned to the sitting room to switch off the light again. "The room is tidy, just as you always insisted it had to be before we went to bed. Now, Mother, perhaps you will let me have the rest of the night for sleep."

She sent the aspidistra a final glare and closed the door solidly behind her.

"Goodnight, our dad," she nodded to her oak-cased clock at the foot of the stairs. "Help me bring our Gerard home. I don't think I can do it on my own."

She climbed the stairs and settled back into bed. Rani turned three turns round her blanket before flopping down on it, then the light went out and the darkness closed in around them and restful, dreamless sleep embraced them both for the rest of the night until the milkman delivered to the doorstep the milk for their early morning cup of English breakfast tea.

Chapter 22

"My dear boy you worry too much. Of course, it is all right," Aunt Gwendoline answered her telephone. "Why don't you come for tea as usual and then stay for dinner again? I have some fish fillets and I can always do more potatoes."

It was no surprise to her to receive his call. She had been out shopping in anticipation of it that very morning.

Gerard, in contrast, was not so certain as he walked down the quiet street to his great-aunt's house. He still felt ashamed of himself for unloading the full, brutal details of Janet Brinsley's murder on to her during his last visit. He rationalised that she was, like his Chatterwood vase, only apparently frail but in reality strong enough to survive two world wars and a lot else besides. But he also acknowledged that, like the vase, she was old. It had not been right to keep her up so late piling his anxieties on to her fine china constitution, and it had not been right to call her two days later and invite himself around to see her, even though he was worried about her. He occasionally wondered what devastating blow would eventually finish her off. He hoped that, when it did come, he would not be responsible for it and that it would be as unheralded and instantaneous as his golf club going through the porcelain of his late great-aunt Alice's vase. But he did not want to think about it. So, in spite of initiating his present invitation to dinner he resolved not to mention anything more about Janet and Mark Brinsley and simply enjoy an afternoon and evening chatting over irrelevancies with his most treasured of relatives.

His resolution was short lived. Dainty tomato and cucumber sandwiches, Earl Grey tea and rich fruit cake greeted him when he arrived, and as the fragrant brew was poured the ambiance of Aunt Gwendoline's sitting room embraced him as it always did. He relaxed and felt himself at home again. He looked up to thank her as she passed him his cup and instantly her steady, blue eyes told him she was not interested in any introductory chat. She was waiting to hear the rest of his story, just as he suddenly found he was anxious to tell it. It seemed that even Rani was eager to hear what he had to say. He smiled and organised his thoughts.

"Mark and I tried to find out why the case against Billy and George Crater had folded so dramatically," he began. "Sergeant Chak told us the Craters' barristers had found a legal technicality which had resulted in all the evidence against them being declared inadmissible in court. With no admissible evidence to consider there was no case for them to answer, and so that was the verdict. It wasn't much of an explanation and it was scarcely believable, but it was all we got. Billy and George Crater walked out of court free men, to have their photos taken later on that evening in one of their nightclubs, surrounded by scantily clad women, disco lights, coloured streamers and bottles of champagne. The pictures were spread all over the pages of the tabloid press the next day.

"Mark was shattered. He had held himself together quite well during the months between the Craters' arrests and their trial, believing absolutely that some justice would be delivered for the way in which his Janet's life had been ended. Now, he was lost. It was not that the Crater brothers had been declared not guilty. Although that would have been against all logic, he could probably have dealt with it as a denial of justice. It was more that all the evidence of what they had done to Janet during the hours over which they had abused and eventually killed her was never going to be seen in the light of day, and that without a public airing of that evidence then all she had suffered and endured counted for nothing. I followed him as he left the court.

"'Gerard, please,' he said. 'You're a good friend but, please, I just need to… I just need to be alone for a while.'

"He walked off.

"'You know where we are, any time,' I called after him, but he did not turn around.

"Fortunately, it took the press hounds a few seconds to get round to our side of the building so they did not see him go, and the next instant a mob of them had surrounded me and were hammering me with questions.

"I didn't see Mark for a week after that. I tried to talk to Sue about what had happened but she wouldn't engage. She took the Craters' acquittal very badly. I tried to tell her that the Craters were not interested in us. There was nothing in their arrest or trial that had involved us, we had not been witnesses for the prosecution and we had made no public statements against them. We had never been into their world, so they had no reason to come out of it and look for us to do us harm.

"'It's not that,' she said.

"'Then what is it?' I asked.

"But she wouldn't, or couldn't, give me an answer, and every time I suggested I call Mark to see how he was, and perhaps invite him over for a meal, I was met with a very frosty response.

"'I don't want him around here,' she insisted. 'Don't ask me why. I just don't want him near us or near you.'

"It got so that we couldn't talk. Every time I tried to say something I would see her go immediately on guard in case I mentioned Mark. Yet at other times, she would be so loving. I remained totally confused by her."

Aunt Gwendoline clenched her teeth. An irritating noise had begun humming in her ears. It sounded faint and far away and she could not say whether it was real or just her ears playing tricks. She looked down at Rani and saw the dog was standing on the alert and sniffing the wind as if trying to locate something in the distance as yet unidentified. Aunt Gwendoline shook her head gently to try and clear the irritation. Whatever it was, the sound had a vague familiarity about it and there was no comfort in it.

"I was very worried about Mark throughout this time," continued Gerard. "I tried to call him at home, but all I ever got was his answering machine. Then, after a week, it seemed that all my concerns were unwarranted. He turned up at the university as if nothing had happened and buried himself in his laboratory.

"It was holiday time so there was no lecturing to do. The time the undergraduates are away is useful to all of us on the staff. We can get on with our writing and research, so I was not surprised I hardly saw him. But I kept up with enough of the gossip to know he was working very hard, perhaps too hard if the talk was to be believed. He was always at work before his postgraduate students arrived and was still there after they left, which to all intents and purposes meant he never went home. A few of us did ask what he was doing but all we got from his research assistants was some technical mumbling about novel organic syntheses, so we didn't ask again. We got the impression they didn't really know either.

"Mark did go home, of course, just occasionally to shower and change his clothes, but he was always straight back to his laboratory afterwards. The security staff put in a safety report about him being alone in his lab throughout the night and finding him asleep at his desk, but his head of department decided to do no more than just keep an eye on him. Everybody knew Mark's story. It was generally assumed he was throwing himself into his work as a way of occupying his time and getting through his grief, and that sooner or later he would come out of it. And we seemed to be right. After about a month the lights went out in his laboratory and he appeared mid-morning the next day, all freshly washed and brushed, entering the front door of the Chemistry Department as if he was on his way to start a normal working day.

"I saw him arrive from my office window and immediately rushed out to see him. He turned and gave me a wave and waited for me to catch up. He was looking tired and thin and a bit grey, but otherwise he seemed to be all right. He wasn't dishevelled or unshaven or anything like that. In fact, he was very neat just like the Mark of old.

"'Hello Gerry,' he greeted me. 'Been neglecting you of late I'm afraid. How are you and Sue?'

"I didn't know quite what to say except that I was pleased to see him and that I had been worried about him. I suggested we meet for a sandwich at lunchtime, to have a chat and catch up with things.

"'I'd like to Gerry,' he replied, 'but I've got a lot to do. I've been letting things slide a bit. I have to prepare for the start of term, otherwise I'll have no wisdom to decant into the undergraduates when they turn up at my lectures. Give me a week or so and then ask me again. I should be well into what I have to do by then.'

"'Yes, of course,' I replied. 'I'll tell Sue. She'll be ever so pleased you're back in circulation. You'll have to come around for dinner.' He smiled but didn't answer."

The noise sounded in Aunt Gwendoline's ears again. This time it was slightly louder. It could be a large vehicle grinding its way along the quiet suburban street that passed by her front door.

"I can't describe it, but there was something about Mark's departure into the chemistry building that left me puzzled," Gerard continued. "I still have no idea exactly what it was. There didn't seem to be any particular inflexion in his tone or expression on his face as he spoke, and I thought afterwards that maybe I had just imagined it. But on the other hand, I suppose I could have picked up some sense that he wasn't quite right, some forewarning of what was going to happen over the next few weeks."

"Some forewarning of what was going to happen?" Aunt Gwendoline echoed. "That sounds very dramatic. What exactly did happen?"

"Mark Brinsley got drunk," he replied. "Very drunk."

Her mind raced ahead of his reply. Mark Brinsley got drunk and after he became sober again Miss Susan smashed sister Alice's vase and walked out of Gerard's life while blazing stars fell from the skyfire in her dream. There was a thread linking them if only she could find it. And the strange noise she could hear in her ears was getting louder. Now it was like the deep growling of a dog informing an intruder of its presence. It was a sound intended to threaten, to warn of

85

the damage that could be done if the threat was let loose and it worried her with its menace.

"Goodness me, that is dramatic," she agreed. "You had better pour us both a sherry and we can sip it while we go and cook dinner. Come along, Rani. It is dinner time for dogs too and I'm sure there is something nice for you."

She rose to her feet, picked up the tray of dirty teacups and carried it out to the kitchen without further ado.

Chapter 23

"Fish on, potatoes on, and I have some fresh runner beans from the market stall. I hope that is all right."

Aunt Gwendoline fussed around the meal preparations and organised Rani's dinner bowl while Gerard watched the fish under the grill. He had been a little startled by the abruptness with which she had interrupted his story when he was feeling so much into his stride with it, but he shrugged and assumed that he had temporarily filled his elderly aunt's mind with all the details and that she needed a break. She showed no inclination to listen to any more of his story while the dinner cooked. Indeed, he sensed a determination in her not to do so. So, the potatoes boiled, the beans blanched and the parsley sauce was stirred in an all involving way until finally Aunt Gwendoline dished up everything on to warmed plates ready for eating.

"There we are," she announced. "Could you carry them into the dining room for us?"

The chatted generally until their plates were cleared, and afterwards, "I have some chocolate cake for desert," she offered.

"You know my weakness too well," he replied with a grin.

"Cream?"

"I cannot imagine anything nicer."

He had become completely relaxed to the point where, as his mouth filled with his favourite flavour, his world began to look very peaceful again. He began to have second thoughts about telling the rest of his story. There was nothing much left to relate. Mark was back working in his laboratory at the university and Billy and George Crater had returned to their underworld, vanishing off the front pages of the newspapers and out of the thoughts of all law-abiding citizens without a

87

ripple being left to remind anyone of their transient appearance above the surface of their criminal pond. Susan was gone. He still thought about her and he still felt sad about her leaving. They had shared some very close times together, and given how intense their feelings had been for each other it was surprising that her presence in his life should have become so thin after such a few weeks. Aside from that Aunt Gwendoline still served dainty cucumber or tomato or smoked salmon sandwiches with fussy cakes and Oolong tea at three o'clock on Wednesday afternoons if he cared to call round, which he always did if he was not overseas. There really was nothing more to add. The last mouthful of chocolate icing slid down his throat, a soothing balm that covered all that had happened since that terrible night when Janet Brinsley was murdered.

"Do help yourself to some tea," Aunt Gwendoline's voice cut into his thoughts. "And would I be right in thinking that Susan had always felt comfortable in Dr Brinsley's company before his wife was murdered?"

The question jolted him and he was grateful that he had the excuse of swallowing his last mouthful of cake before he had to answer it.

"She always seemed to be," he replied somewhat puzzled. "We often went out together, and I would have said we were all very good friends. Mark and I tended to talk together while Sue and Janet swapped 'girly gossip' as they described it. It was to Sue that Janet first mentioned her hopes about starting a family, only a few weeks before she was murdered. Talk like that could only mean they were close friends."

"Perhaps so," replied Aunt Gwendoline. "But that is Susan and Janet. What about Susan and Mark?"

He dredged his memories again. "I can't recall anything to suggest they were not good friends. Sue never hesitated when Mark asked her to dance at university social evenings and she always leaned forward to receive a peck on the cheek from him at the end of it. They chatted and joked easily together. I suppose that is what made her subsequent attitude all the more puzzling to me. We were good friends, all four of us, and when you have friends like that you don't just drop them when they are in trouble. I can understand some of Sue's reaction immediately after Janet was murdered. It was a frightening thing to have happened, but after that I would have thought she would have rallied round with support. Mark was helpless in the face of what he had to deal with. I just don't understand how she could turn against him as she did."

Aunt Gwendoline watched the discomfort triggered in him by her question and she became aware of the distant purring, growling sound in the background of her thoughts again. It was less like a dog's growl this time, more like something mechanical.

"I think we might move back into some easy chairs," she smiled across the table to him. "We can leave the dishes until later and I am sure my elderly bones will feel a lot more comfortable on some supportive cushions. Would you mind passing me my cane? Then you can tell me what happened when Dr Brinsley got drunk."

She stood and was surprised how free she felt from her earlier stiffness. She looked down at her forearm. There was the sensation there that a hand was guiding her, drawing her towards her favourite carved rosewood chair, and the distant engine noise in her ears abruptly ceased.

"I suppose in retrospect, the reason for Mark getting drunk is fairly obvious, although it did take us all a bit by surprise," Gerard resumed after they had settled. "Those of us at the university who knew him all thought he had come through his traumas extremely well. He had some time off, but he soon found his way back to work. He was not as dynamic as before, but that was accepted. There was no doubt that the verdict from the Craters' trial hit him very hard and we all thought the judge's conclusion was frankly off the planet. But Mark seemed to get through even that disappointment by throwing himself intensely into his work, coming out of it a month later exhausted and drained but at peace with himself."

"All very plausible," commented Aunt Gwendoline.

"But he had changed," Gerard continued. "He was more solitary, and while those who worked with him said he was still an outstanding chemist in a cerebral sense, he was now hardly ever seen tinkering at his laboratory bench. All that was left to his students. He still delivered his lectures and attended the usual departmental and faculty meetings but gradually the recognition grew on all of us that he was different.

"I found him quieter. I don't doubt that he put immense value on our friendship, possibly because most of his other so-called friends had dropped him off their address books, not knowing how to deal either with him or what he had been through. But he and I still had our sandwich lunches together and he always seemed pleased when I called him and suggested a coffee. We chatted as we always had, although I would have to say it was mostly me doing the chatting. He could still be immensely stimulating when we got on to the topic of some of the collaborative work we were doing and he even began talking to me about Janet. He told me about some very private moments they had shared together, which I took as a good sign. It was consequently a big surprise to me when one afternoon I arrived at the staff club to find the whole place raucous with talk about him.

"'He wasn't exactly shickered but he was awfully tongue-tied when he tried to pronounce the names of some of his chemicals.'

"'I'm surprised you didn't smell the fumes when you walked in to give the next tutorial.'

"'There's good air conditioning in that lecture theatre.'

"'Even so, you could smell the whisky all the way to the back row by all accounts. The students thought he was hilarious.'

"'That is utter nonsense,' I protested. 'Mark doesn't drink whisky. He doesn't like the stuff. He never has.'

"'I'm only repeating what the students are saying and they were there. And they would certainly know the smell of whisky when they came across it.'

"'And it wouldn't be the first time that unfounded rumours have been started by mischievous students with no sense of responsibility,' I stormed at them. 'It was more than likely just the smell of one of the chemicals from his laboratory clinging to his clothes.'

"'Something that smells like whisky and makes your speech slurred? I'll buy a gallon of that.'

"They all collapsed in laughter.

"I dismissed it as a single event, but it worried me again when a few days later the rumour mill proclaimed that one of the students had caught Mark replacing a half empty whisky bottle in the top drawer in his office desk. A couple of days after that one of the cleaners found an empty whisky bottle inexpertly hidden in his waste paper bin.

"'Mark, this is serious,' I said to him. 'We all know that the university turns a blind eye to the occasional bottle of red or half dozen beers when a department is celebrating a success, but hard alcohol on the university, apart from what you use in your chemistry laboratories, is absolutely forbidden outside the licensed bar areas. You could end up in serious trouble.'

"'I've already had a visit from the chief of security acting as proxy for the dean,' he grinned.

"'Take it seriously, Mark, for goodness' sake. You know that keeping half empty bottles of whisky in your desk drawer is a bad sign under any circumstances. Please, Mark, for friendship's sake, have a care.'

"I could see he was listening to me.

"'It's all right, Gerry,' he shrugged. 'I just felt like a drink, that's all. Thanks for being such a good friend, but I promise you I am quite all right.'

"I mentioned it to Sue later that evening. She immediately withdrew behind a shield of anger or caution or something.

"'Don't get involved,' she demanded. 'You have done enough now let him get on with his own life. Stay away from him and let him go his own way.'

"'I can't do that,' I argued. 'He is a good friend and so was Janet when she was alive. You don't ditch friends just when they are trying to get their lives back together.'

"'If he has a problem with alcohol, then he needs professional help,' she insisted. 'Keep out of the way and let the professionals deal with it.'

"'For goodness' sake, Sue, he doesn't have a problem.'

"'How do you know?'

"'Because he told me so,' I fired back. 'He's been through a bad time and he just felt like a drink. That is all. There's nothing wrong with that. We all do it. It's not something that happens every day and at least he hasn't taken up smoking.'

"I shouldn't have added that last bit but her lack of sympathy towards Mark got to me. Both he and Janet had been good friends, to Sue as well as me. Her attitude was not right.

"'I'm sorry,' I ended. 'Let's just step back and take a breather. I'm sorry.'

"She did not answer but only stood rigid and silent in front of me. I could not read what was in her face. Some of it looked like fear, but surely she would know she had nothing to fear from me. I saw her later in the hallway looking at Aunt Alice's vase on its stand and I stopped to say something to her, but before I could do so she turned to me and looked up at me and was soft and tearful again.

"'Ger,' she whispered. 'Be careful. Please, for both our sakes, be careful.'

"I had no idea what she was talking about and was too confused to answer her."

Chapter 24

Aunt Gwendoline was confused too. She again paced through her thoughts seeking the thread that was winding Susan and Gerard into a sinister tangle around Mark Brinsley. Susan had smashed sister Alice's vase and had done it for a reason. She had tried to tell Gerard what that reason was and had tried on more than one occasion, but each time she had been unable to do so. Whatever it was centred on Mark. So, what was it that she could see and Gerard could not? Or perhaps it was something that she could not see but could only sense, so could not explain. Susan, Mark and Gerard. Three friends. Three stars falling from the skyfire, falling and flaring suddenly and burning out before their time, and all centred around Mark Brinsley and the unspeakably brutal murder of his much-loved wife. She waited for the roar and fire of the blazing Zeppelin to appear in front of her, or the curious engine sound she had heard earlier to buzz in her ears again, but neither did. Not one of her thoughts triggered their response.

"I gather then, from what Miss Susan said, that there was more mischief to come from Dr Brinsley," she nudged gently.

"Most definitely, yes," Gerard confirmed. "A great deal more, but I will say right away that he did settle down eventually."

The certainty of his reassurance surprised her and simultaneously collapsed most of her thinking.

"Nothing much happened for a couple of weeks after Sue and I had that row except that I began hearing more and more rumours about Mark and his drinking," he continued. "I barely saw him, but I wasn't overly bothered by his lack of communication. I felt that if he was really in trouble, he would call or contact me in some way and we could take it from there. I was right as it turned out, though not in the way I expected.

"Very quickly, the rumours became really wild. Mark was arriving late for lectures and, although not drunk, he was usually described by the students as being 'in his cups' or some similar phrase. They all thought it hilarious. Some said they had seen him wandering erratically down the main night club strip in the city in the early hours of the morning. Another, who had a part-time job as a barman in one of the night clubs, swore he had served Dr Brinsley several large scotch whiskies one night to the point where the bouncers had to be called to escort him off the premises. Then a second empty scotch bottle was found in his office waste paper bin, and one day he didn't turn up for lectures at all and nobody knew where he was. At that point, the head of the School of Chemistry was instructed to read him the riot act, which he duly did, and everyone waited for Mark to return to his senses. Unfortunately, he didn't and the stories just kept multiplying.

"Nobody had any real idea about what was happening to him during this time. He was living alone and he called nobody. I don't know whether he spoke or wrote to his parents in Canada, or whether Janet's parents heard from him. If they didn't, then it was probably just as well. According to the gossip he was beginning to make a serious nuisance of himself. I tried to call him at home but all I ever got was his answering machine. At work his phone was sometimes answered by one of the people in his laboratory or else just left to ring. I gather his staff got fed up with saying that Mark wasn't there, that they didn't know where he was or when he would be back, and they could take a message but all the messages from the previous week were still sitting on his desk waiting to be answered.

"I talked to Sue about my increasing concerns one evening and, to my surprise, she remained very calm. She listened to what I had to say, held my hand and seemed understanding. She had become more relaxed as contact between me and Mark became less. She had stopped smoking, at least around the house, and I noticed that we began sharing jokes again about everyday things when we talked. But towards Mark, she remained implacably hostile. He was not to come near our house under any circumstances.

"'Be there for him if you must, Ger,' she said, 'but remember, you cannot help him. If he has hit the bottle, then he is not the same Mark as we used to know. He has changed, and if he is going to come out of it, he will require more support than you can ever give him. He is going to need professional help. He is a different man, and you are going to have to leave him to go to his own hell in his own way and come out of it in his own way too. You will not be able to stop him and if you try, he will only take you with him. He is not your friend any more, Ger. He is a different Mark. Let him go.'

"It was very strong and powerful stuff and utterly damning, and she was quite forceful about it. And it was a message she repeated to me over and over again through the following days. She was prepared to be sympathetic to Mark from a distance but she was not going to have him anywhere near us. That was all there was to it as far as she was concerned."

"It certainly sounds as though your friend had gone over the edge," Aunt Gwendoline agreed. "And I suppose it should not have been a surprise. After all that had happened, there was probably very little in his life at that moment to hold him on the right side of rationality. Maybe that is what Susan was trying to tell you, although breaking your Chatterwood vase does seem a melodramatic way of doing so."

Gerard paused and forced a deep breath into his lungs. He had forgotten about Aunt Alice's vase. He looked at his elderly aunt sitting quietly with her spaniel peacefully chin on paws at her feet and wondered whether all of his story, apart from the breaking of his vase, had not simply passed straight over her head.

"She didn't smash it then," he answered patiently. "That came later. Aunt Alice's vase did not get smashed until Mark sobered up. He did recover, and it was only then that Sue swiped it off its pedestal and walked out."

95

Aunt Gwendoline nodded, but she could not accept the reassurance that her grand-nephew clearly felt. Nothing stirred in the room around her to tell her why the story he was telling her was not harmless and it was that absence of any shiver in her surroundings that bothered her. There should be something, some ripple somewhere to indicate the nature of the danger that was approaching him. But there was nothing. No skyfire shedding its stars blazed in front of her, no engine noise buzzed in her ears, and only a yawn escaped from Rani lying at her feet. She cast a sideways glance at the aspidistra.

"You're a good girl, our Gwen. Keep the family together for me. Look after them."

"You're not helping, Mother," she muttered silently to it.

She returned to her grand-nephew. "Gerard, dear boy, I do appreciate your indulging an old lady with your story and I hope you will stay until you have finished it. But in the meantime, perhaps we can have another pot of tea to help settle our dinner. Orange Pekoe, I think. Will you help me with the tray?"

She rose cautiously to her feet, stiffened once more by sitting for so long, and Rani and Gerard followed her out to the kitchen.

"Poor Dr Brinsley," she fussed as she filled the kettle. "It does make one wonder how best to help the poor man. He must have suffered terribly."

Three incandescent five-pointed stars falling to earth pressed their way into her thoughts, but she brushed them aside.

"Violence is a terrible thing and it does terrible things to people," she continued. "And drink is no answer, of course."

Images of her father switched on in her mind, pictures of the much loved figure swaying on the doorstep, finally home from the workman's club where he had gone to try and drown the demons left behind in his imagination by his time in the trenches of the Great War.

"Poor men," she sighed. "Poor, poor men, all of them."

She froze in her setting of the tea tray.

"All three of them," she repeated, quietly startled. "All three of them are men."

She had no idea where the thought came from, but the force of it left her with no room for doubt. The look on Gerard's face told her that she was not making sense.

"Now why did I say that?" she smiled to him. "It must be the lateness of the hour."

But she was suddenly certain Susan was not among the three flaring stars burning out before their time. They were all men. She indicated the tray.

"If you can carry that in for us, we can continue with your story, because from what you keep telling me Dr Brinsley did eventually recover from his experiences unscathed. Am I right?"

Chapter 25

"Seemingly so," Gerard answered as they resettled in their chairs. "And the key word is 'eventually'. In the short term, he was quite definitely scathed. As I said, I had very little idea of what Mark was doing during this time. He didn't return any of my calls and while I don't think he was deliberately avoiding me I certainly didn't see anything of him. That was until very late one night, sometime after midnight, Sue and I were suddenly woken by a disorganised hammering on our front door.

"We were completely startled and both awake in an instant. I switched on several lights and went to see what on earth was going on. Sue grabbed a dressing gown and stayed back in the safety of the bedroom.

"'Who is it?' I shouted through the door.

"There was more hammering and I heard my name called out in a muffled reply, so I opened the door and there was Mark. He was obviously drunk, barely holding himself up against the door frame and with an inebriate's grin on his face. He was dishevelled and disorderly with mud all over his shoes where he had walked across the garden beds.

"'Hello, Gerry. Hi there, Sue,' he shouted out in a cheerfully slurred greeting that must have been heard by all the neighbours. He then took a step forward and collapsed full length on the hall carpet.

"Sue had followed me to the door once she had heard Mark's voice and she was clearly not amused. She did not say anything. She just looked down at him with an angry stare, and then at me without changing her expression. She gave a shiver although it was not cold, then wrapped her dressing gown more firmly around herself and strode back to our bedroom where she very solidly shut the door.

"I did what I could for Mark. He was stinking of whisky but I managed to haul him fully inside. He was not unconscious but his legs wouldn't hold him, so he was no help when I tried to stand him up. In his drunken state he seemed to think the whole business very funny. I dragged him into the bathroom where I dunked his head unceremoniously in some cold water and finally dumped him on the bed in the spare room with a plastic bucket and some old towels all around him. At one o'clock in the morning, I could only agree with Sue that he was being more than a nuisance.

"Sue was rigid when I got back into bed. I could hear from her breathing that she was fiercely awake. I tried to say something to her but she turned over without uttering a word. Later on, I heard Mark go to the bathroom where he was strenuously sick, then I heard the running water as he tried to clean up after himself. I dozed off after that, so I don't know whether Sue got any sleep or not. All I know is that she was very silent over breakfast and was smoking again.

"Mark appeared just as we were finishing. He was very pale and shaking and gave a good impression of being hugely sorry for the trouble he had caused. Sue was distant with him but did manage to smile at him like an aggrieved friend rather than as an avenging angel.

"'I made a bit of a mess, I'm afraid,' he said. 'I hope it's not too bad.'

"'Gerry cleaned it up,' she replied. 'For which you had better be grateful because if it had been me who had to do it one of us would not now be sitting here at this table.'

"Mark grinned sheepishly to her and sipped at his coffee. He made a superb effort of looking for all the world like a contrite schoolboy grovelingly grateful for escaping his just punishment. I took him home on my way to work and had a stiff word with him.

"'It's gone far enough, Mark. You have to stop. You're getting a stinking reputation around the university and you're becoming a laughing stock. For God's sake, how do you think Janet would react if she knew what you were like at the moment? She'd be disgusted. You'd never do it to her so why are you doing it to us? She loved you, Mark, and you're letting her down. I don't know what she would say if she was here.'

"'That's the whole point,' he answered, suddenly belligerently sober. 'She's not here. Those bastards took her away from me and they took our baby away from us too, from both of us. And they got away with it. They had "no case to answer" if you remember. They raped and killed her and the law said it didn't matter, they had no case to answer. If they had, then I wouldn't have to be doing this. But they didn't and she's not here. And if she was here, she wouldn't have to say anything to me. But she's not, and if she is looking down at me at this moment, then she knows and understands. So don't tell me what she'd say, Gerry, because you wouldn't know.'

"With that he seemed to run out of steam, and he sagged where he stood.

"'I'm sorry, Gerry,' he finished. 'You're a good friend, the best, and probably the only one I've got at the moment that I can rely on. I'm sorry, and I didn't mean to do that to you, to get angry with you I mean. I'll try for it not to happen again, but don't tell me that Janet and our baby were nothing. I'm sorry.'

"'Pull yourself together, Mark,' I urged him gently. 'This isn't the way to get over things and you know it. If you need help at any time, you know you can call me. You know that. But only you can sort out whatever it is that is burning you up for yourself. I can't do it for you. All I can do is help. I can't tell you how to live.'

"He nodded an acknowledgement and I left him to go and sleep off his hangover. I didn't see him again for a good few days after that and I resisted the temptation to call him. The whole incident had disturbed me deeply and I tried to come to terms with what was happening to him. It was obvious that he had tried hard to get through his grief and anger at Janet's death. He had doggedly faced the world and the press tribe immediately after her murder and he had hung on as long as he could to the hope that a just verdict would be delivered against her murderers. And when that did not eventuate he tried to exhaust himself in his work. But in the end, none of it was enough. I began to realise how deep were the scars that had been inflicted on him.

"'If she was here, she wouldn't have to say anything to me. But she's not, and if she is looking down at me at this moment, then she knows and understands.'

"It was those particular words of his that kept coming back to me. I don't know why they worried me so much and in the end they didn't matter, because he did eventually sober up and go back to being the respectable university senior lecturer in chemistry that he was employed to be. But I can still remember him saying them to me as if they had some deep significance for him, which they probably did at the time. I only wish they had seen the end to the whole business, but they didn't."

Chapter 26

"Aunt Gwendoline, are you all right?"

"Yes, dear," she answered. "Quite all right. I have just been sitting for too long. It happens when one gets older."

She was tired and was beginning to think it was time for her bed, but she had suddenly felt cold down one side of her body and the weight of the hand was once again pressing down on her left shoulder. She shivered and tried to brush it off with her right hand and her fingers felt the familiar, swollen knuckles that had spent a lifetime scrubbing and cooking to keep the family free from all manner of want and harm even through the most desperate of times. It demanded that she sit still and pay attention and she acknowledged in its grip the same determination that had shaped its life, the refusal to be bowed by circumstance and be denied a few brief moments of begrudgingly offered joy during the three score and seven years it knew. She looked down at Rani. There was a knowingness in the dog's eyes that looked unblinkingly up at her, so much so that she had to avoid their gaze. She tightened her shawl around her and accepted the hand, and sat more straight in her chair.

"So, that first night on which you experienced your friend's drunkenness was not the only occasion it happened," she summarised. She felt the grip relax and the warmth return to her body.

"No, it was not," confirmed Gerard. "And it got a lot worse before it got better. Sue went back to smoking in the house and all the easing of tensions that had come from the previous weeks when Mark had been physically distant from us evaporated the instant he fell in through our front door. I suggested to Sue that we start planning our next holiday and I collected some brochures from the travel agent. But although we looked through them together, she remained indifferent to them and strangely sad as if it was all irrelevant and not going to happen. I might be confusing memories here because that is what did happen in the end. She smashed Aunt Alice's vase and walked out and we never did go on our holiday.

"Mark disappeared from our lives for a few days but he was soon back. The telephone rang at seven thirty one morning, just as we were finishing breakfast.

"'I'm sorry to bother you so early but we have a friend of yours, a Dr Mark Brinsley, down here at the police station. He has given us your telephone number as someone who could come and collect him.'

"'It's for you,' said Sue.

"The police sergeant at the desk was very polite but formal as they brought Mark up from the detention cells where, apparently, he had spent the past few hours. He had been delivered there after causing a disturbance outside a night club in the city and he was still breathing thick whisky fumes over everyone.

"'Your friend is a very lucky individual,' the sergeant advised me while focussing on Mark that stare that policemen and head masters learn as part of their trade. 'The proprietors of the establishment where he caused a ruckus last night have decided to be forgiving on this occasion and not press charges. So on this occasion, and I stress it will only be on this occasion, we too will let the matter rest with a word of caution. But next time it may well be very different. Sign here if you will, sir.'

"Mark signed for his belongings and followed me unsteadily out into the world again. I was furious with him.

"'What the hell do you think you're doing, Mark?' I began.

"'Thanks for coming, Gerry,' he replied. 'I couldn't think of anyone else.'

"'But what the hell were you doing, getting so drunk you get into a fight outside a night club? For God's sake, Mark, that's not you. What's happened to you that I get a call at breakfast time to come and collect you from the police station?'

"'Look on the good side, Gerry,' he smiled to me. 'At least I held off giving them your telephone number until breakfast time. If they had it their way, you would have got the call at around three this morning.'

"'Very considerate of you I'm sure,' I stormed. 'But don't imagine I feel any gratitude to you for such a small mercy. Next time you may find I will not answer the phone.'

"He stopped and turned to me pleadingly. 'I'm sorry, Gerry, truly sorry, but it was necessary.'

"'What was necessary? You getting drunk and ending up in a fight in the early hours of the morning? You can push friendship too far, you know.'

"He could see I wasn't feeling very forgiving.

"'I know, Gerry, I know. But please stay with me on this, will you? You're the only true friend I've got at the moment. It is important and it won't go on forever, I promise. With your help I will get through it, if you can give me a little more time.'

"He was looking very pale and grey and he was already starting to lose weight as a result of his new lifestyle. I could only shrug. This was Mark and I could not believe he was being insincere.

"'Come this way,' I answered him. 'We're not going in my car with you drenching everything in whisky fumes. I'll walk you home. In case you don't realise it, I would be very surprised if anyone could stand being in a confined space with you for the rest of the day so you'd better keep all doors and windows wide open wherever you go.'

"We set off across the park in the bright morning air, and something began to niggle me.

"'I thought you didn't like whisky,' I challenged him.

"'It's an acquired taste,' he grinned, and said no more."

Chapter 27

"It was only a few nights later when the telephone rang again, this time in the dark hours. I recognised the desk sergeant's voice as soon as he spoke.

"'Sorry to bother you, sir,' he began in his official tone. 'I am calling to advise you that we have Dr Brinsley in the cells again, having picked him up about an hour ago in a state dangerous to his health. We were wondering if you could come and collect him and take him home, sir. We are rather busy, so it would be better for him to go home with you rather than have us look after him for the rest of the night.'

"It was two thirty in the morning.

"'Yes, yes thank you, Sergeant,' I answered. 'I'll be there shortly, as soon as I can.'

"'Don't you dare bring him here,' muttered Sue fiercely.

"She was fully awake and sitting forward in bed ready to take on anything that walked in through the door.

"'I'll do what I can, Sue. Go back to sleep. If he is in a fit enough state, I'll take him back to his own place.'

"'And if he's not?' she challenged.

"'Then I'll think of something else,' I answered.

"I was only just awake and still getting my thoughts together while I pulled on some clothes.

"'Why the hell are they calling us?' she demanded. 'Why don't they call Alcoholics Anonymous or someone who can take care of him?'

"'Probably because the police sergeant has our number and he knows we are Mark's friends.'

"'But why the hell does he always have to call you?' she persisted angrily.

"'Because, as I said, we are Mark's friends.'

"'No, we are not,' she shouted back. 'I'm not his friend, you are. It's you he calls, not me. Whenever he gets into a fix he calls you and he drags you into whatever mess he is in. And you always go. Why can't you let him go and sink in his own stew? You are not part of it, Ger, you didn't create it. Why do you have to go? Don't go, Ger. Let the police look after him and hand him on to someone competent to deal with him tomorrow. I'm begging you, Ger, don't go. Don't go to him. You don't know what you're getting into. It's too…, it's not…, Ger, don't go.'

"Two thirty in the morning is not the time to be having such a conversation and Sue was verging on hysterical.

"'I have to go, Sue,' I replied. 'He's a friend and he's in trouble, and he has asked for my help. Go back to sleep and I'll go and see him home and we'll talk tomorrow about where we go from here. I might be a couple of hours so don't worry. I'll see you at breakfast and we'll talk then.'

"She flung herself back on the bed and gripped the bedclothes tightly around her. She was shaking and crying, presumably with anger, and she didn't respond to the kiss I gave her as I left. I don't imagine she went back to sleep.

"The desk sergeant seemed pleased to see me in an official sort of way. He was having a very busy night and his holding cells were all full, so I suppose freeing one of them was going to be helpful to him. A constable brought Mark out and held him up against the counter while the paperwork was produced. He could hardly stand so I signed for his pocket contents.

"'Thank you, Sergeant,' I managed. 'I'm sorry you had to be troubled by whatever led to this.'

"'That's all right, sir,' he replied. 'We know Dr Brinsley very well and we know you are a good friend of his.'

"He then leaned across the desk to me while I took Mark's weight off the constable.

"'And you might like to believe it, sir,' he continued more quietly, 'but here in the police station we too like to think of ourselves as good friends of Dr Brinsley, particularly after what happened to his wife and the bastards that did it to her.

All of us here remain deeply upset about it and we are inclined to agree that it is enough to drive any man to drink. But I'm afraid Dr Brinsley has been making an increasing nuisance of himself and it can't go on. An awful lot of flexibility has been applied to the procedures to keep him out of any serious trouble, but he has to get himself sorted out now or else those procedures which have so far been held in check will no longer be able to be contained. I'm sorry to tell you this, sir, and if we can be of any assistance to you, we will be. But as I'm sure you understand, there is a limit to how far we can keep turning a blind eye.'

"'I appreciate that, Sergeant, and thank you for your advice, although I'm not sure what I can do about it.'

"'I don't know either, sir, but I thought it only fair to warn you' he finished. 'Goodnight, sir, and have a safe trip home.'

"I hauled Mark out of the station and into the fresh air, and tried to get him to stand.

"'Hello, Gerry,' he slurred. 'Sorry to trouble you.'

"I didn't answer him. I was too busy trying to work out the best way of getting him home. I doubted a taxi would have stopped for us and I certainly wasn't going use my car. We had just got to the park gates when he suddenly broke away from me.

"'Sorry, Gerry,' he choked, and promptly started to throw up all over the pavement.

"He hung on to the park railings and retched and retched for five minutes or more, all over his shoes and the front of his clothes and was utterly, utterly revolting. The smell almost made me sick too and it was impossible for him to do it quietly. A couple of cars slowed to gawping speed as they passed and some early, or late, pedestrians decided it was safer to cross to the other side of the road to get past him. Eventually, he stopped vomiting and wiped his mouth with a handkerchief and managed to stand up on his own. He looked awful. I handed him some tissues from my pocket to help with the clean-up.

"'Sorry, Gerry,' he repeated. 'It's the bloody whisky. It's awful bloody stuff, I hate it.'

"He looked at me with very glassy eyes.

"'If you hate it so much, then why do you drink it?' I asked. I was too tired to be angry.

"'Because I have to,' he replied. 'It has got to be whisky. Can't be anything else.'

"'What the hell do you mean by that?' I demanded.

"'Nothing,' he answered. 'Nothing at all.'

"He waved a dismissive end to the conversation with an unsteady hand and began staggering off in the direction of his home. I saw him in, loosened his belt and took off his shoes and collapsed him face down over the end of his bed, and there I left him to come round and finish cleaning himself up in his own time. Aunt Gwendoline, do you want me to stop now?"

She had dropped her forehead on to her hand and shivered again, although this time not with cold but with fatigue.

"I don't know that I can do it, Mother," she muttered silently. "I'm getting old. I must rest."

But the hand on her shoulder still held her, more tenderly but still insistent. She heard Gerard repeat his question.

"No, my dear boy," she replied. "I was just resting. You must continue. Please do so."

Chapter 28

"I arrived home just a Sue was finishing breakfast," Gerard resumed cautiously.

He was not sure he should tell any more of his story for the moment and it was only his great-aunt asking him to that led him to continue.

"She poured me a cup of tea but said nothing. We just sat in silence, tiredly looking at each other across the table. The only thought in my mind was that I must not tell her about what had happened.

"'Well, how was he?' she asked eventually.

"'Not good,' I replied. 'But I think you're right. I'll have to call Alcoholics Anonymous and get hold of someone to give him some professional help. He's drinking himself into oblivion, and he's drinking whisky which he doesn't like. He'll end up self-destructing if it goes on. And you are right, I can't handle him on my own. Even drunk he retains the same charm and friendliness he has always had and I find it very difficult to be firm with him. Upset, sad, angry with what he has been through, yes, but I cannot sustain any anger towards him to the point where I can give him a sustained telling off.'

"'You care for him very much, don't you?' she commented.

"'He's a friend, Sue, and we have done some good work together. And Janet was a friend too, to both of us, so I feel some sort of obligation to try and care for him in her absence.'

"She cleared away part of the dirty dishes and half busied herself for a few seconds putting them in the sink. She then turned back and leaned across the table to me.

"'I care about you too, Ger,' she said. 'But I am frightened about what you are getting into. Get on to Alcoholics Anonymous or whoever you have to, and do it today. Then hand Mark over to them and don't go near him anymore. I'm frightened, Ger. There is something about him that frightens me. The whole situation frightens me.'

"I remember thinking that 'frightened' was very strong word for her to use and it puzzled me. Drunk or sober, Mark was never frightening. Violence was not in him, and when legless he was just a grinning, charming, friendly, vomiting nuisance.

"'I'll think about it,' I replied.

"'Don't think about it, Ger,' she insisted. 'Do it!'

"I neither saw nor heard from Mark for a couple of days, and then on the third night we got another telephone call.

"'No!' screamed Sue the instant she heard the ring. 'Let him go. Don't answer it.'

"I did answer it, of course, and scrambled to put on some clothes and find my car keys. Sue rolled over and curled herself up under the bedclothes.

"'Don't go, Ger, don't go,' she kept repeating.

"She was sobbing. I tried to reassure her and hold her for a few moments but she would not bend to me. She lay rigid under the blankets in a tight ball, the corner of the sheet screwed up and pushed into her mouth with her fist. It was as if she had woken from a nightmare and was still terrified by the images of it, and she began shaking too hard for her to tell me what it was about. All she would say was 'don't go, please Ger, don't go'.

"'Don't worry,' I told her. 'Nothing is going to happen.'

"I arrived at the police station a short while later and was approaching the desk sergeant when a voice called out to me.

"'Gerard, I'm pleased you've come. Could I have a word with you? It won't take long.'

"It was Sergeant Chak. He had clearly been waiting for me and, before I could answer him, he led me into one of the side rooms where we would not be disturbed. I was pleased to see him again, although puzzled that he should want to see me.

"'Gerard, how much do you know about Dr Brinsley's drinking?' he began.

"'Only that he's having a rough time of it. I'm assuming it is part of his way of dealing with his wife's murder and the failure of our wonderful criminal justice system to extract any penalty from her murderers.'

"I answered a little bitterly then realised I was being unfair. Sergeant Chak and the police generally had done a wonderful job of identifying Janet's killers and collecting the evidence for their trial.

"'I'm on the point of calling Alcoholics Anonymous to see if I can get some help for him,' I continued more reasonably. 'I know he is being a bit of a nuisance to you people and I'm sorry about that. You've been more than understanding.'

"He nodded, and paused as if thinking about what to say next.

"'It's a bit more than that,' he replied, 'and if it doesn't stop, he could be in for some very serious trouble.'

"I looked at him. The delivery of the warning had not been threatening but there was no question he was deadly serious.

"'Your desk sergeant did tell me there was a limit to how far you could stretch the procedures to shield Mark from the consequences of his behaviour,' I replied.

"'That is certainly true,' he replied. 'But I think it might be advisable for you to have some additional information. Gerard, what I am about to tell you is strictly off record and must go no further. I am stepping outside my authority in telling you this, and if it becomes known that I have spoken to you, I could be in serious trouble. It is absolutely confidential. Do you understand what I am saying?'

"I nodded.

"'Have you wondered why we have not yet charged your friend Dr Brinsley with any offence?' he asked.

"'I assume it was because you and your colleagues have been extremely tolerant and understanding of his circumstances,' I answered.

"'In part,' he agreed. 'What happened to Janet Brinsley did shock us all, as did the failure of the court to convict Billy and George Crater. But you are missing my point. We can be

111

flexible within fairly wide limits when faced with what are really minor incidents of affray, but the public is not generally quite so tolerant. In particular, the owners and managers of businesses that are disturbed if not damaged by the sort of behaviour Mark Brinsley has engaged in tend to take a very dim view of it. In general, they have no hesitation in lodging formal complaints against the offender and filling out the forms to prefer charges against them. When that happens, we have no option but to act.

"Now, when you consider that over the past month or so Mark Brinsley has been spending his time parading up and down the main night club drag of this city, entering establishments and being abusive to the staff, tipping up tables and generally upsetting other law-abiding customers, breaking more than the occasional drinking glass, bottle and bar mirror, and on several occasions creating a fracas to the point of fighting with the club security, you do have to wonder why no complaint has been lodged against him.'

"I was aghast. 'What? Mark has done all that? I had no idea. I thought he was just getting drunk. Are you sure? No, that's a silly question, of course you're sure. It just doesn't sound like anything I would ever have imagined him doing. Has there been much damage?'

"'Yes, there has been damage, and in a couple of cases quite a bit,' he answered. 'And no, in all cases there has been no complaint, the damage has been covered by the owners of the establishments concerned and Dr Brinsley has not had to cough up any money to pay for it.'

"'So, there have been no official complaints and no bills for damages in spite of all the trouble he has caused?' I repeated. 'Why? It doesn't make sense.'

"'Exactly,' he nodded. 'You are beginning to see my point.'

"He let me have a few seconds to digest the information.

"'It gets more interesting,' he continued. 'If Mark Brinsley was simply intent on getting himself plastered to try and erase the memory of what happened to his wife, and there are a number of us here who would understand that and be as accommodating as we can with him, then any old pub or drinking hole would suffice. But Mark's watering holes have not been randomly selected.'

"'What on earth do you mean?' I asked.

"'Let me explain. Criminal organisations generally run a line of legitimate businesses as a front to hide their illegal activities from public view and provide them with a means of laundering the money they make from those activities. The Crater family, as we know, is one of the biggest crime families in this city and their illegal activities include all the usual lines of drugs, bent gambling, prostitution, people trafficking, fraud and all the nasty offshoots of all those activities plus a heap of others, which is why they have been on the books of the Major Crime Division for a long time. The front they use for all this illegal activity is their legitimate clubs and drinking dens found along the main nightclub drag of this city. And it is in these specific establishments that your pal Mark has been getting drunk.'

"'Oh, shit!' was all I could think to say.

"Sorry, Aunt Gwendoline, but I suddenly came out in a cold sweat at the implications of what Sergeant Chak was telling me.

"'Let me understand this,' I asked. 'Mark has been getting drunk and getting into fights in nightclubs owned by the Craters? He must have lost his mind. What on earth is he up to?'

"'That's what we want to know,' he answered. 'And if you have any information that might help us answer that question then give it to me and give it to me quickly. Let me make this quite clear to you, Gerard. Mark Brinsley is being a problem to the Craters. They have clearly instructed their club managers to hold off from taking any official action against him following his rampages, probably because they fear that, if they do, some junior journalist going through the court proceedings will connect Mark Brinsley's name with theirs and Janet Brinsley's murder will be back on the front pages of the newspapers all over again. They do not want that. They only just got away with her murder and they want to keep it that way. A low profile is what they are after because that is the best way for them to stay off our radar.'

"I was beginning to feel sick.

"'But it cannot go on,' he continued. 'Mark's drinking binges are becoming increasingly public, and so the possibility arises that the same junior journalist will sooner or later notice them anyway. And if that happens, the link between the Brinsley and Crater names will be made and banner headlines reminding the world of Janet Brinsley's murder become likely. So, the Craters have a problem. They are damned if they take action against Mark and damned if they don't. If they do take action, they put themselves in the spotlight, and if they don't take action and he continues being a nuisance to them, he does it for them. Either way they have got to stop him causing trouble.'

"'You think Mark might have realised that, and is deliberately getting drunk in the Crater's night clubs to generate publicity?' I asked.

"'It has crossed our mind,' he agreed. 'But if that is his game, then it is a very, very dangerous one. I cannot stress too heavily that the Craters are an extremely nasty crowd. When they have a problem, they do not usually come to the police with it, they deal with it themselves. And when they do that problem always disappears. It might be a few days or weeks before the disappearance is noticed, but when it does there will be no evidence of a trail to anywhere, no body, no crime scene, no weapon or means of dispatch, nothing, and certainly nothing to point a finger in the direction of the Craters. It will be as if the problem had never existed.'

"I almost threw up on the spot.

"'I can only think that Mark doesn't realise what he is getting into,' I protested. 'As far as he is concerned, Billy and George Crater murdered his wife and got away with it and he is angry. Getting drunk is his way of dealing with it and gravitating towards the Craters' establishments is a natural course for him because that's where his mind is focussed.'

"Even to me my words sounded like wishful thinking.

"'I really cannot imagine Mark is up to anything more than impotent rage,' I persisted. 'He has never been violent. I cannot imagine he would have even the first idea of how to look after himself in a real fight.'

"'By all accounts, he has been easy to handle by the professionals,' smiled Sergeant Chak. 'But that is not the point. The Craters will see his kicking up a fuss in their establishments as the threat to their peace and quiet, however trivially he may be able to damage them physically. It is the threat of publicity they will want to stop.'

"I thought of Sue and her premonition and gulped in a deep breath.

"'Don't go near him,' she had said. 'I'm frightened, Ger. The whole situation frightens me.'

"I was beginning to think she was right.

"'Thanks for telling me, Sergeant. I'm sure Mark has no idea what he is doing. He really is a decent bloke, just someone who has temporarily gone off the rails.'

"Sergeant Chak nodded. 'I hope so Gerard, but stop him before the Craters run out of patience. We will eventually get them, but in the meantime, we have no special brief to watch over Dr Brinsley so there is not much we can do to look after him. And the last thing we want at any time is a misguided amateur cutting across our investigations. So stop him for all our sakes, Gerard, and remember this conversation never happened.'

"'Of course not, Sergeant,' I nodded in return. 'And thanks.'"

Chapter 29

Aunt Gwendoline felt cold again and her sitting room seemed darker than it had been earlier. Gerard was still talking but she was having difficulty concentrating on what he was saying.

"I collected Mark and his pocket contents from the desk sergeant, a procedure that was becoming uncomfortably familiar to me, and then I walked him home," he recounted.

She brought forward in her mind the image of the skyfire and its falling stars and focussed her tired brain on that.

"I gave him a good tongue-lashing and this time I really ripped into him with the gist if not the actual words of what Sergeant Chak had told me."

She tried to convince herself that what she was thinking was nothing more than an old woman's imagination. All nothing and nonsense and of no consequence whatsoever as she silently wished it to be. There were six stars originally. The first one was for Janet Brinsley which left five and then the five separated into three and two, and the three burned more brightly and died before their time. Three stars for three friends, Gerard, Mark Brinsley and Susan, except that Susan is not among them. All three stars are men. Gerard, Mark Brinsley and Sergeant Chak perhaps.

"I don't know how much of my telling-off registered with Mark and I don't believe it did much good anyway. He just sat quietly and smiled at me, still half cut from the booze of the previous night. All he said at the end of it was 'thanks, Gerry', so I left."

She wanted to believe that everything around her was perfectly normal and reasonable. Gerard was sitting in his chair opposite, talking away and obviously fit and safe, but the weight on her shoulder was telling her all was not well.

"I have to admit I was more than a little scared walking home and I didn't dare tell Sue what had happened," he finished.

"Gerard, my dear boy," she interrupted him. "It is very late and way past my bed time. Interesting though your story is, I do hope you will forgive me if I call a halt to it now. I don't know that my old brain can take in any more for one day. It is such a pity because there is so much more to tell. Do you think you could come to tea tomorrow and finish it for me? You did say it was holiday time at the university, didn't you? Would you be able to come?"

"Of course," he replied without hesitation. "Of course I will, although there really isn't much more to tell."

He smiled at his elderly aunt and was mildly shocked to see how tired she looked, and he immediately felt guilty for keeping her up so late yet again.

"Good," she confirmed. "Because I have still to find out why my late sister Alice's vase came to be so decidedly broken."

"I will tell you that tomorrow," he smiled.

He shrugged and gathered his coat ready for leaving.

"You have been wonderfully patient listening to my ramblings. I do appreciate it, Aunt Gwendoline. It has been good for me to be able to unload so much that has been on my mind. I can only say that everything turned out all right in the end so there is no need to worry. Have a good night, and sweet dreams."

He gave her a gentle hug and waved to her from her garden gate before striding off with his usual confidence up the road and into the night, grinning and shaking his head as he went still bemused by his great-aunt's focussing on the tiny matter of his smashed Chatterwood vase.

Behind her solidly locked front door Aunt Gwendoline leaned against its frame and looked tiredly up into the face of her oak-cased clock.

"Oh dear, our dad," she sighed to it. "I don't know that I have the stamina any more. I am an old woman so how am I going to stop a family of gangsters harming our Gerard?"

117

The clock looked back at her, firm and proud, a constant in her life that had always given her strength. There was hope. The skyfire had not reappeared and that the mysterious engine noise that had disturbed them earlier had not returned. But it did not have to be nonsense. Premonitions were not of the present. They were of the future. She looked down into the quizzical eyes of Rani and managed a smile.

"It is all nonsense and I shouldn't worry myself into so much of a knot over it, should I, Rani?"

The dog swished her tail stump on the carpet and gazed back at her in understanding.

She shuffled into her sitting room to clear away the tea things and caught the aspidistra on the edge of her vision.

"There is no need for you to look so smug," she fired at it. "I knew there was something not right about Miss Susan for our Gerard. They were not suited to each other, and to her credit she too had reached that conclusion and was going to leave him. She even got as far as putting her clothes out on the bed ready for packing after Mark Brinsley first went home following his wife's murder. But she stayed."

The plant did not respond.

"Of course, our Gerard does not know she was going to leave him but then that is not surprising," she muttered, tidying the tea tray. "In spite of how much I have tried with him he can be quite blind to what is happening around him. Give him a potsherd or something from five thousand years ago and he can create whole vistas of cultures that nobody has heard of for millennia. He can see all that. But give him the present, living, world and he is utterly hopeless. He is a worry. But should I tell him that Susan was going to leave him regardless, do you think?"

Not a leaf flickered.

"It doesn't really matter," she sighed. "But it must have been very upsetting for Miss Susan to have Janet Brinsley's murder cut across whatever plans she had to leave. She could not have expected that. And after it happened she then stayed with our Gerard even though there was a lot in the situation that was very frightening to her. She has courage, that young woman, and decency too. She must have cared for him very much to stay with him under those circumstances, so we will not think too badly of her will we, Rani? But I do wonder what it was that especially frightened her."

She picked up the tea tray and gave the aspidistra a final glare.

"I know you have a hand in this, Mother," she addressed it irritably. "And as usual you will not make it easy for me, will you? If you are going to ask me to look after the family, you might give me a little assistance occasionally. Why did Miss Susan break our Alice's vase?"

The plant remained doggedly uncommunicative.

"Come along, Rani," she sighed again. "I am too tired for any more thought tonight."

She left the tray in the kitchen and dragged her feet up the stairs to bed.

"Goodnight, Rani," she called out into the darkness as the bedside light was extinguished.

"Goodnight, our dad," she added softly as her oak-cased clock reminded her of the extreme lateness of the hour.

Her thoughts paused briefly on the aspidistra in its ornamental pot in the sitting room, but after the fleeting moment she turned over and ignored it. She certainly was not going to wish it a pleasant night's sleep.

Chapter 30

She was walking along a path. It was a sunny and hot afternoon and the path was packed earth worn smooth by the tread of workmen's boots on their way to and from Felderby Pit and made rough by the stones that poked up through its surface. There was a ditch on one side lined by a hedge and on the other side was the quilt-work of allotments where the men of Low Felderby dug and planted and harvested their vegetables in their spare time. Mother was walking ahead on the path, panting a little and sweating. In the crook of her arm she cradled some freshly pulled greens and in her other hand she carried a tin bucket half full of potatoes. Alice was learning her colours at school and was running back and forth with each new flower she picked from the hedgerow.

"Look, our Gwen, this one's a pretty blue, and this one's a red one and this one is white."

From her toddler's height some of the allotments appeared as a forest of cabbages, early cauliflowers and Brussels sprouts, but where the path humped she could see over these to the flags of torn newspaper fluttering on the tangles of pea sticks with the last of their summer crop. In some places she could see even further, to the crossed poles that supported house high stands of scarlet flowered runner beans, but mostly all she could see were the closer rows of carrots, onions and potatoes.

"Come along, our Gwen. You must keep up. I can't carry you as well."

Mother's tone was sharp, but then she was always sharp when they went up to the allotments. Some of the allotments had gone to weeds, but not her dad's. It was Uncle Jack and Granddad that tended her dad's allotment, keeping it dug and tidy with its crops because Dad was away at the War. At the start of the War it had been pronounced unpatriotic of an employer to turn a man out of his home if he was away doing his duty in the trenches instead of his job at the Pit or the Works, so his house remained for his family to live in and for him to return to, and one way or another his allotment remained productive. It had been Uncle Jack who had dug the potatoes and left them under a sack for collection as needed.

But if the man was killed, or wounded so badly he could not work, then his allotment went to weeds. Soon after, his family left the village and a new one arrived. Mother put her head down and walked more quickly past the allotments that had gone to weeds.

"Keep hold, our Gwen," Mother snapped. "You keep a tight hold and don't fall. I can't carry any more than I'm doing."

She sought Mother's side opposite the swinging bucket and gripped the skirts more firmly and it was her young ears that first heard the sound coming up behind them. It was very faint, a low purring, growling sound like a dog announcing its presence to an intruder, only more mechanical and not quite natural. She sensed its threat and turned to see what it was but she could make out nothing against the brightness of the sky. Mother had not yet heard it and neither had sister Alice who was occupied in her flower collecting.

"Alice!" screamed Mother.

Potatoes and greens scattered themselves across the path and the darkness of Mother's shawl enveloped her. She heard sister Alice yell and then Mother's arms wrapped tightly around her and she was carried falling and helpless into nowhere to land somewhere with a jolt. She fought the shawl that clamped her hard against Mother's shoulder and threatened to deny her breath while Alice screamed and Mother howled back in terror at the roaring, growling, fearful thing that split the sky above them. And then in an instant it was gone, its roar leaving them as suddenly as it had come, fading away to nothing in the distance.

"It's all right, my pet. It's all right. You keep hold now. I've got you. If only your dad were here."

121

Mother hugged and trembled and cried and rocked them both. Sister Alice mewled in fear but around them again there was only peace and the protective sides of the muddy ditch and the clear blue sky above.

On her blanket beside her mistress' bed Rani looked up quizzically into the dark in the direction of the cry that had brought her to her feet. Her mistress was face down in her pillow and murmuring something and bedclothes had wrapped themselves restrictingly around her as she twisted in her dream. Rani put a paw against the blankets but there were no commands she could understand. She sat quivering and alert, watching in the dark while the dream rewound itself in her mistress' mind.

It was a hot, sunny afternoon, and the path was packed earth with stones poking through it. There was a ditch on one side lined by a hedge and on the other side were the allotments where the men of Low Felderby grew their vegetables. Dad was away at the War and Mother was walking ahead carrying an armful of greens and a tin bucket half full of potatoes that Uncle Jack had dug. Mother was sweating and anxious as she always was when up at the allotments. Sister Alice was skipping ahead, collecting wild flowers from the hedgerow. And then she heard the low, menacing sound, far off but coming up behind them.

Mother screamed. Bucket, potatoes and greens flew everywhere, and Mother's shawl was flung over her head as she was carried bodily down into the ditch where sister Alice was already howling and shaking in fear. But this time she was prepared for the tumble, and she raised her arms so that the shawl should not cover her face. She heard the roar split the sky above her and she felt the cold as a monstrous black shadow raced fleetingly across them. The shadow was sharp and solid, not like one made by a cloud, and Alice was crying and Mother was rocking her and reassuring her.

"Keep hold now, our Gwen. I've got you. It's all right."

She herself felt no fear as she listened to the shadow's voice fading away into the distance and she twisted around, struggling against Mother's protective hug.

"Don't let go, our Gwen. Keep a hold. It'll be all right. Stay with me."

But she did let go. She twisted and stretched to release herself, and she reached up to the monster that was creating the shadow. She let out a laugh as she realised she was suddenly free, flying up and away, streaming along in the clear sky behind the snarling beast that had frightened them all.

It was a flying machine, the first any of them had ever seen, and she thrilled to the wonder of it. She flew higher so she could look down on it as it raced over the ground, dragging its shadow beneath it.

"It's one of ours," she called out as she saw the red, white and blue decals of the Royal Flying Corps on its upper wing. "There's no need to fear. It's one of ours."

She laughed joyfully at the sight of the harmless toy-thing, and she raced to follow its fragile grace as it threw itself through the air. She flew down, dropping behind it and to one side of it, and decided to come up to it mischievously as it had tried to do with her and Mother and sister Alice. It took no effort and in no time at all she was broadside on to it with the wind rushing in her face.

The pilot looked pleasantly dashing, slim and youthful with his white silk scarf streaming out cheerily behind him. She decided he might even be handsome. He had a broad grin on his face that stretched his smartly clipped moustache, and a deep scar that raked across his forehead. It was a ferocious scar. It started at his left eyebrow just where it joined the bridge of his nose and it slanted backwards and to the side until it disappeared into his hairline. She had only ever seen scars like it on men who had survived accidents at the Pit, and like those scars it could only have been a signature dashed in an instant upon the line that separates life from oblivion.

She raised a hand to wave to the pilot but hesitated as he turned to look at her. His grin was not one of joy. It was only *a mechanical grin sculpted on his face by the wind in the cockpit pulling at his cheeks. It did not reach his eyes and it was his eyes that held her. They were like her dad's eyes as she had seen them when he had first come home from the War. They saw her, but they looked at her as if through a film that allowed through no emotion. They offered her no threat or greeting but only noted her presence as an item in the stream of an existence that flowed before them. Her dad's eyes had looked like that until, months later, he had begun to believe in life again.*

She dropped back, and as she did so the pilot reached down into his cockpit and held up a bunch of papers like the pages of a notebook but without a cover. There was writing on the loose sheets, although she could not see what it was. He waved them vigorously at her with his left hand as if determined that she should see them. He spoke no words to her but there was a message in his gesture.

"I've got it," he signalled to her. "I've got it all worked out."

And with that he turned his head forward and raced off. She did not follow him and in the next instant she was back in Mother's arms being smothered and rocked and soothed.

"It'll be all right, my pet. Your dad will be back soon. Please God let him be back soon. You'll see, it'll be all right. I'll not let you go."

Mother was crying and sister Alice was sobbing, and she looked round at the damp, gritty walls of the ditch and the stagnant mud clogging around Mother's boots, and suddenly she too felt afraid.

She woke with a cry, her hand grasping in the darkness for the switch on her bedside light and Rani standing with her forepaws on the bed covers whimpering anxiously.

Chapter 31

Aunt Gwendoline decided she was feeling remarkably fresh and alert in spite of her disturbed night. The afternoon tea was Darjeeling, the sandwiches smoked ham and cress and the cakes were fussy angel cakes full of fresh cream from one of her favourite bakeries in town. There were also some chocolate biscuits which Gerard was devouring down to half their number.

"So, continue with your story," she prompted him. "Dr Brinsley was becoming habitually drunk and Sergeant Chak had told you he was doing so in clubs and bars owned by the Crater gangland family, after which you saw him home."

Gerard nodded. "I didn't dare tell Sue about what Sergeant Chak had told me, about how Mark was being a nuisance to the Craters," he mumbled around a mouthful of cream. "She was in a nervous enough state when I got home and I couldn't in all conscience scare her right out of her mind. She was standing in the hallway when I arrived back, looking at Aunt Alice's vase. It seemed almost strange that it should still be there with all the turmoil going on in our lives. Sue didn't say anything and I went and lay down on the bed for a couple of hours before heading off to my office at the university.

"In hindsight, it was not a good idea not to tell Sue what Sergeant Chak had said to me," he reflected. "Because it was less than forty-eight hours before Mark and the Craters were back in our life again. Sue and I were asleep in bed when we were both woken by the sound of a car engine revving its way along our road. We both sensed something was wrong as the car's tyres screeched in a tight turn and the noise of the motor drew up outside our house. There was a brief sound of running footsteps followed by a short hammering on our front door, then a car door slammed and the engine roared away again. It was just after one thirty.

"Sue was immediately hysterical. Lights went on in a couple of the neighbours' windows but it was clearly us who had been the focus of the attention.

"'Don't open it,' she screamed as I went to unlock the door.

"I looked out, and at first I could see nothing except a couple of neighbours standing in their front doors in their dressing gowns. Then I heard a faint groan in the darkness and made out what looked like a heap of old clothes trying to get up. It was Mark. He was bloody about the nose and face and had obviously been damaged in other places too. He was vomiting furiously. His clothes were muddy and he tried to stand, but he couldn't manage it and collapsed back on the ground groaning loudly.

"'Call an ambulance,' I shouted to Sue.

"I tried to calm Mark as best I could and Sue brought out my coat and some blankets to cover him.

"'I'll get some clothes on and then you can get dressed while I watch him,' she said. 'You'll need to go with him in the ambulance and I'll follow in your car.' I was surprised how calm she was.

"I had just finished pulling on some clothes when an ambulance and the police arrived. I told them the victim's name was Mark Brinsley and the police officers nodded knowingly and reported the information straight away. They then started knocking on neighbours' doors, much to the annoyance of those who had only just got back to bed. Nobody had seen anything, of course. Meanwhile the ambulance people loaded Mark on to a stretcher and drove off with lights flashing and sirens waking up anyone who might have missed the excitement.

"I did not go with Mark in the ambulance. Sue drove me to the hospital about half an hour later. I was pleased to have her with me even though we travelled in silence. By the time we arrived, Mark had been processed and dealt with through Accident and Emergency and was on a trolley waiting to be wheeled to a bed in one of the observation wards. Various tests had been ordered but Mark himself was asleep or unconscious, presumably sedated, and was looking a lot cleaner for all the attention he had received. He still smelled strongly of whisky but even so he managed to give the appearance of the innocent asleep in angelic repose. It was unbelievable how untroubled he looked. One of the doctors came and gave us what sounded like an extraordinarily long list of significant injuries he had sustained, and ended by saying they would know more after the radiologist had examined the x-rays. Sue had still not said anything.

"'Let's find a coffee,' I suggested, and under the unforgiving lights of the hospital cafeteria I told her what Sergeant Chak had told me the previous day."

Chapter 32

"'Why didn't you tell me earlier?' she asked calmly.

"'Because I didn't want to scare you,' I replied.

"'Scare me?' she repeated, and I could see she was very near to tears. 'I am already scared, Ger, scared out of my mind. What do you think I have been trying to tell you these past few weeks? I've been scared witless. I knew something like this was going to happen. Ger, what have you dragged us into? You realise you're next, don't you?'

"'Don't exaggerate, Sue, I'm nothing to the Craters. I am simply Mark's friend.'

"'Then why did they dump him on our front doorstep?' she demanded.

"'Because they are looking to you to help them solve their little problem. Hello, Gerard, Sue.' Sergeant Chak sat down beside us with his coffee. 'Well, I did tell you that Mark Brinsley was due for a warning,' he smiled ruefully. 'And now they've given him one.'

"'It was quite a beating,' I agreed.

"'No it wasn't. It was just a light dusting.'

"'It looked pretty severe to me,' I argued.

"'That's because you have never seen a really good kicking delivered by the likes of the Billy Crater. If they had really intended to do your friend damage he would at this moment be in intensive care fighting for his life, not in an observation ward. He would have bones broken all over his body, his hands would have been mashed, his skull fractured, his spleen would be ruptured and most likely his liver as well, and his kidneys would have been split open from the outside. He would have been lucky to come out of it only paraplegic. Believe me, he got a light dusting, that is all. And he was not dumped out in the middle of a park to freeze to death overnight. He was brought to a place where it was known he would get immediate care and attention, namely to your doorstep. I'm sorry, Gerard, but he has now received the warning that I was afraid was on its way to him. He had better take notice of it.'

"'And we're part of it,' said Sue.

"'Only indirectly,' he replied. 'You are obviously Mark's friends and so by leaving him with you the Craters are telling you that if you don't look after him, then next time they will. It's a friendly gesture on their part.'

"'That's not how I would describe it,' I answered. 'It's bloody scary.'

"'And it's not over yet,' Sue added quietly.

"'Why do you say that?' asked Sergeant Chak.

"She did not answer.

"'Was it Billy Crater who beat him up?' I asked.

"'No. It was just a couple of employees from the Purple Heaven nightclub. Your friend tanked up in one of the Craters' other clubs before going on to the Purple Heaven where he demanded to see the boss. The bouncers recognised him, of course, but they had their orders to treat him gently so after some argument they called the manager.

"'That's not who I want,' your friend argued, 'I said the boss, the man in charge, Mr Crater no less. I want to see Mr Crater.'

"When informed that Mr Crater was busy and not available, your friend insisted that he wanted to make an appointment.

"'What business do you have with Mr Crater?' he was asked.

"'That is between me and Mr Crater,' he replied. 'I want him to look me in the eye while I tell him what pigs his sons are and what they did to my wife. He owes me that. That's what I want, to have him look me in the eye while he hears it from me what his sons did, and he owes me the opportunity of telling him. You tell him that. And if he doesn't let me tell him to his face then I'll keep on telling the whole world, and everyone will know what cowardly pigs his sons are. You tell him that too. And after I've told him, then I'll go away. But not before. Once I've told him to his face and seen him look me in the eyes while I tell him, then I'll go away. So, make sure you tell him that too. That's what business I have with Mr Crater, now when is my appointment?'

"And with that he asked for another drink, which was refused. By this time he was shouting, getting very red in the face, and threatening to upset the enjoyment of all the other customers in the club, whereupon the manager nodded to the bouncers and Mark was taken out the back door, lightly dusted over and delivered to your doorstep.

"'You have very good information about what happened,' commented Sue.

"'The Craters are of special interest to us,' he replied.

"'Is anybody going to be charged with Mark's assault?' I asked.

"'Our information isn't that good.'

"Sue put her head down into her coffee and I saw her shiver. 'I'll go and wait in the car,' she said, and drifted off.

"'None of this sounds the remotest bit like Mark to me,' I shrugged after a pause. 'It's just not like him to be aggressive and confrontational, at least not under normal circumstances. Tell me, Sergeant, why wasn't the evidence to convict Billy and George Crater allowed in court? That's the issue that's bugging Mark. If he could only have seen some accounting for what they did to his wife, he wouldn't be like this now. He feels immeasurably let down by the entire system that is supposed to deliver us a sense of justice when we have been wronged, especially wronged like he has been. You seemed so certain about getting a conviction. All the evidence was there, you said, and it was irrefutable according to what you told us. And we believed you. So why did it all fall apart?'

"'It's a sore point,' he answered, shifting uncomfortably. "'You're right, we did have the evidence, good, solid forensic evidence, not based on the testimony of frightened witnesses. We had enough evidence to convict them both twice over on rape, assault, murder plus a whole lot of lesser charges if we wanted to.'

"'So what went wrong?'

"'The decision was made high up near the end of our investigations that the case should be handed over to the Major Crime Division, and in court the defence counsels were able to argue that, in the handover, the chain of evidence was broken. Major Crime were not able to demonstrate that the evidence they wanted to present against the Craters was the same evidence that we had collected at the crime scene and handed over to them. We don't agree. As far as we are concerned we can identify every scrap of it through every step of the way into court, but the Prosecution was not able to carry the argument against the massively expensive briefs the Craters employed. As a result, none of the evidence could be used.'

"'In other words, someone goofed,' I summarised.

"'My team did not goof. We were rock solid,' he responded angrily. 'As I said, it's a sore point. We don't like losing either.'

"'You're not on duty at the moment, are you?' I said to him.

"'No,' he confirmed. 'I got a call from one of my team at the station and came straight here.'

"'Your wife couldn't have been very happy about that,' I suggested.

"I was thinking of Sue waiting in our car.

"'Divorced,' he replied. 'It's an occupational hazard. But I do have two lovely kids and their mother and I still get on very well, so there's no conflict. It was just that being a policeman's wife is a job she couldn't live with, so it was better we lived apart.'

"I did not have any real argument with him. Right from the start he had been hugely supportive and a friend, and I could see he was as frustrated as we were by the turn of events.

"'Thanks, Sergeant,' I sighed. 'Thanks for coming in.'"

Chapter 33

"I went up to the ward to find Mark clean and comfortable in his hospital bed, and conscious.

"'I did tell you,' I began. 'I don't know whether you remember it because you were still more than half cut at the time, but I did tell you. Sergeant Chak said you were headed for a beating and now you've had one. So, now will you listen? It's got to stop, Mark. You can't go on getting drunk and worrying the Craters like this. You were lucky that this time they decided not to bury you without trace, but next time they might think differently. And it's not just you that's involved, it's me and Sue too. You are putting us at risk too simply because we are your friends, or trying to be, and that's not right. Take the warning, Mark. Take it and let this drunken madness go. It's not going to bring Janet back and the police have not given up on the Craters. They will eventually get them for something. So, let them get on with their job and you get back to your own life, for all our sakes.'

"He didn't look at me. He just remained still and quiet, propped up on his mound of pillows, but then I suppose he was probably stiff and sore all over. All he could manage was a smile and it was not an easy smile given the bruising to his face and the stitches in his upper lip, but I'm convinced it was real.

"'You're right, Gerry,' he wheezed at last, trying not to move his mouth too much. 'It is time to bring it all to an end.'

"It seemed a very strange way of putting it but it was the answer I wanted. Aunt Gwendoline, are you all right?"

Aunt Gwendoline tensed in her chair. The silver and black skyfire was shimmering in front of her, exploding and burning, breaking and crackling silently in the middle of her sitting room in the space between her and her grand-nephew.

She could feel its heat and she was afraid she might pass out as she watched three bright stars fly from it, waving and flailing in agony, getting brighter as they fell until they seemed to explode silently in mid-air and disappear into blackness before reaching the ground. At that moment the noise of a biplane screamed overhead and cracked the air around her. She winced with the pain of it, the shock of it hammering her into her chest, and she panted momentarily with the fear it spread in its wake. And then it was gone and all was quiet, and she became aware of Rani standing up against her, whimpering and pawing at her leg. She put her hand down to reassure her and heard Gerard's voice once again.

"Aunt Gwendoline? Aunt Gwendoline?"

"Yes, I'm all right. Would you be a dear boy and get a glass of water for me?"

"Yes, of course."

He hurried out to the kitchen. His hand shook and the glass rattled against the tap as he filled it. He was having difficulty breathing too. He had never seen her in such a state. He rushed back to the sitting room and was relieved to see she was still breathing and not collapsed or fallen out of her chair.

"Thank you, dear boy," she said as she took the glass.

Her colour returned, and with it the cosiness and security of her sitting room. Gerard allowed himself to take a deep breath.

"Aunt Gwendoline, are you sure you are all right?" he asked. "I kept you up very late last night and the night before. I can finish my story another day if you'd rather. There is not much more to tell and it will keep. It's all just history now anyway."

"I am quite all right," she reassured him. "It was just one of my turns. Old people get them, you know, and by the time you have reached my age you feel yourself perfectly entitled to the occasional dizzy spell if you feel like one. But we get over them. You must finish your story for me. My late sister Alice's vase is still intact and I need to know the exact circumstances under which it met its end. I insist on it."

133

Gerard watched her cautiously, and helped her as she rearranged herself in her chair. "Very well, if you are sure you are not too tired," he queried.

"Continue," she instructed.

Chapter 34

"There really is not much more to tell," he sighed. "I drove home with Sue and she was very quiet. Apart from a 'how was he?' she said nothing more for the rest of the night. I told her I had read Mark the riot act again and that he had said he really was going to behave himself from now on. She didn't believe it and I don't think I did either, but I didn't feel that there was anything more I could do. With Mark tucked up in hospital we could at least get a couple of hours uninterrupted sleep before facing work the next day, and probably get a few nights of completely undisturbed rest while he recovered.

"It was not to be. Unknown to us Mark discharged himself from hospital that morning around breakfast time. I only found out when I went to visit him on my way home after work and was told by the ward sister he was no longer there. I was surprised he was able to move after the pasting he had been given. I called his home but only got his answering machine, and then I called Sue. She was not pleased to say the least.

"We were both totally worn out from the disturbances of the previous night and so, after an early dinner, we went to bed. We were sound asleep by nine o'clock and it was just after midnight when we were both woken by the insistent hammering and ringing of our front door bell. We had both been in very deep sleep and had taken some waking. Sue sensed straight away that it was Mark.

"'No, no, no!' she screamed and began pounding at the pillows. 'Don't answer it. Don't open the door. Tell him to go away. No, Ger, no!'

"'It may not be him,' I answered. 'I have to go and see who it is.'

"'It is him,' she shrieked. 'It is, it is. Don't answer it. Don't let him in.'

"Tears were pouring down her face.

"It was Mark and as soon as I saw him I knew he had gone straight back to his drinking. He was just managing to hold himself upright on the door frame and was reeking of whisky as usual.

"'Hello, Gerry,' he smiled at me. 'Sorry to trouble you but I didn't think I would be able to make it home to my own place. Hello, Sue.'

"'Get him out of here,' she shouted. 'Call the police, call Alcoholics Anonymous, call anybody but get him out of here. Get him away from here.'

"Mark stood swaying on the threshold smiling drunkenly as if pleased with himself, and even managed to look hurt by Sue's response.

"'Mark, you're drunk,' I said. 'Stay there while I put some clothes on and I'll drive you home.'

"'Don't think I can make it home,' he slurred. 'That's why I came here.'

"With that, he slid down the door frame and ended up sprawled full length in the hallway. Sue looked terrified but at the same time furious enough to explode.

"'Sorry, Sue,' he called up to her from the floor. 'It's the legs. They just gave way. They always do. But this is the last time. I won't be any more trouble, not after this, I promise. This really is the last time.'

"She stared down at him and then at me, and then on the verge of tears she stormed back into the bedroom and slammed the door very firmly behind her. I had the feeling that if she had been able to lock it and bolt it, she would have done so. I dragged Mark inside.

"'Gerry, it's all right. I have finished, I promise. It won't happen again. Tell Sue it won't happen again, won't you?'

"I was in no mood to discuss it with him. His clothes were stinking of rotten fish where might have rolled, or been rolled, in some rubbish. The stitches holding his top lip together had split and he was bleeding down his chin. I stripped him off in the hallway, more to protect the carpets and bed linen than anything else, and dumped him on the bed in the spare room to sleep it off. I had come to the end of my patience and at that moment I could wish him very little by way of good will.

"Next morning, Sue was icy. She sipped her tea and projected the mixture of anger and fear I had come to associate with her whenever Mark was in the house. She was pale and drawn and I could see she was nearing the very end of her tether too.

"'What are you going to do?' she demanded exhaustedly.

"'I'll call Alcoholics Anonymous and get some counselling for him and hand him over to them. You were right, Sue. I can't manage him and I have had enough too.'

"'That won't stop him coming round here,' she countered.

"'I'll see what the counselling services say,' I answered. "'I have no experience in handling situations like this. He may still need the support of friends to get over it.'

"'Ger, he is not your friend,' she growled at me, showing the full force of her anger. 'He is not the Mark we knew in the Mark and Janet days. When will you accept that? He has changed, he's different, and he is dangerous.'

"I did not want to argue with her.

"'I've said I will get some advice,' I replied as patiently as I could. 'But I don't agree that he is not the same. Underneath, he probably is. He has just gone through a lot more than it is reasonable to ask anyone to deal with.'

"'Stop making excuses for him, Ger,' she shouted. 'He's had gangsters beat him up and dump him on our front garden. And you've been told he's trouble by your police friend. What more do you need to see that he is not safe to be around? A petrol bomb through the letter box? I'm scared, Ger. I can't explain it any better than that. I'm scared out of my life. There is something about him that scares me. I have tried to tell you, but you won't listen.'

"She stopped and hid her face in her hands and I reached across to her.

"'He will get over it,' I tried to reassure her. 'He has already told me he wants to. He told me in the hospital and again last night when he arrived that he wants this to be the last time.'

"'He's an alcoholic, Ger. He cannot keep a promise. He will tell you anything and go right back to being drunk the next instant. He can't help himself any more. Let him go, Ger. He is no longer your old friend. He is danger.'"

"What did she say?" interrupted Aunt Gwendoline.

"Let him go, Ger. He is no longer your old friend. He is danger," he repeated.

"She didn't say 'he is dangerous'?" she queried.

"No," he replied. "She said 'he is danger'. But you must remember we were both tired, so a certain sloppiness in speech was not unreasonable."

"Perhaps," mused Aunt Gwendoline.

Chapter 35

"I knew something had to be done," Gerard continued. "We couldn't live too much longer with disturbed nights and unknown, and quite possibly real, threats coming at us from out of nowhere. We had to make life go back to normal and I knew it was up to me to make it happen. But before I could say anything more the kitchen door opened and Mark was standing there.

"'Sorry to disturb you,' he greeted us.

"We were so intent on arguing with each other that we both jumped at the sight of him. His sudden appearance startled us, but it was how he looked that surprised both of us more than anything else. He was freshly showered and shaved with his hair neatly combed. His jacket and trousers were also clean and only mildly creased rather than crumpled and filthy, and it was difficult to imagine his shirt and tie had been dragged through the rubbish with him the previous night. His shoes did not have a high polish but they had at least been brushed free of mud and his folded raincoat which he held over his arm no longer carried the stink of rotten fish. True, he was pale and as he held out his hand it shook a little, but apart from that he looked for all the world like a normal, freshly scrubbed man popping his head round the door to say goodbye before heading off for work. He must have spent hours cleaning himself up and all without us hearing him.

"'I know I have caused you two a bit of trouble over the past few weeks and I really cannot say how sorry I am that I did,' he began. 'It wasn't easy for you, I know, and what you both did went well beyond all I could ever ask from a friendship. I want you both to know how much I appreciate it and that I could never in my dreams have wanted a pair of better friends than you two. You have been absolutely wonderful. I want you to know now that all the trouble I have caused you is now finished and that there will be no repeats of any of it in the future. I know you probably won't believe me, what with the way I have been lately, so all I can do is ask you to give me some time and I'll prove it to you. I won't let you down I promise, not this time. I've got everything sorted out, I really have, and I can only say again that I am truly very, very sorry about the past few weeks and I hope that in a short while we can go back to being the friends we were before all this happened.'

"We could say nothing in answer to him. The whole presentation left us gaping. It was not just Mark's words. It was also the fact that his speech was clear and free from any suggestion of a boozy night out. He was as diffident and polite as he had always been before Janet's murder, and apart from a slightly bloodshot look about his eyes it was almost as if he had never been drunk. Of course, if we had measured his blood alcohol, we would probably have found him still running on a full tank and way over any legal limit. But we just looked at him open mouthed and said nothing.

"'I'll be off now,' he ended. 'I want to get into work early. I'll catch a bus so don't offer me a lift Gerry. I'll be better off walking in any case. You finish your breakfast in peace. Thank you both once again for being such good friends. I could not have managed the last few weeks without you and I really can't thank you enough. And I will make it up to you, I promise.'

"We heard the front door close gently as he left and we still could not say anything to each other. And that was it. It was over. He had come back to his senses, sobered up, and was ready to start living rationally again. I could not contain the feelings of relief that ran through me at that moment although I still thought it wise to reserve final judgement for at least a few days until it was clear he was not going to renege again. But I felt sure that this time he meant it and was back to normal. He had not mentioned the Craters in his little speech, or Janet or what had happened to her. All he had done was apologise and that most sincerely. I felt certain he was over his problems.

"It has now been over two months since that last drunken night and there has been no sign of him drinking since then. He is back at his chemistry bench doing well with his research, being taken seriously again by his students, and all gossip about him around the university staff club has tapered off to nothing. He has made a complete recovery. It is as if none of it had ever happened."

"And what about your vase?" asked Aunt Gwendoline.

"Ah, yes. Aunt Alice's vase," Gerard smiled. "After Mark left Sue remained stony faced and disbelieving and sitting at the breakfast table. She barely said another word as we both got ready for work. I left about an hour later, leaving her finishing off her make-up, and when I got home Aunt Alice's vase was smashed into a thousand pieces all over the hallway. She had taken out one of my golf clubs and side-swiped it off its pedestal, swinging with such force that the impact made a dent in the wall opposite. And she was gone, as were her clothes from the wardrobe and her other possessions from the cupboards and drawers. She has not been back and I have not seen her since. She has not returned any messages I've left, but from other people I know she is all right. She is a lovely girl and I still miss her at odd moments, but apart from that I don't know how I feel about her or about what she did to Aunt Alice's vase."

"I'm sure you don't," agreed Aunt Gwendoline. "But it is very odd. Of all the things she might have broken as she ended your relationship, she chose my sister Alice's vase."

Gerard watched his elderly aunt turn over her thoughts. He was pleased to see she was looking quite recovered from her earlier dizzy spell.

"Gerard, my dear boy," she announced at last. "You are absolutely correct. We did have a very late night last night and I do have to admit that it has left me feeling exceptionally tired. It is quite unceremonious of me I know, but I am going to bustle you on your way and take myself off to an early night. Thank you so much for telling me your story but I fear that if I do not say goodbye immediately, I shall not make it up the stairs without falling over. I do believe I have done all the thinking and listening I can manage for a long time."

"Of course," he smiled back to her.

He pulled on his coat and leaned over and gave her a long hug and a peck on the cheek.

"Thanks, Aunt Gwendoline. Thank you for everything. It has been good telling you about Mark and Janet and Sue and all that. You've no idea how much better I feel."

"That is what great-aunts are for," she answered.

She waved to him from the step then shut the door solidly against the failing light.

Chapter 36

"Well, Rani," she declared. "That was an anti-climax, wasn't it? Do you think it was worth all the effort?"

The dog sat quizzically at her mistress' feet and wagged her tail stump in hesitant answer.

"It would appear that our Gerard's Susan smashed our sister Alice's vase in nothing more than a fit of pique. She wanted to leave him but he was too engrossed in the affairs of his friend to notice. So, in the end she just left, smashing the last thing she saw on her way out in frustration which just happened to be our sister Alice's vase. I do despair sometimes at the lack of self-control displayed by the young people of today. Still, we mustn't be too hard on them, must we? Not given the sort of escapades my younger sister Lizzie used to get up to, getting me and Alice into all sorts of trouble as she invariably did. She was nothing but a worry from the moment she was born. But at least we can now relax, the whole business is at an end."

She nodded firmly and hauled herself off the timbers of the door frame, and the tread of her oak-cased grandfather clock sounded into the silence of the hallway and held her. She looked up into its face and searched it questioningly for a few seconds.

"Do you believe that is all there is to it, our dad?" she asked.

She listened to its unvarying, answering beat and after a few seconds sighed deeply.

"No, I don't believe it either."

She wandered into her sitting room.

"Janet Brinsley was murdered by Billy and George Crater, who got off scot-free at their trial," she summarised. "Mark Brinsley threw himself into his work and then got hopelessly drunk, annoying the Craters. Finally, he sobered up and went back to his life as if nothing had happened. Then, and only after everything was back to normal, Miss Susan finally felt she was able to leave our Gerard. She smashed our sister Alice's vase on her way out as a signal to him that their relationship was irretrievably at an end since nothing else seemed to be getting through to him. How does that sound, Rani?"

The dog showed no more enthusiasm for this version of events than her grandfather clock did for the earlier one.

"You're quite right," she sighed again. "It does not explain why our sleep has been disturbed by dreams of blazing Zeppelins and young pilots in biplanes buzzing us on our way back from our dad's allotment. It is all very confusing, and yet everything does now seem back to normal. I really am too tired to worry about it anymore. Such a fuss being made over a smashed vase. It was not as if it was Ming, was it Rani?"

So chattering, she tidied the sitting room before wearily climbing the stairs to settle herself and Rani down for a much anticipated, undisturbed, long night's sleep. It lasted until half past one.

Chapter 37

"Oh my goodness."

Aunt Gwendoline slumped back on her pillows. She had difficulty moving in the twisted bed sheets. It was dark and her heart was racing. She was panting and sweating profusely and her roiling mind carried no cohesive thought.

"Just a moment, Rani," she called. "Just give me a moment."

The dog was standing whimpering with her forepaws on the bed, obedient as ever to the instruction never to jump up.

Aunt Gwendoline wrestled with the tangled bedclothes hopelessly knotted around her. After a couple of attempts she succeeded in freeing a hand and reaching out to the bedside lamp, then she rested again against the pillows while her heartbeat dropped back to somewhere near its normal rhythm and her eyes became used to the sudden brightness.

"Goodness me," she wheezed. "The bed looks as though it has been hit by a thunder storm. I shan't be able to get back to sleep in it like this, shall I?"

Cautiously, she lowered her legs over the side and stood up. With careful lack of haste, she collected her pillows and pulled the blankets and sheets back into some sort of order.

"There, that looks better. But seeing that I am up I could really do with a cup of tea. Some Orange Pekoe I think, and while it is not usual to be eating at this hour of the morning I do think a small biscuit might be in order while I try and sort out exactly what is going on. Would you agree with that, Rani? I certainly need something."

The dog wagged her tail stump and followed her mistress downstairs. A glare of tested patience was sent towards the slumbering aspidistra as the closed sitting room door was passed, and a few minutes later the fumes of the piping hot

Orange Pekoe tea were being inhaled and savoured while the rational, if early morning, world re-established itself in the kitchen.

"It is all most odd," Aunt Gwendoline declared shaking her head. "I thought we had dealt with the Zeppelin and its falling stars. It was nothing, a nonsense, just the ramblings of an old woman, which is what I am. Nothing happened in the end, did it? Janet Brinsley was murdered but her husband, Miss Susan and mercifully Gerard himself are all well. Even the Crater brothers are well, for which we can give no thanks to our justice system. But that is not our concern, is it? No. At the end of our Gerard's story, the point at which Miss Susan broke our sister Alice's vase, everyone was back to normal. So, why am I still dreaming about Zeppelins and a strange young man in a biplane buzzing us as we walk back from our dad's allotment?"

Rani listened attentively to her mistress' voice, trembling gently and enjoying the break of nocturnal habit. She had scored a tiny piece of biscuit.

"When the young man flew over us all those years ago, he was simply exhibiting high spirits on his way back to his home airfield," Aunt Gwendoline reminisced. "There was no malice in him. True, he did scare Mother and we did end up in a ditch. But aeroplanes were a very rare sight in those days. Indeed, it was the first one we had ever seen. But why should I be dreaming about him now?"

She tapped the table top quietly with her fingers.

"First, there was a Zeppelin and six fiery stars," she recapped. "And then Gerard's story ended and it was at that point that the young man in his biplane decided to come up behind us and fly low over us and give us a fright, just as we were on our way home and thinking we were safe. It was something we were not expecting."

The words brought her up with a start.

"Something we were not expecting," she repeated. "Oh, dear."

She focussed on them more deeply and pursued the conclusion they were leading her to.

"Mother was frightened by the aeroplane because it was something she did not understand and it surprised her. But I heard it coming before either she or sister Alice did. I knew it was coming then, and I heard it again earlier this evening, didn't I, Rani? A faint growling, purring noise like a truck rumbling up the road outside heard through the walls of the house. It was while Gerard was finishing his story and I heard it coming, something that no one else has yet heard, something unexpected, something threatening, trying to sneak up behind us to frighten us. Oh, my goodness, Rani. I don't like these thoughts at all."

The dog sensed her mistress' deepening concern and put a paw up on to her knee in gentle reassurance.

"If I am right, then the whole business of Janet Brinsley's murder is not yet at an end. There is something more to come, something unexpected and something frightening. Which brings me back to the stars that fell from the burning Zeppelin and the three that flared and burned out before their time. Three stars for three men. One is almost certainly for Mark Brinsley. Susan said of him 'he is danger'. That is what she said. Gerard was quite clear on it. And a second star must be for our Gerard or else why would I be being bothered by all this dreaming? But who is the third one for? It is not Miss Susan. It has to be a man, and so far we have assumed it is our Gerard's new policeman friend Sergeant Chak."

She sipped her tea and made a final attempt to put the puzzle in her mind into its proper order. From the distant hallway of her small home she heard her oak-cased clock strike three. Three strikes and three stars. She registered that over an hour had passed since she had woken in turmoil and that her tea had gone cold.

"I wonder who the pilot was in our dream?" she asked. "Could that be Sergeant Chak? He is certainly someone who has seen a lot of violence, and that regrettably is a fair description of the work of our police these days. And I did call out 'it's one of ours' when I saw the biplane with its Royal Flying Corps markings. 'There's nothing to fear, it is one of ours,' I said. And Sergeant Chak is one of ours, isn't he, Rani?"

Sergeant Chak, the young man in his biplane, on patrol to defend them against undeserved and unasked for violence, unwittingly and unexpectedly exposing his friends to danger while he pursues the Crater gangland family for their crimes. The picture sat inextinguishably over her thoughts. If it was true, she had no idea what to do about it. But she had to save Gerard's star.

Her companion pawed once again at her knee.

"Yes, you are quite right, Rani," she finally acknowledged. "And thank you for reminding me. It all comes back to Miss Susan breaking our sister Alice's vase. It was not chosen randomly and it was not broken out of spite. Something was frightening her and Gerard hasn't been able to tell us what it was, has he? So we will have to ask her ourselves. That was a most useful reminder, Rani."

She reprised her thoughts one final time but was far too tired to trouble them any further.

"We must rest for a day or two and catch up on our sleep," she sighed. "And then we must go in search of Miss Susan and ask her what it was that was frightening her so much that she stayed with our Gerard and then smashed his vase as she left. Come along, I think we can both go back to bed now. It is almost morning and we have a lot to do."

A final quarter of biscuit was caught deftly from mid-air and, delighted by the result, Rani followed her mistress back up the stairs to the placid atmosphere of their bedroom.

"Sleep well, Rani," called her mistress as she extinguished the bedside light.

Rani turned her customary three turns around her blanket and also settled down to undisturbed slumber for what remained of the night.

Chapter 38

Aunt Gwendoline found two day's rest remarkably recuperative, so it was late on the third morning by the time she had carefully applied a minimum of face powder and lipstick, ensured that she had on her most comfortable town walking shoes, fastened the tail of the fox fur collar of her overcoat into the animal's spring-clip jaws, and adjusted her simple but elegant hat with its peacock's feather standing proudly erect at the front.

"One has a tendency to let one's self go as one gets older and that would never do for us, would it?" she explained to Rani. "We will be smart."

Rani's coat was adjusted, and after a final review of them both in the hallway mirror Aunt Gwendoline collected her horn handled walking cane from the hall stand and they left at a leisurely pace to catch the bus into town. There was, after all, plenty of time.

The journey was pleasant and sunny on a fine autumn day, and alighting in the town centre Aunt Gwendoline immediately turned right in the direction of a particular tea shop.

"Oh, I'm sorry," apologised the young woman coming around the corner in the opposite direction and almost colliding with her. "Gosh, I'm sorry, oh hello, it's Aunt Gwendoline."

"Good morning, Miss Susan," Aunt Gwendoline beamed to her. "What a pleasant surprise. I must say you are looking well."

"Thank you, I am," Sue stammered in return.

She was momentarily flustered by the unexpected encounter. It had been more than two months since she had walked out on Gerard and a confusion of memories and guilt

149

suddenly surged forwards in her that she could not immediately control.

"I'm just on my way to my lunch break," she blurted out with no particular thought in mind.

"That is capital," smiled Aunt Gwendoline. "There's a small café around the corner here which does a nice fresh pot of tea and home-made scones with jam and cream. I was just thinking of having some. I'm sure they also do more substantial food if that is what you are looking for. Will you join me?"

Sue looked into Aunt Gwendoline's steady and clear blue eyes and could not help smiling back to her. She did not know that she wanted to be reminded of uncomfortable events so recently in the past, but Aunt Gwendoline was such a refined old lady and not directly a part of them.

"That would be lovely," she replied.

"'Cool', is the current idiomatic response I believe, is it not?" Aunt Gwendoline asked.

"Not quite," laughed Sue. "But close enough."

There was a pleasant table situated in from the window where they could watch the passing crowds and enjoy the sunshine without being on display, and they ordered their food and drinks. A silence followed in which Sue's feelings of awkwardness returned and she wondered whether it had been a good idea to have a snack lunch with Aunt Gwendoline and why she had been so quick to agree to it. Some memories still coiled disturbingly within her but somehow it seemed unforgivably ungracious to say 'no' to the powder soft old lady sitting opposite her.

"How's Gerard?" she began cautiously.

"He's fine," answered Aunt Gwendoline. "He told me that you two were no longer close friends."

"He's a nice person, Aunt Gwendoline, really lovely. I didn't want to hurt him or cause him any upset, but we couldn't have gone on as we were. He didn't do anything wrong or anything like that, you know. It was me really. I just felt there was nothing left in our relationship and that all it could do was end in tears. So, I thought it was best to break it off while we were still friends."

She realised she was explaining too much but the words tumbled out of her.

"He'll get over it," smiled Aunt Gwendoline. "He is robust and will no doubt soon be off to the jungles of Southeast Asia on another one of his earth moving expeditions. But how are you managing? I gather you were on the point of leaving him just before that terrible business of Janet Brinsley's murder occurred. Its timing must have been very difficult for you."

Sue could not hide her surprise.

"Did Gerard tell you that?" she asked.

"Good gracious, no. He had no idea. He never said anything."

"We weren't suited, you know."

"I know that, Susan dear. It was never going to last, but Gerard had not got to the point of discovering that for himself. You didn't do anything wrong. You merely came to the conclusion before he did and acted upon it. Ah, here is our tea."

"You must think me a terrible butterfly," smiled Sue sheepishly.

"On the contrary, I have the highest regard for you. Your relationship as you call it was at an end and you did what you had to. But when trouble erupted you put your plans on hold and stayed with Gerard to give him support. I can only consider that very kind of you and it is certainly not something that I would reproach you for. In his own way Gerard understands that too, although he is a little puzzled about the manner of your departure."

"You mean me breaking his vase," Sue replied, shifting awkwardly in her seat. "Yes, I'm sorry about that. I know it was rather special to him. It came from one of his Aunts, I believe."

"My late sister, his great-aunt Alice."

"Oh, dear," Sue answered. "I didn't know that. That makes it doubly embarrassing for me. I did like it, really I did.

It was special to me too although I don't know why. Was is very valuable? I know Ger's mother thought it was Ming."

Aunt Gwendoline chuckled. "No, it was not Ming," she assured her. "And Gerard and I have already had that conversation. It was not particularly valuable and he should be able to replace it easily enough."

"That's something at any rate," concluded Sue.

She looked out at the sunshine, taking a few seconds to organise her thoughts.

"Aunt Gwendoline, does it make sense for me to say that I do not know why I broke Ger's vase?" she asked.

Aunt Gwendoline waited.

"It was special to me. I felt somehow drawn to it, and when Ger and I couldn't see eye to eye about things I would go and stand in front of it in the hallway and look at it. It was silly I suppose."

"It was only an old vase," agreed Aunt Gwendoline.

"I know," answered Sue. "But it was strange how as things blew up between us, particularly after Janet Brinsley was murdered, I would spend hours just staring at it and even talking to it. Can you imagine that? I talked to Ger's vase. Things were very tense between us and I suppose I was looking for answers. And I felt that something that had lived as long as that vase just had to have some answers in it somewhere."

Aunt Gwendoline did not reply.

"I was really rotten to Ger," Sue continued quietly. "It's very kind of you to say so but I don't know that I really gave him much support. I even took up smoking again just to annoy him. I was difficult, and if I'm honest I was hoping that we would end up in a blazing row so that I could walk out and leave all the blame with him. But Ger isn't like that. He's too nice. He wouldn't argue or lose his temper with a fly. He is just too gentle."

"He did make a lot of excuses for you," Aunt Gwendoline confirmed.

"Oh dear, that makes me feel worse. Did I hurt him badly? I didn't want to but I just had to get out of what was happening. Aunt Gwendoline, does it sound crazy if I say that after Janet was murdered I became more and more scared?"

Aunt Gwendoline did not move. The young woman sitting opposite her was looking piercingly at her, pleading for answers to the questions they both had inside them.

"A lot of how I felt straight after Janet's murder can be explained by what was done to her," continued Sue more calmly. "It was terrible, but after the immediate shock of what happened had died down, I wasn't worried by her memory. I didn't really think the Craters would come back to get us and it wasn't Ger that scared me. He would never have hurt me and he was wonderful at listening to me and trying to understand how I felt. But somehow I couldn't feel that I could tell him what was going on in my head, so I wasn't able to tell him why I was so scared."

She wrestled with her thoughts and looked out at the sunshine again. It was not easy recreating how she felt but Aunt Gwendoline seemed to understand.

"It wasn't Ger that I was scared of," she repeated. "But I began to feel scared when I was around him. I couldn't tell him about it because it was all so irrational. I couldn't explain it to myself, never mind to him, and yet I got to feeling so frightened, especially when Mark was around. I began to think I was going mad."

"So you talked to Gerard's vase instead," Aunt Gwendoline prompted.

"Yes, I talked to his vase," Sue smiled. "But please, Aunt Gwendoline, please don't think that Ger ever did anything to frighten me. He didn't. He is the gentlest man I know. That's what made it all so insane. I couldn't be frightened of him. If I was really honest, I would have to say it was Mark who frightened me."

The words jumped out of her and she winced at their release. After so much time and denial they could only sound like a betrayal.

Chapter 39

"We were all such good friends together," Sue continued, listening carefully to her own words as if she was hearing them for the first time. "Neither Ger nor I had ever seen any anger between Mark and Janet. He was only ever the loving husband and she adored him. It was inconceivable that any woman could ever feel anything but safe in his presence. And yet it was after Janet's murder that he began to frighten me."

Aunt Gwendoline reached out to the flaming Zeppelin and its falling stars, and to the young man with dead eyes flying his biplane arrow-straight on a mission. Both images were too far away to discern very much about them. Rani stirred momentarily against her feet under the table.

"It's easy to say that Mark went off the rails and temporarily lost touch with reality, and so I became frightening," Sue reasoned. "Janet had been horribly murdered so it is not surprising the shock sent him out of his mind. But he changed in a way I can't explain. He changed quite suddenly, and especially after that aborted trial of the Craters. He became different. Does it sound weird, Aunt Gwendoline, to say that one day I suddenly found I could not look at him without seeing a sort of fog hanging around him? It's too dramatic to say it was like a dark cloud that went with him wherever he went, but that was the general feeling of it. It was like an aura that was never there before. It was not there in reality, of course. It was just in my imagination. But it frightened me."

She paused while she considered her words.

"I couldn't explain it to Ger," she resumed. "I couldn't even explain it to myself. It's never easy to try and explain the irrational so I couldn't tell Ger that his friend was getting darker and darker and more and more sinister. It got worse and worse all through the time when Mark was trying to work himself to death and later when he tried to drink himself out of existence. Oh God, they were terrible times. I desperately hoped Ger would see the change in Mark too and that I wouldn't have to explain it. But he didn't, or couldn't, and he is very loyal. But what worried me more and more was that whatever it was that was surrounding Mark seemed to be reaching out to Ger whenever the two of them were together. It was totally insane. Even to that last morning when Mark poked his head around the kitchen door looking all spick and span and ready to say 'goodbye', that evil mist thing hung round him. It was so menacing. I thought I was going completely round the twist."

She sniffed and reached for her handkerchief as two tears fell off her chin to scatter the scone crumbs on her plate.

"I knew then that I had to get away," she sighed at last. "I knew it on that last morning when Mark said that it was all over and that he had given up drinking and that everything was going to go back to normal. I couldn't believe him. Even as he spoke it was as if he was talking to me through his mist, and it scared me to the point where I couldn't look at him. Ger couldn't see it, and Mark himself didn't seem to be aware of it. And I knew it wasn't there really, which is why I really thought I was going mad."

She sniffed into her handkerchief and looked across to Aunt Gwendoline though tear filled eyes.

"I had pleaded with Ger to let Mark go, to hand him over to professional help and have nothing more to do with him. But Ger couldn't leave his friend and I couldn't give him any rational reason why he should, other than that I was scared of something that didn't exist. In the end, I waited until he had left for work and I packed my things. On my way out, I passed his vase sitting on its pedestal in the hallway. I stopped and looked at it and suddenly wanted to ask it what was happening to me, and for it to tell me why I was feeling like I was. That really did send me into a panic. I was asking a vase why something that didn't exist scared me. It was a vase. How could it answer me?"

"It couldn't," replied Aunt Gwendoline. "But that doesn't mean that talking to it was unreasonable. Gardeners are well known for talking to their plants."

Sue felt the sound of Aunt Gwendoline's voice break through the armour of her agitation and a faint smile stopped her tears.

"Ger told me you sometimes talk to your aspidistra," she said.

"Did he?" responded Aunt Gwendoline in some surprise.

She had not realised it had become so obvious. She would have to be more careful in future.

"Well, if I do at least it gives me the satisfaction of being able to have the last word, and I can also be sure it will not gossip afterwards."

"Yes, there is that," smiled Sue. "But even so, I couldn't leave Ger's vase where it was, not with it knowing so much. So, I took one of Ger's golf clubs out of the cupboard and smashed it so hard that it could never be put together again. I didn't do it to hurt Ger, Aunt Gwendoline. Really I didn't. I did it because I had to. And then I walked out."

Aunt Gwendoline waited while Sue blew her nose and dabbed her eye make-up and wipe her face one last time with a clean corner of her handkerchief.

"I suppose the only question is," she commented after a pause, "did you feel better for having smashed it to smithereens?"

Sue raised her head from her hands in another smile.

"Yes, I suppose I did," she replied.

"Well then, that's really all that matters, isn't it? I would hate to think you went to so much effort not to feel some benefit from it."

Sue paused and looked at the wonderful old lady sitting across the table from her.

"Aunt Gwendoline, you really don't think of me as a butterfly for planning to leave Gerard as I did, do you?" she asked sheepishly.

"If I do, I don't see that it is something to be at all concerned about. I was a young woman during the Second

World War and there were an awful lot of fine looking young men in uniform about the place, our own boys, of course, but also a good number of Canadians and Americans as well, not to mention a few continentals, mostly French and Polish if I remember correctly. Indeed, it is not every young girl who can boast that she was taken home after a dance in a tank transporter."

"A tank transporter?" echoed Sue incredulously.

"Yes. The young gentleman was in the Tank Corps and it was the only vehicle he had available. It made a terrible noise grinding all the way from Catterick Army Camp and along the main street of Low Felderby at one o'clock in the morning. It woke everybody up and my mother gave me a terrible tongue lashing about it next morning."

"It sounds absolutely wild," laughed Sue.

"Mind you, they were dangerous times," Aunt Gwendoline continued, waving for the bill. "My mother never stopped drumming it into me that if a soldier so much as put his hand on my knee, I would end up pregnant, and my elder sister Alice was forever reminding me that I was in grave danger of getting myself talked about. And she was mostly right. I was, after all, the first girl in our village to wear nylon stockings, and very daring they were too. They were more than enough for me to get myself talked about."

Sue pushed her handkerchief back into her eye sockets, this time to soak up the tears of laughter. Rani stirred, stood up and yawned. Lunch was over.

"Aunt Gwendoline," smiled Sue as they stood briefly outside the café before going their separate ways. "Thank you so much. I've not told anybody about how I ended up after Janet's murder so it's been wonderful talking to you. I can't thank you enough. I'm so glad we ran into each other, and if you see Ger…"

"I shan't say a word," interrupted Aunt Gwendoline. "What you young people get up to is your own affair and you certainly don't want us older folk poking our noses into it. Now off you go. It was a pleasure meeting you again Miss Susan and have a safe journey back to your office."

Sue could not stop herself. She leaned forward and held the old lady in a close and deeply affectionate hug and kissed her warmly on each cheek.

"Thanks again, Aunt Gwendoline. Thank you so much for everything."

She skipped off, leaving the old lady smiling after her.

"I don't know, Rani, but the young people of today have no idea of self-restraint, do they? I think it is time we went home before we get ourselves talked about all over again."

There was determination in Aunt Gwendoline's step as she and Rani found their way back to their bus stop.

Chapter 40

"So, Rani, I was right," Aunt Gwendoline declared as she sank gratefully into her favourite Victorian rosewood grandmother chair with a freshly brewed cup of Prince of Wales tea in hand. "It is not just me. Miss Susan saw it as well. As our dad would have said, 'There's trouble at Pit,' and there certainly is. About that there can no longer be any doubt."

She stirred her tea and helped herself to another biscuit while Rani wagged her tail stump in anticipation.

"Something which frightened her, that's how Miss Susan described it. It was something which made her fearful, not of Gerard but for him. That confirms our conclusion that there is some mischief yet to come and that our Gerard's friend Mark Brinsley is at the centre of it, whatever it is."

She gave a shudder. All she could think of was the three stars from her dream, three young men being extinguished before their time. Gerard, Mark Brinsley and the young pilot with his emotionless eyes coming up behind them in his biplane. She recreated the image of the pilot in her mind and shuddered again.

"'I've got it. I've got it all worked out'," she repeated. "That is what he signalled to me and it is certainly something a policeman might say before moving in to arrest his quarry. And he might very well wave his notebook as he did so. I'll have to ask Gerard if Sergeant Chak has a scar on his forehead."

She sighed. "But I am still no further forward in determining what thuggery is around the corner, am I? Whatever it is, Mark Brinsley annoying the Craters and Gerard getting caught in the crossfire because he is Mark's friend, and it all being triggered innocently by Sergeant Chak doing his duty, we can't let it happen, can we?"

Rani sat looking up at her mistress and quivering with unquestionable intelligence. Aunt Gwendoline stood up, too agitated to rest in spite of her tiredness, and took a couple of paces across the floor.

"Susan tried to tell our Gerard about it. She even talked to our Alice's vase about it."

She stopped short in her pacing and turned towards the aspidistra.

"All of which points to you having a hand in it," she admonished it firmly.

Not a leaf twisted, not a stem turned.

"You had no right to do it. You realise that, don't you, our mam? You had no right at all. Using our Alice's vase like that, you frightened the living daylights out of that poor young woman. She thought she was going mad. I suppose you would say that you had no other option, that you had to get the message through to our Gerard somehow. He, bless his little cotton socks, would never have noticed the precariousness of his situation on his own. And neither he did, did he? And he still doesn't, does he? You were very lucky that Miss Susan was able to notice, even if in the end our Gerard didn't listen to her. She was going to leave him, you know, even before the whole business of Janet Brinsley's murder came up. You were very lucky she stayed. She is a young woman of considerable courage but you terrified her to the point where she thought she was losing her mind. Really, Mother, that was unconscionable."

The plant remained unmoved under the barrage of remonstrance piled against it.

"So where does that leave us?" she continued. "Susan smashed our Alice's vase, which makes you responsible for that too, and that then became the starting point for our Gerard telling me his story. So you did get that bit right, although I would seriously have to question your methods. You don't make things easy for me, do you? But then there is nothing new about that, is there? You never made things easy for any of us, except Lizzie. I am an old woman now, not a child with boundless energy. You asked me to look after the family and I have always done that, but this present set of circumstances is too exhausting for an old body. You have to give me a little more help and show me some consideration."

She returned to her chair and eased herself tiredly into it once more.

"It's all right, Rani," she soothed. "I'm just an old woman ranting on, and a little tired after our trip into town, that is all. There is so much to do and so little to work with. I have no idea what it is I am supposed to do."

The precise ticking of her station clock beside her bookcase insisted there was no hurry, that the timetable was set and all trains were running on time.

"Miss Susan thought she was going mad talking to a vase," she sighed. "And here am I arguing with an aspidistra."

The tut-tutting of her ecclesiastical clock added its admonition that she should calm herself and that becoming het up over things she could do little about would achieve nothing.

"I wonder what Susan would think of a silly old woman talking to an aspidistra?" she mumbled.

And over them all the solid and constant, familiar and never-failing tread of her oak-cased grandfather clock cast its beat to steady her and bring her rest and comfort.

"Bless you, our dad," she whispered to it. "You always were our strength."

Her eyes closed and her body relaxed. There was still the mystery of what trouble there was in the mist or whatever it was that surrounded Mark Brinsley. She must tell Gerard that Susan was right about being frightened, that she had been a better friend to him than perhaps he realises, even though she broke Alice's vase and is not the girl for him. She must tell Gerard that he must distance himself from Mark and his new police sergeant friend, although being Gerard he would find that difficult to do. He had always been a very trusting boy, extremely loyal, right to the end.

Her clocks pressed their message. There was time. The schedule was set and the stars would fall as they had to. She could not stop them. All she had to do was be there to catch the one that was Gerard's. She would look after the family as she had promised Mother. There was the matter of how she was going to catch Gerard's star and stop it burning out before its time but at least she would not be alone. Our dad would come home from the War and he would spread wide his big, strong arms and hold them all and make their world solid again. And Mother would be happy once more and give the aspidistra its weekly polish and complain about our dad leaving his tobacco plugs on the soil to keep them moist. And sister Lizzie would get her and Alice into trouble as she always did because she was the youngest and she had a bad heart and they all let her get away with her mischief because none of them knew what a short time it would be before she would no longer be with them. But at least she would give them the line that would lead to our Gerard. And Gerard would go to Southeast Asia and dig his archaeological holes in the ground and come back with some more honey. And young men in biplanes would fly over them and protect them from raids by Zeppelins.

Rani settled down beside her mistress to rest watchfully over her nodding sleep.

Chapter 41

On Wednesday, Gerard called to say he had visitors in his department and that he was unable to come over for afternoon tea, so over the next three days Aunt Gwendoline caught up on a lot of sleep. She took Rani for extra walks in the late year sunshine and also managed a little shopping in town. On Sunday, she enjoyed a relaxed day with one of her friends at an antiques auction where she successfully bid for a small snuff box.

"You're not taking snuff on the quiet, are you?" asked the friend.

"No," smiled Aunt Gwendoline. "But nobody seemed interested in it so I thought I would give it a home."

Engine-turned, about 1840 and the work of Nathaniel Mills of Birmingham. It was a bargain.

So, Aunt Gwendoline waited for the clockwork of the universe to turn, for the days to pass and the hours to strike according to their schedule. She rested and recouped and it was late on Tuesday morning that her telephone rang.

"Gerard, my dear boy. What a nice surprise. Yes, of course, you can come over. Right away? No, I'm not busy. Is there something the matter? You sound a little agitated, if you don't mind my saying so. Very well, I'll put the kettle on and you can tell me over some tea and lunch. I'll see you in a short while."

As she cradled the receiver she thought she heard the faint sound of an engine revving in the distance. It was far away but coming closer. She cocked her head to try and locate it.

"Do you hear it, Rani?" she asked. "Do you hear it with your dog's sharp hearing as opposed to my dull old human ears?"

Rani sat in front of her looking up expectantly, only tentatively wagging her tail stump.

Gerard arrived a few minutes later, so clearly agitated that he barely said 'hello' to his great-aunt and almost ignored the tea she offered him.

"I'm not sure how to begin," he started as soon as he settled into his customary chair. "It's this whole business of Janet Brinsley's murder. It just keeps coming back. I thought it was all over when Billy and George Crater were arrested, but it wasn't. Then I thought it was all finished with when Mark finally came to his senses and sobered up, but it's not. It's back again, except that I'm not sure that I have anything more than a lot of empty suspicions that have grown up out of nothing. I think I am becoming paranoid."

"I hardly think so," responded Aunt Gwendoline firmly. "You are far too relaxed. I have seen paranoia in some of the men from Low Felderby who, like your great-grandfather, managed to make it home from the First World War. I can assure you, you are not paranoid."

Gerard felt himself respond immediately to the ageless certainty in his great-aunt's voice. He sucked in a deep breath and held it while he calmed himself.

"Dear Aunt Gwendoline," he thought. "Don't ever die. I don't know what I would do if you did."

"I had hoped that Janet's murder was now in the past and that we could all forget about it and get back to being as normal as it is possible to be after such an horrendous event," he resumed more calmly. "If you look at it rationally, Janet was killed a year ago, Billy and George Crater were brought to trial for her murder six months ago, Mark went through his binge drinking period three months ago, and since then everything has been very, very quiet. I haven't seen anything of Sue since she left, and from what little contact I have had with Mark he is getting on with his work, lecturing to his students and doing his research. In short, everything has settled back into its proper place and life is going on more or less as it should."

"And it is not?" prompted Aunt Gwendoline.

"I'm not sure," he replied. "Mark told me something on Sunday night that I can't get out of my mind. He could have been joking and it was very late. In fact, it was dawn by the time we had finished talking and we had knocked off a fair bit of wine with dinner and brandy afterwards. But what he said was so plausible that I cannot be sure. If it was a joke, then it was a very sick one, but then Mark has changed from who he was during the Janet days. He is quieter now, less driven, more cynical, and I can't read him like I used to. On the other hand, if it was not a joke then I don't know what to think. It is all so monstrous."

Aunt Gwendoline watched her grand-nephew closely. He was more upset than she had ever seen him. He had left his chair and stood up with his tea cup in his hand and was pacing backwards and forwards as he spoke. He looked out of the window, wandered all about the room, then he stopped in front of the aspidistra and studied it for a few seconds before sitting down again.

"I had a dinner on Sunday evening," he resumed. "It was just two couples and me. It was something Sue and I had done in the past, part of the round of casual evenings one gets into in an environment like the university. My friends had been good to me, still inviting me around even though they knew Sue and I had broken up, and I felt it was about time I reciprocated. Just because Sue wasn't there didn't mean I couldn't manage a dinner, so I did and it all went very well."

He paused and Aunt Gwendoline watched while he organised his mind for whatever he was going to say next.

"Mark had been quiet in the two months since he had decided to sober up, so I thought I would invite him as well. I was a bit wary of doing so, particularly as I would be throwing him in with a group of people who knew his recent past and who would not necessarily be diplomatic in discussing it over the dinner table. But I felt it was time he came back into circulation again and he seemed pleased with the invitation, and he accepted it straight away. My fears turned out to be unfounded. The marital problems of some other senior academic are now the gossip of the hour and Mark's past misbehaviour was barely mentioned. When it was, a light, jocular context prevailed and Mark responded with equally comic repartee, and it was clear that the subject had evolved down to the amusing anecdote stage.

"Throughout the evening Mark was as charming and as witty as he had been in the old days with Janet and it was a joy to see him like that again. I kept half an eye on his wine consumption throughout the meal just in case it was still a problem but there was no sign of him losing control, at least no more than the rest of us. We did knock off a good number of bottles of red as I discovered next morning when I put out the empties. But Mark enjoyed himself and his descriptions and impersonations of the late-night life in the city's night clubs had us all rolling with laughter. By the end of the evening, he was being regarded as an obligatory guest at all forthcoming parties. He was back, repatriated and welcome. Up to that point, it was a good evening."

He paused and Aunt Gwendoline watched him as he hauled on his next few thoughts, disciplining them and stopping them racing ahead and churning his story out of sequence.

"Just before midnight one couple left because they had to get home and release the babysitter before the late fees kicked in, and the other couple left soon after," he continued. "That left Mark and me sitting amongst the usual ruins of a successful dinner.

"'That was absolutely superb, Gerry,' he said, smiling broadly to me across the table. 'Thanks for dragging me along. I have been out of circulation for a while and this evening has been a most magnificent return. Thank you so much. You and Sue are the best friends a fellow could ever have. Not that I'm a Fellow yet, that's the next level of promotion in our academic hierarchy. But I hope I make it.'

"We both laughed at the weak joke. We were relaxed, I was not in any great hurry to leave the table and it was clear that Mark wanted to talk on a bit. It didn't bother me. There was the spare room where he could crash out if he wanted to and we had shared a bathroom before in the past.

"'Sit still, Mark,' I said. 'I'll get us some scotch.'

"'Good idea,' he answered, and then looked at me puzzled. 'But not scotch, Gerry. I don't like whisky, you know that. Hate the stuff. But if you've got a decent bottle of brandy, I'm sure we could do that some damage.'

"'Brandy it is, then,' I grinned. 'Two glasses?'

"'I think there is only two of us,' he giggled. 'So, two glasses should be ample.'

"We were only playing, of course. We were not drunk, merely relaxed and acting the part. But it was good to have my old friend back again.

"'So, what do you want to talk about?' I asked him."

Again, Gerard hesitated.

"Aunt Gwendoline, what Mark told me next I still don't know how to take in. Some of the implications of what he said are so terrible, so horrible, so unbelievable that I don't know that they ought to be repeated."

"Continue," insisted Aunt Gwendoline.

"But I have no reason to believe that what Mark said to me is even true. In many ways it is unbelievable, and it could simply have been his now warped sense of humour interacting with a couple of bottles of red wine and some brandy to have a big joke on me."

"Gerard, my dear boy, how many times do I have to tell you that I have lived more than eighty years through what has been the most tumultuous century in the history of our species. Do not concern yourself that I shall find whatever it is you have to say so shocking that I shall call for the smelling salts and hesitate to speak to you ever again. Now please go on."

"I don't know how to," he appealed to her in some desperation, "except in his own words."

"Then those are the ones you must use," she answered patiently.

The buzz of the biplane engine had returned to her ears, announcing itself quietly, purring its threat in the far distance and casting its shadow of unease over her sitting room. It was coming towards them. She scanned her senses to try and spot it with its young pilot, with his trim moustache and scar on his forehead and his fistful of notes in his left hand that he waved at her as he sped away. She brought her focus back to her grand-nephew sitting in indecision in the chair opposite her.

"I require to know every detail of what your friend Dr Brinsley said," she commanded. "Please tell me."

Chapter 42

Gerard braced himself. "I said to Mark, 'So what do you want to talk about?'

"'Para nitroso alpha naphthyl three amine,' he replied.

"I shook my head to make sure I had heard him correctly. "'Para nitro ... that sounds like the name of one of your chemicals,' I answered. 'Either that or one of us has had too much brandy.'

"'You are absolutely correct on the first. It is the name of a chemical and it's not a very nice one either.'

"'It wouldn't be with a name like that,' I replied. 'Para nitrate whatever is a bit of a mouthful to come out with. Couldn't you call it something simpler, like Fred.'

"'Try PNA,' he replied. 'That's its usual abbreviation.'

"'PNA,' I repeated.

"'Exactly, got it in one.'

"'So why do you want to talk about PNA?' I asked.

"'Because it's nasty,' he answered. 'It's just about the nastiest chemical ever to come out of the chemistry division of the weapons research laboratories of our much esteemed Ministry of Defence. It's not a very nice chemical at all.'

"'I suppose it wouldn't be, coming out of a stable like that,' I shrugged. 'What does it do?'

"'It causes cancer.'

"'That is nasty,' I agreed.

"I couldn't see where the conversation was going but I wasn't yet bothered enough to attempt to stop it.

"'Tell me,' he continued after an exaggerated pause, 'have you ever wondered how much of the published medical literature on cancer research has come out of the weapons research laboratories of our Ministry of Defence and its counterparts in the United States, Russia, France, Japan and, for all I know, China and India and a few other places as well?'

"'I've never asked the question,' I replied.

"'Well, I'll tell you. It's a lot, a hell of a lot. In fact there was a period during the nineteen sixties and seventies when more than sixty percent of all literature published on cancer causing chemicals came out of such establishments. They did a lot of cancer research in the Ministry of Defence, a hell of a lot.'

"'It's nice to know our money was being well spent,' I commented somewhat sarcastically. 'I gather they didn't come up with a cure or anything like that, otherwise we would have heard about it.'

"'You're too nice, Gerry,' he replied. 'Far too nice. They weren't interested in curing it. What they wanted to know was how to cause it.'

"He leaned across the table, helped himself to another brandy and gave me such an odd smile it made it difficult for me to gauge what he was going to say next.

"'It was all done with the best of motives,' he continued. 'The argument went "if we don't develop and research these chemicals and find out how nasty they are, then how will we know what to do when an enemy uses them against us?". So they spent our taxpayers' millions creating literally thousands of new and increasingly nasty cancer causing chemicals and testing them to make sure they worked. And that's just what is published in the scientific and medical literature and does not include all the others that are still hidden under the Official Secrets Act and its American, Russian, French, Chinese and so on counterparts.'

"'I suppose they were right in a way,' I countered. 'Whatever the motives for their original research, we have ended up with a heap of knowledge about those chemicals and what they can do. We at least now know what additives not to put in our food; environmental agencies now know enough to make sure that our workplaces are safe; and defunct industrial sites are properly cleaned up before developers move in to build desirable homes that would otherwise give residents nasty tumours. You'd have to agree all that is a good thing'

"'Don't be so bloody naive, Gerry,' he replied shortly. 'These chemicals were created with warfare in mind. It was the mad, military fashion of the time that led to their existence. The generals of the day dreamed about flying aeroplanes over swathes of enemy troops and spraying them with chemicals like PNA so they would all fall down and die of cancer.'

"'So, we can only be thankful that it never happened,' I answered.

"I found the thread of the conversation was beginning to make me feel uncomfortable and I was trying to defuse it. And as he spoke Mark became different to how he had been earlier on in the evening. He became buoyed up, but irrationally so. He gave the impression of being triumphant and pleased with himself to the point of being belligerent, or at least boastful as he pressed on with his argument. If I hadn't known him better, I would have said he had just snorted something except that I knew that all he had consumed all evening had been red wine and by now a quarter of a bottle of brandy.

"'You mentioned the sixties and seventies,' I said. 'Do I take it that all this cancer producing weapons establishment work ceased after that?'

"'Just about,' he nodded. 'And for two reasons. In the first place, military fashions change just like everything else. By the mid nineteen eighties it had occurred even to the military minds of the day that cancers take time to develop, so spraying enemy troops with cancer causing chemicals was not going to stop an invading army in its tracks. The enemy troops might eventually get cancer, but in the meantime they will still have knocked out most of your tanks and infantry and clobbered your air force as well. What was needed was something faster acting. It was at that point that some bright spark dangled nerve gases under the noses of the generals and they went for them like a shot. All funding for chemical weapons research was diverted into creating compounds that instantaneously turn human beings into writhing heaps of fused nervous systems and chemical carcinogenesis was left to wither on the vine.'

"'Not a very nice picture of our species,' I commented. 'But you said there were two reasons why the work stopped. What was the other one?'

"'PNA,' he grinned.

"'You mean that nasty chemical you mentioned at the start of this conversation?'

"'Exactly,' he beamed. 'It's a ridiculously simple chemical, which is why it was just about the first one to be discovered in the research. It's very easy to synthesise. My first year undergraduates could do it almost blindfold except that I would never let them try. A year later they would all be riddled with some of the most aggressive and untreatable cancers known to medicine and be dying like flies. PNA has never been tested on humans, of course, at least not intentionally or as far as anyone is prepared to admit, but it proved so ferociously lethal in laboratory rats that it wasn't considered necessary to test it on any higher animal.'

"'It's sounding more ghastly by the minute,' I commented.

"'It's more than that,' he continued enthusiastically. 'It is the best. It has remarkably innocent looking crystals, long and needle-like and faintly tinted with yellow. Looking at them you wouldn't think that they could harm a fly. Yet they dissolve in water, are tasteless, have no smell, and the amount required to kill you is minimal. Imagine six grains of sugar on a spoon, that would be enough. And twenty five years after it was first made, with millions and millions of pounds, dollars, roubles and yen spent on creating and testing literally thousands more previously unknown cancer producing chemicals, nobody managed to come up with anything more lethal than PNA. It was the gold standard. Nothing was more effective, and by the end of the nineteen eighties the weapons research establishments all over the world had just about given up all hope of improving on it. So the research ground to a halt.'

"I was beginning to feel quite nauseated by his commentary.

"'So we've got the king of the cancer causing chemicals. I suppose that's some sort of achievement for mankind,' I concluded.

"'It most definitely is,' he laughed. 'Especially when you know how it works.'

"'Do I really want to know this?' I asked.

"'Yes, you do, Gerry my friend. Because it is important.'

"He was looking at me so intensely his eyes were sparkling, and not just with the brandy. He was excited in the way that, under other circumstance, always made him a joy to work with. But these were not those other circumstances.

"'Then you'd better tell me,' I replied. 'But be quick about it because I want to go to bed.'

"He leaned slowly back in his chair, took a large swallow of brandy and beamed at me.

"'If you swallow some PNA,' he expounded, 'or even touch some of the crystals, it goes straight into your bloodstream. Twenty minutes later, I could analyse your blood until the cows come home and I wouldn't be able to find even a trace of it. I could take bits of your tissue from any of your organs, kidneys, lungs, stomach, anywhere, and I still wouldn't be able to find any. It would be gone. And since you wouldn't have been aware that you had swallowed it then, after twenty minutes, there would be no evidence that it had ever existed in your body.'

"'It's untraceable,' I summarised.

"'After twenty minutes, yes,' he agreed. 'That is unless you knew what you were looking for. But by that time it would be too late.'

"'How do you mean?' I asked.

"'It would not really have disappeared, of course, but it would have been changed inside your body. As I said, it has never been tested on humans but the best guess is that, within ten minutes of you swallowing it, it will have entered your cells. By eight hours it will have become incorporated into your DNA, and once part of your DNA it sets a clock ticking, tick, tick, tick, tick, and it cannot be stopped. And the first thing you would know about that clock would be some six months later when you went to your doctor because you were not feeling well. There would be the usual tests which would take a few more days to weeks, and what they would eventually show would be that you had well advanced cancers in your gullet and stomach. If you left it another month before you went to see your doctor, the cancers would have spread to your kidneys and liver. Another month and they would be in your lungs and after that everywhere. You would be dead within a year. Gerry, Gerry old pal, I'm sorry. I seem to have upset you.'

"'You're not exactly describing fun and games on bonfire night,' I choked.

"'Gerry, please. I am sorry. I wasn't thinking. I didn't realise it would upset you so. Maybe I have gone a little over the top. Here, have another brandy. You're the dearest friend I've got so please don't be upset. I don't know what I would have done this past year if it hadn't been for you and Sue. Sorry, sorry old chum, truly I am. Please forgive me.'

"'I'm going to make some coffee,' I replied. 'Do you want some?'

"Any thought I had of finishing the evening and going to bed was gone. My thoughts were racing in all directions. It wasn't only what Mark had been saying about cancer causing chemicals that upset me. I had never thought about it before, but being a chemist I suppose he would have to know a fair bit about them for safety's sake, his own and his students. But it was the way he told me about them that disturbed me more than anything else, particularly the one he called PNA. There was a fire in him that I found particularly unsettling. Its intensity was frightening."

Aunt Gwendoline noted her grand-nephew's distress. His conversation with his friend had not been pleasant. Indeed, she had found it more than worrying herself. She looked down at Rani and saw she was sitting up, alert, sniffing the air and poised to point in the manner of her breed. Something was approaching. She strained every nerve to listen. If only she

174

still had the young ears she had all those years ago, then maybe she would hear it coming too. But nothing reached her over the ticking of her clocks and the shaking tones of Gerard's unsettled voice.

Chapter 43

"I believed him when Mark said I am his dearest friend, Aunt Gwendoline, and I still do," Gerard sighed. "Our friendship is important to him and I could not regard him in any other light. He is a friend, a very dear friend. He just shocked me very much with what he had said. When I returned with the coffee, he was calmer and had poured us both another brandy.

"'It's true,' he continued. 'I really don't know how I would have managed the last few months without the help of you and Sue, particularly those last three or four weeks when I was sozzled most of the time. By the way, where is Sue? I noticed she wasn't here this evening. Is she away on one of her courses?'

"'She is not here anymore,' I replied. 'She left. We've separated and gone our separate ways.'

"'Gerry, no. I'm so sorry, I didn't know. I've been out of circulation for a while. When did that happen? She didn't leave because of me, did she? I know I caused a bit of trouble but surely she would have seen that it was only temporary, didn't she?'

"'She didn't leave because of you, Mark, even though you did, as you say, cause a bit of trouble,' I answered. 'In fact, it was more than a bit, it was a lot. And, no, it was not obvious that it was only temporary. To be blunt, we were seriously discussing how to get you into long term care for your alcoholism.'

"'Oh, Gerry, I am sorry. You two were my best friends. I wouldn't have done that to you for the world. Tell me she didn't leave because of me.'

"'You didn't do it, Mark. Sue and my relationship had come to an end and our interests were drifting apart. The ruckus you caused might have provided an excuse for the final split but it was not the reason for it. Now let the matter drop, will you?'

"'Do you still see her?'

"'No.'

"He was quiet for a few seconds while he drank some coffee and swallowed some more brandy. It was difficult to see what was going on in his mind but he seemed genuinely upset by the news.

"'You were seriously thinking about how to get me into care for my alcoholism,' he said at last. 'That's real friendship. You could have just dropped me like all my other so-called friends. I must have been very convincing.'

"'What the hell do you mean, convincing? You were smashed, night after night. You turned up drunk to your lectures, half-empty scotch bottles were found in your desk drawer in your laboratory, more empties were found in the rubbish, and when you turned up here you were reeking of whisky. It was coming out of your every pore. And I thought you didn't drink whisky anyway.'

"'I don't,' he replied. 'I can't stand the stuff.'

"I stopped, puzzled. I was still angry with him but the casualness with which he agreed with me silenced me.

"'Then why on earth did you decide to go on a class A bender every night for weeks on end by drinking scotch whisky?' I finally asked him.

"'Because that is what the Craters' drink,' he replied.

"'Jesus Christ,' I said.

"Sorry for the blasphemy, Aunt Gwendoline, but I had no other reply to give him. His logic escaped me. I didn't know where the conversation was heading, what he meant, or anything. All I knew was that his answer was the last one I expected to my essentially rhetorical question. I was stunned."

Rani stood up in a heightened state of alert, sniffing the air more vigorously as if trying to locate a quarry, her tail stump stilled in concentration. Aunt Gwendoline sat rock still in her chair. She waited for the noise of the biplane or the heat of the blazing skyfire to manifest itself but she heard or felt neither. Nothing stirred in her sitting room.

"What happened next?" she asked calmly.

"Nothing, immediately," answered Gerard. "A silence fell between us until at last Mark spoke and for the next couple of hours I just sat and listened. It was a long and frequently interrupted monologue. At times, Mark was crying as he told his story and it wasn't only because of the wine and brandy. At other times, he was angry. There was a lot of anger in what he said. And at yet other times, it seemed as if he was crowing, laughing in a triumphant manner before plunging back into the depths of despair. It was not a pretty story and I'm still not sure how much of it I believe or even want to believe. But it was a huge and horrific switchback of a two hour ramble that he embarked upon and I just hope that a lot of it is not true."

"So what did he say?" prompted Aunt Gwendoline.

Chapter 44

"He began by saying, 'I can't forget her, Gerry. I can't forget how she was when I last saw her. You didn't see her, Gerry, and be grateful forever that you did not. You didn't see how they tore her. You didn't see her broken teeth and bruised lips where they forced a bottle of brandy into her mouth and made her swallow whatever nasty little pills they had it in mind to dope her with. You didn't see the cuts they made down her thighs, deliberately while she was still alive, to make her thrash around and give them more pleasure while they were having her. You didn't see the score marks they made down her ribs and round her breasts and belly for the same reason, to make her writhe and squirm so they could get even more excitement yet out of her as they were fucking into her. You didn't see the bruising around her throat where they half strangled her, trying to get yet more orgasmic pleasure still as they screwed her, or the pillow they used to half suffocate her with the same end in mind. And you didn't see her final moment of terror, frozen for all time in her eyes in the instant she died. You didn't see any of that, Gerry. Be grateful for it, because I did.

"'It's Billy Crater who is the psychopath. He's the vicious brute with no conscience whatsoever, and he's the one who finally killed her. George is the younger and he adores his older sibling, admires him beyond all reason, hero-worships him, so whatever Billy does George follows and does exactly the same. That's why whatever terrifying bestiality Billy unleashed on Janet she had to go through it all over again a second time at the hands of his slimy little toad of a brother. Even now I cannot imagine everything they put her through.

"'It was Billy's twenty-second birthday and the two of them decided to go out and celebrate. They started off getting well drunk on alcohol and goodness knows what else by way of so-called recreational drugs at one of their family establishments, then they drove around randomly out of their usual territory and ended up in our street. It was nothing more than that. It was a random, mindless, drug and alcohol fuelled opportunistic celebration of Billy's birthday that brought them into our street and led them to knock on our door. Damn it, Gerry! Why couldn't they have gone somewhere else? It wouldn't have upset the statistics of the universe if they had found someone else's street and knocked on someone else's front door. Why did they have to end up on our doorstep?

"'I didn't know she was pregnant, Gerry. I didn't know until I found out at the inquest and the pathologist announced it so casually as part of his report. I suppose they all thought I knew, but I didn't. Janet hadn't yet told me. When Billy and George Crater forced their way through our front door she had just got out of the bath. She was in her dressing gown and making a special effort to be extra special for me when I got home. She was smelling all nice and clean and she had put on the very best of her perfume, and all her special clothes were laid out to put on for me, because that evening was going to be special. She was going to tell me she was pregnant; that the family we both wanted and looked forward to had started; that she was carrying our child inside her; that we were going to have our baby. She was going to tell me when I got home and we were going to celebrate. It was going to be such a special evening. But she never got the chance. Billy and George Crater knocked on our door first.

"'After the abortion of their trial, I was gutted. I couldn't believe that they would walk away free, out into the world again as if nothing had happened. Something had happened. My Janet had happened, the woman I loved, the woman who made me laugh, the woman who was carrying our baby, she had happened. And suddenly it was as if she hadn't happened at all. Suddenly, she could be killed by animals like Billy and George Crater and nobody and nothing in the whole universe was ever going to notice. The police, the legal system, even the Craters themselves, were all back smiling, shrugging, "oh well, on to the next one" attitude. You saw the prosecution barrister turn and shake hands with the defence silks, congratulating them on their result, "interesting case, some interesting points of law" and so on, and all the time all of them knowing full well what Billy and George had done. They had murdered my Janet in the most bestial, sex and drug crazed manner possible, and not just her but our baby too. They had killed them both and now they were going to walk out into the sunshine as if nothing had happened because of a legal technicality. No one was ever going to do anything about it. They had "no case to answer".

"'I didn't know what to think when I heard the judge say those words. There was no doubt about their guilt, yet it seemed as though the question was never going to be put. My Christ! My Janet and our baby had been murdered and there was no case to answer. I didn't know what to do. I just had to get out of the court and go somewhere in the fresh air and throw up. I remember asking you to field the press pack for me, which you did and for which I am still very grateful. But apart from that I just too numb to think. I couldn't breathe, I couldn't swallow, I couldn't talk, nothing. I know I walked off and after that I just walked and walked and walked for God knows how long before I finally had to sit down. So, I found a café with an outside table and ordered a coffee.

"'I had been thinking all the time I was walking, of course, not consciously or deliberately but somehow on autopilot in the back of my brain. It seemed to me that it could not be right that Janet and our baby should be dismissed like that. There had to be some accountability somewhere. They couldn't just let her die like that and nothing happen, although clearly that was the intention of our ponderous and idiotic criminal justice system. And without realising it I began to get what at first seemed like a crazy idea. I got to thinking that if I could get to speak to old man Crater, Billy and George's dad, and tell him what his boys had done, what animals they were, what they were capable of, then perhaps he might do something. I didn't expect him to kill them or anything like that, but boys generally respond to their fathers. And whatever his

181

reputation as a gangster he was at bottom a businessman, and businesses of all descriptions, even illegal ones, must depend on good relationships between people, so having a couple of murdering loose cannons around like Billy and George is not going to help any business run smoothly. I thought I could tell him that. And after that I would tell him exactly how his two sons had killed Janet, how they had doped her and cut her and raped her and strangled her, and make him see what evil they had done. And then I would leave it to him to sort them out in the way that a father can, so they knew that what they had done was wrong. I didn't want revenge. Life's too short for that. I just wanted to sit across a table from him and see his face change as I told him the full horror of what his sons had done to Janet and our baby. And at the end of it I wanted to hear him say "I'm sorry, Dr Brinsley. Leave it to me, I will deal with them".

"'It was naïve thinking, of course, and I wasn't really myself as I sat there at the café table. As I found out later, the Craters, the whole family from the old man downwards, don't have any human feelings like the rest of us. They are criminals and violence is the standard currency in which they deal. But I didn't know that then. All I knew was that I wanted to hear one of them say "sorry". I wanted to get to see the old man and have my say, and then hear him say "I'm sorry for what my two boys have done". I wanted him to acknowledge that my Janet and our baby had once had some existence and some meaning in the universe, that she couldn't be done away with like that and nobody notice. Anyway, I was thinking all these things when a young woman came up to my table.'"

Chapter 45

"'Dr Brinsley?' she asked. 'I'm Amanda' something-or-other, I forget her surname, 'from', and she mentioned one of the provincial newspapers.

"'Go away,' I replied.

"'Dr Brinsley, please. I don't want to disturb you, particularly at the moment when you must be suffering terribly from the shock of what has just happened in court, but I was wondering if I could help.'

"I didn't want to talk to her. I just wanted to be alone but I was so shattered that I didn't have the strength to push her away. She looked very young and her approach was not polished or confident, although that was what she was trying to be. She was on her own as far as I could see. She had no camera and she didn't thrust a recorder on to the table in front of me, and when I smiled at her there was a good deal of relief and nervousness in her answering grin.

"'You're new at this, aren't you?' I said to her.

"She nodded. 'Yes. My first big story. Do you mind if I have a coffee?'

"She gulped it down as soon as it arrived.

"To cut the story short, Amanda was very much a junior on her newspaper, an inexperienced assistant sent out by her news editor to be a coffee fetcher for the one whose job it was to get the cover on the courtroom story. When she saw me escape from the crush outside the court, she slipped her leash and followed me, and did so for the whole two hours and more while I wandered aimlessly around trying to sort things out in my head. It wasn't until I sat down at the café table that she finally plucked up the courage to approach me and blurt out her introductory words.

"Maybe I did fall for a slick, innocent approach but, like you Gerry, I have dealt with enough students to separate those who are genuine from those who think they can fool you. She was genuine, and I think she was just out of her depth and overwhelmed by her own gall at seizing an opportunity that luck had dropped in her way.

"Once she sat down, she didn't know how to proceed. I found her uncertainty touching. She was like a student who has suddenly seen the implications in an idea you have just presented to them and whose vistas are now so wide that they have no idea in which direction they should start running first. It's the joy of teaching, isn't it, Gerry? It's the one thing that keeps us hammering away with our words of wisdom to tribes of bored undergraduates week after week. It's that single moment when you see the light flash in the eyes of one of them when they find they can suddenly see a further horizon. That's the opium of it, isn't it? That's why we do it.

"Anyway, I'm afraid I was a bit of a bastard to her. I needed to know about the Craters and how to get to see them and she wanted a few words for her paper on how I felt about the dismissal of Billy's and George's trial. I gave her a few words, and in the process I got out of her as much about the Craters as she could remember from the contents of her newspaper's archives. She remembered quite a lot. She told me about old man Crater and his three sons. There was Frank, the eldest, who we had seen in the public gallery at the trial. He had been groomed to take over the family's businesses and had been kept scrupulously clean as far as the law was concerned for that purpose. He was the bright one. He had gone to university and studied business and law. She told me also about Billy and George who, it seems, were little more than hoodlums from the time they were born. They were never given any responsibility in any of the family's businesses because everything they touched they wrecked in short order. Consequently, they lived lives of protected criminal idleness, literally, with nothing to do except enjoy themselves and cause chaos and havoc wherever they went. They were a constant source of worry to the old man and a good deal of the Craters' resources were spent keeping them out of trouble. That was important because it was through Billy and George that the police saw their most likely chance of getting into the Craters' organisation and destroying it. There was no mention of a Mrs Crater, although presumably there was one somewhere.

"Amanda also told me about the Craters' various businesses, both legal and illegal, and she gave me a list of the nightclubs they owned in the city. It seemed that one called Purple Heaven was the one they mostly used as their office. And then she told me the most trivial thing in the archive, the most trivial of all the trivia. She told me what the Craters drank. According to her newspaper's files all the nightclubs they owned had to keep a bottle of a particular scotch whisky handy in case old man Crater felt like a drink during one of his visits. She couldn't remember the name of it, only that it was a single malt. It wasn't the most expensive whisky on the market or an especially difficult one to come by. It was simply the one he drank and a bottle of it had to be kept under the counter in the bar of all their establishments.

"I never checked to see whether her editor liked her words enough to use them. I hope he did and that she got a timorous toehold on the first slippery rung of the ladder to respectable journalism. She was a nice girl and she had shown me a way of getting through the Craters' front door and up their stairs into their office. I knew it wasn't going to be easy but I had to face them. I had to tell the old man what his two sons had done and I had to hear him or someone from his family say "I'm sorry"."'

Chapter 46

Aunt Gwendoline took a deep breath. She had become stiff from sitting for too long, although part of her stiffness she knew was reaction to what she was hearing. Rani remained alert at her feet, looking up at her and watching as if also taking in every word.

"It would appear that your friend Dr Brinsley was far more disturbed than you supposed," she observed quietly into the pause.

"I would have to say the state he was in did upset me," sighed Gerard. "I had thought he was almost back to the Mark of old, easy-going and sociable, ever ready with a grin and a laugh. But underneath he seemed not to have resolved anything at all. I couldn't begin to fathom the depth of the anguish that clearly still racked him. The madcap scheme of his to face the Craters was pure insanity. What could it achieve? He more or less admitted he wasn't thinking straight when he dreamed it up. I was long past being able to understand how he was thinking and what he was trying to do, so all I did was sit and listen to him. It was around two o'clock in the morning by this time and he showed no signs of calling it a day."

"I take it he did get to meet the Crater gang?" Aunt Gwendoline queried.

"Yes, he did," Gerard nodded. "And by his own account, it took some doing. I still don't know how far what he told me really happened or whether it was just his imagination running wild under the influence of all the stress he had faced and the alcohol he had consumed. But he was certainly plausible, and that is what worries me."

"Gerard, dear boy, you are not making much sense. Would you take your story more slowly so that I can follow you?"

"Sorry," he replied. "I was jumping ahead a bit.

"Mark said he worked out very quickly that meeting the Craters would not simply be a matter of ringing them up and making an appointment. He knew he would have to get through a number of minders, bouncers, bodyguards and so forth, all capable of extreme violence, so he lit on the strategy of going to the night clubs the Craters owned, getting mildly drunk and making a minor nuisance of himself.

"'You mean the whole drunken thing was deliberate?' I challenged him.

"'I had to be convincing,' he replied. 'I had to build up some sort of track record of a man going off the rails because he had lost his wife. I couldn't have just walked into the Purple Heaven nightclub, got plastered and demanded to see the boss. That would have put me in the closest rubbish skip in no time.'

"He reasoned that if he was seen to be an inoffensive drunk not capable of hurting anyone, then the bouncers would regard him as someone they could take in their stride and not get too heavy with him. If at the same time he kept giving them the message that he wanted to see old man Crater, and would go away and be a good boy once he had done that, then eventually the old man would agree to see him just to get rid of him. It all sounded very innocent and naive even as he described it, and no doubt in his emotional turmoil at the time it probably seemed quite reasonable. So, he started to get drunk.

"'Mark, you bastard,' I exploded at him. 'You mean to say it was all a big act?'

"'Oh, no,' he countered. 'It wasn't an act. I really did get drunk and in a big way. It was ghastly. Surely you remember that morning when you collected me from the police cells and I threw up all over your shoes? I had some real blinders of hangovers. You can be absolutely certain they were no act.'

"I could not believe what I was hearing.

"'I don't care how you try and justify it, Mark, but you turned into a major problem. Sue and I thought you were in genuine trouble. You have no idea what you did to us. And we did it because you were a friend and we wanted to help you. And now you tell me it was all a big act, a ploy just so you get close to the Craters?'

"'Don't be angry, Gerry.'

"'What the hell do you expect me to be? You caused merry hell in our household. You scared us until we could not get to sleep at night, Sue in particular, and now you are telling me it was all deliberate. Mark, this is the end of whatever friendship you and I ever had. It is too much to ask anyone to accept, even allowing what was done to you.'

"I was furious with him.

"'Please, Gerry. I couldn't have done it without you,' he protested. 'You're the best friend a fellow could ever have, to put up with me through all that. And you did help. You helped enormously. You were totally convincing. Don't you see I couldn't tell you? Your concern had to be genuine otherwise the Craters would have twigged I wasn't kosher. They have all sorts of lines of information going back to them. You were wonderful to me and they noticed it. That's what helped me convince them I was genuine. It was your friendship, just about the closest and most important thing in the world to me.'

"'You used us,' I roared at him. 'And what about Sue? You put her through hell too.'

"'I know,' he nodded contritely. 'And I'm truly sorry. I hadn't intended there should be quite so much trouble for you two. I knew there would be some, but not so much that it couldn't be patched up afterwards. But then you did say that you and Sue were breaking up anyway, that you had come to the end of your relationship and that it wasn't all my fault, didn't you? So you can't put it all down to me.'

"'You don't get out of it that easily,' I growled at him. 'What you put us through was indescribable and unconscionable.'

"'I know, Gerry, I know, and I'm not trying to get out of it. Still, I don't suppose I'll ever see Sue again to apologise. So, if you see her perhaps you could apologise for me?'

"'Like hell I will,' I assured him. 'I wouldn't even approach the subject with her. I have no reason to suppose she would ever want to speak to me again anyway after what you've just told me.'

"'Stay friends, Gerry,' he pleaded. 'I've got nothing else left now. I need you as a friend. Please stay friends.'

"I wanted to believe him, Aunt Gwendoline. I wanted to believe in the memory of the Mark I knew. You don't drop a friend just because he is going through a bad patch, and there was no doubting by this time that he was still going through about as bad a patch as it is possible to find yourself in.

"'So, you got drunk and annoyed the Craters. What happened then?' I asked."

Chapter 47

"'It wasn't easy annoying the Craters,' Mark smiled. 'I thought that after a couple of nights when I'd made a nuisance of myself, they would have me hauled into their office, let me have my say, then packed me off with a gangster-type warning making it clear that if I persisted they would take me for a swim in the river wearing a concrete overcoat, or something similar. End of story. But it didn't happen.'

"'That's because the Craters had instructed their bouncers to go easy with you,' I answered.

"'How do you know that?' he asked.

"'Sergeant Chak told me. Apparently, the police have their lines of information too. The Craters told their staff they were to do no more than make sure you didn't do too much damage to the property, or upset too many of the club's customers, then slide you quietly out the front door on to the street while they called the constabulary to look after you until you sobered up.'

"'But why would they do that?' he persisted.

"'Because all they wanted was to go back to their quiet life of making their criminal millions. Pressing charges against a drunken Dr Brinsley after they had murdered his wife, with the whole story then becoming headline news all over again, was not consistent with their idea of having a life below the level of the police radar. You were obviously too convincing in your act as an inoffensive drunk. You probably left them thinking that if they ignored you for long enough, then you would eventually get tired and go away on your own accord.'

"'So that was it,' he shrugged. 'I did wonder. It puzzled me as to why they should treat me with such soft hands for so long. In the end, I decided I had no option but to increase my nuisance quotient or whatever you want to call it, which is what I did. I'm afraid it had the effect of stringing out the whole operation for a lot longer than I had originally planned, but I couldn't stop once I had started. God, I got drunk. All that scotch. I was really ill.'

"'I know,' I replied. 'Sue and I cleaned up most of it.'

"'I know you did, Gerry, and I say again I am sorry, truly I am. But it did go on a lot longer than I had intended. The bastards wouldn't react.'

"'You still haven't told me why you got drunk on scotch,' I reminded him. 'If all you wanted to do was annoy the Craters, you could have got drunk on anything. Why choose scotch when you don't like it and you know it makes you ill?'

"'I have told you that,' he answered. 'It's because that's what the Craters drink. And I had a bit of luck there one night. I had gone into one of their clubs and started to get mellow according to the pattern I had established, and lo and behold but one of my students was working there as a part-time bar tender. He shouldn't have been, of course, it being against university rules. I pretended I didn't recognise him but I could see he recognised me. All to the good I thought, because that will get around the university pretty quickly and add to my cover story. Anyway, after a few drinks I started to get fussy about the quality of the scotch he was serving and demanded he find me something special, like something from under the counter. He was cautious about it at first and I saw him catch the eye of the bouncer, but at the same time I suppose he wanted to keep on the right side of his senior lecturer in chemistry who would be marking his papers at the end of the year. So, he pulled out a bottle from under the bar and showed it to me. It tasted just a foul as all the other scotches as far as I was concerned, but I memorised it instantly in spite of having a little trouble with my focus. It was called Glen Cona, a single malt, and if my little journalist friend was right it was the scotch that old man Crater drank. I was elated and nearly smashed the bottle in my excitement, and probably would have done if the bouncer hadn't intervened.'

"'But why the focus on the specific brand of whisky that old man Crater drank?' I asked. 'Surely it wasn't that important.'

"'Ah, yes,' he replied, and looked down at his empty brandy glass. 'It was important, and I haven't quite come to that bit yet.'

"He poured himself another measure of brandy and offered to top up my glass. I waved it away. The night was starting to fade, but I did hope to do some work during the following day."

Chapter 48

Gerard paused once again to rein in his thoughts and bring them back to order. Aunt Gwendoline too churned the questions in her mind, trying to bring the pieces of the puzzle to a cohesive whole. She could sense it was coming together, but interesting though it had been so far it had still not provided her with an answer to the question foremost in her mind. Susan had smashed sister Alice's Chatterwood vase so she could break free from a peril that Mark was dragging Gerard into. What she wanted to know was the nature of that peril and how it was going to take three young men and burn them up before their time. Gerard, Mark Brinsley and Gerard's detective sergeant friend Sergeant Chak. Three men and three flaring stars, and the time was running down to when she would have to know which star was Gerard's so she could be in position to catch it. She looked over to the aspidistra sitting in a shaft of afternoon sunlight on its corner table.

"By this time, I was barely recognising my old friend Mark anymore," Gerard continued. "I couldn't forget all that Sue and I had gone through on his behalf, the looking after him, the caring for him, the picking him up out of the gutters and cleaning up after him. I couldn't forget the rows we had when I defended him as Sue shouted at me to forget him. And now to be told that his drunkenness was all deliberate on his part, a big act so he could get up the noses of the Craters, it was too much to take in. It looked as though Sue was right all along and that I had just been a blind fool, except that this was Mark. Only it wasn't. It was someone else I didn't know, someone who seemed set on a course to God knows where with a determination that ignored everything else around him.

Even his grin seemed artificial, forced, with no real humour behind it."

Aunt Gwendoline felt her heartbeat skip. An added tenseness sprang into Rani's stance while the image of the young pilot flashed across her mind. She refocussed on her grand-nephew's words.

"'I gather you did get to see old man Crater face to face, judging by the way you were dumped out of a passing car and on to our front doorstep late one night,' I challenged him.

"'Yes,' he shrugged with a smile. 'I did, but not on that evening. I gather they weren't at the Purple Heaven that night but somewhere else. But it was a good evening. When I woke up in hospital I knew I was getting close to them, that they were finally getting the message that they would have to see me. It didn't happen that night. They simply got a bit more heavy-handed with me than usual and gave me a good belting in the back alley before delivering me home.'

"'Sergeant Chak said it was a light dusting,' I informed him.

"'He wasn't on the receiving end of it,' he countered. 'The bullies were very good, mostly left my face alone, but didn't half give my ribs and kidneys a going over. They knew what they were doing and, God, I was sore next morning. Even breathing hurt.'

"'You still discharged yourself from hospital and went back for more,' I argued.

"'I had to, Gerry. I knew I was close and that one more little push and I would be through. And it had to be the next night, so they knew beyond all doubt I was serious and that they would have to see me. So yes, I went back to the Purple Heaven that next night ready to see them.'

"'The whole scheme sounds totally screwball,' I snorted. 'And highly dangerous.'

"'It was screwball and dangerous,' he agreed. 'But that was the beauty of it. It was so unbelievable to them that I, a respectable university lecturer with no criminal connections and not even a speeding ticket to my name, should present them with any physical threat. I was a man who could not cope with the murder of his wife and who had taken the age-old path to the bottle to get over it, and if I didn't get over it then what was it to them anyway. But in the meantime, I was being a nuisance and insisting in seeing them face to face to give them a few choice words. And since the most aggressive thing I have ever done is argue with a neighbour over where to put the dustbins out on rubbish collection night, then the chances were that, once I had delivered my abuse, I really would go away. And if I did go away, their problem would be solved. And if I didn't, well, they still had the swim in the river wearing a concrete overcoat as an option. I was impotent as far as they were concerned. They had nothing to lose from giving a broken drunk thirty seconds of their time.'

"'You had it all worked out, didn't you?' I snorted.

"'Yes, I had it all worked out,' he fired back angrily. 'But remember, I was doing it for Janet. For Janet and our baby. They had killed them both and had got away with it, and nobody wanted to know or take any notice. They had "no case to answer", remember? I couldn't let Janet go like that. Somebody had to acknowledge that she had existed and that they had killed her. Somebody had to say "sorry". You bet I had it all worked out.'"

Aunt Gwendoline gripped the armrests of her chair as she felt her heart thump in her chest again. "I've got it. I've got it all worked out." That is what the young pilot in his biplane had signalled as he waved his fistful of notes at her before he sped away, a young man with a grin on his face that was not a grin, set on a course with a determination that ignored everything else around him. "Some sort of fog that surrounded Mark and was reaching out to Gerard." That's what Miss Susan had said. She forced breath into herself and desperately tried to concentrate. "Help me with this, Mother. I can't manage this on my own. Help me, our dad." She heard Rani's quietly anxious whimpering. Her heartbeat fluttered again then steadied, and she was able to take a deeper breath.

"And did his plan work out?" she panted.

"That's exactly what I asked him," Gerard continued.

Chapter 49

"'Is that how it happened?' I asked.

"'In part,' Mark sighed, calming down a bit. 'I went to the Purple Heaven that night and I sensed there was something up straight away. I was expecting to have to argue with the bouncer on the door to let me in but he hesitated only briefly, blocking my way for only a second before waving me through. No doubt the message went upstairs fairly quickly that I was on the premises.

"I had a couple of whiskies at the bar and had just ordered my third when I became aware of two hoodlums just behind me.

"'Good evening, gentlemen,' I greeted them, raising my glass to my lips.

"I hadn't caused any trouble up to that point but I could see immediately that these two new heavies were not the ordinary front of house security. These were real commandos. I hadn't heard them coming up behind me and I was fairly certain that if they had wanted me not to see them I wouldn't have known anything more that night or forever. They were truly terrifying.

"They waited until I had finished my drink then moved in close behind me. One of them said very quietly, 'Come this way, sir. Mr Crater would like to see you.'

"I wasn't given any option and was literally frogmarched between them out through a discreet door behind the bar and up a flight of stairs without my feet touching a single step. They were really big blokes. There was no way I could have resisted even if I had not had the "light dusting" the night before.

"We stopped at the end of a short corridor in front of a solid door and I was frisked, my wallet checked and replaced inside my jacket, and the bottle of whisky I was carrying removed from my overcoat pocket. One of the minders then knocked shortly on the door and it was opened by George Crater. The minder handed him my bottle of whisky then they both marched me into the office. They stood me in the middle of the carpet, turned and closed the door behind them as they left. I was rather dishevelled and the three whiskies I had drunk were beginning to make me sway a bit, so I don't doubt I presented as a clean shaven but slightly scruffy and rather sorry sight. George Crater looked at my bottle of whisky, grinned and showed it to Billy.

"'What's this?' said Billy taking it from his younger brother and grinning broadly himself.

"'Just put it on the desk, Billy,' ordered Frank who did not move from his chair.

"Billy obeyed instantly. All four of them were there. The old man was behind the desk. I had not seen him before but he sat very dignified, old, silver haired and the picture of a gentle grandfather letting the world pass him by in the twilight of his life. I know stereotypes are difficult to avoid but anyone looking less like a ferocious gangster was impossible to imagine. Under other circumstances, you could almost see him covered in grandchildren, telling them stories while holding them gently on his knees. He was just the sort of person you could talk to, open your heart to and receive a comforting and understanding pat on the hand when you had finished. Maybe under other circumstance that is exactly what he would have been, but then it might just have been the whisky going through me that made me think like that. But throughout the whole meeting, he didn't utter a word. He didn't appear to move apart from the occasional blink. He certainly didn't say anything, even though it was him I mostly addressed when I spoke. It was Frank who did the talking.

"'Well, you're here,' Frank began, with just enough threat in his tone to let me know that this was not social.

"He stood up and walked towards me.

"'You've caused enough nuisance to get yourself in here,' he said. 'You've drunk to excess, on more than one occasion you've upset some of our most highly regarded guests and you've caused not a small amount of material damage. So now you're here. You've said you have something to say to us so say your piece.'

"I swayed a bit and tried to gather my thoughts. The three whiskies I had consumed downstairs were beginning to have their full effect.

"'Well?' prompted Frank.

"'You, you killed my wife,' I stammered out.

"'That is a slander, Dr Brinsley,' he cut in immediately. 'And there are laws in this country against slander. You could find yourself in serious trouble if you go around saying things like that.'

"I tried to focus a bit more.

"'Not you, Mr Crater,' I slurred at him. 'Not you. Nor you, Mr Crater, sir,' I addressed the old man. 'No, sir, not you. But your two boys here…'

"I saw Billy tense and George tense. I spoke quickly.

"'These two here, Mr Crater, sir. Your two boys, Billy and George, they did it.'

"'Watch it,' threatened Billy.

"'They did it, Mr Crater, sir. I have no quarrel with you, sir, but you must know what your two boys did.'

"'Shut him up,' shouted Billy.

"'Yeah, shut him up,' echoed George.

"'Dr Brinsley,' interrupted Frank sharply. 'As I said before that is a slander and there are strict laws about slander in this country. You should be very careful about repeating it. As you well know there was an allegation against my two brothers, William and George, involving the unfortunate and regrettably unsolved death of your wife. But the evidence was brought to court and duly considered and the court found that evidence to be invalid. As a result, the court ruled that my two brothers here have no case to answer. That was the verdict. They have no case to answer. Now as far as we are concerned that is the end of the matter. They had nothing to do with it.'

"'But their DNA and footprints…' I attempted.

"'Were all reviewed by minds far less addled than yours, Dr Brinsley,' Frank finished for me.

"'Yeah, less addled,' giggled George.

"'And they found on sober review…' continued Frank. He emphasised the "sober" and George giggled again. '…That my brothers were not involved. So that is an end to it.'

"'But they were there…' I tried again.

"'Oh, for Christ's sake, shut him up,' snapped Billy impatiently. 'He's just a snivelling drunk. Get rid of him.'

"'Yeah,' chimed in George. 'Kick him in and get rid of him.'

"The old man never stirred and I was beginning to wonder whether or not he was capable of moving.

"'I need a drink,' I muttered.

"I made a lunge for my whisky bottle that was sitting on the desk. I heard George yell, "Watch him!", and then I was face down on the carpet with Billy's knee leaning heavily into my bruised kidneys. I heard Frank shout "Billy!", which I presume saved me from the killer blow. I was in such agony I couldn't have stopped it if it had been aimed.

"'Pick him up,' ordered Frank.

"Billy lifted me bodily to my feet and then threw me against the closed office door, managing a sharp jab into my injured ribs in the process. I slid down the door. I couldn't help it. I was sweating with pain. I looked up and focussed as far as I was able to. Frank was standing with my bottle of whisky in his hand and was examining the label.

"'Dr Brinsley,' he said, addressing my bottle. 'Glen Cona scotch. You are a man of taste as well as of education.'

"He turned to my slumped heap on the floor.

"'All I can say,' he continued, 'is that it would be terrible waste of all the effort you went to in getting that taste and education if circumstances subsequently conspired against you in such a way as you were not able to use them for the benefit of yourself and mankind.'

"He paused for dramatic effect.

"'I need a drink,' I groaned.

"'No, you do not,' he answered sharply and bent down on the floor close to my face. 'You need to sober up. You need to forget about what happened to your wife and anything and everything you think you might know, but in fact do not know, about my two brothers. You need to get back to being the insignificant little university lecturer you have always been and leave us alone. That is what you need, Dr Brinsley. Do I make myself clear?'

"I nodded drunkenly and he stood up.

"'So, to that end,' he continued more reasonably, 'we are going to drink your health, Dr Brinsley. Glasses, George.'

"George stared puzzled at his brother, then chuckled, beginning to see the beginnings of a joke. He pulled four crystal tumblers from the bar unit and placed them on the desk. He grinned broadly as Frank poured out a generous measure of my Glen Cona whisky into each one.

"'We are going to drink to your health, Dr Brinsley, to a man of taste and education,' Frank continued. 'We are going to raise a glass in the certainty that, one way or another, your future will know only quietness and peace.'

"'Yeah, cheers,' echoed Billy, also grinning widely. 'Your health, drunk with your own sodding whisky, you heap of...'

"'That's enough Billy,' warned Frank.

"'Yeah, cheers,' echoed George belligerently.

"Billy and George sculled their drinks in one and burst into fits of laughter. Frank swallowed half of his and savoured it before swallowing the rest. He nodded with approval. The glass placed in front of the old man remained untouched on the desk.

"They all watched my despair at seeing my whisky going down their throats and not being able to do anything about it. Billy, then George, put out their glasses for another measure but Frank recorked the bottle.

"'Yes, Dr Brinsley, we all hope you remain quiet and healthy from now on, don't we Billy, don't we, George?' he continued. 'And we don't want to hear any more slander against our good family name. Your wife was killed, it was a terrible tragedy, but the law has very clearly stated that we had nothing to do with it. Remember that, Dr Brinsley. We had nothing to do with it. Understand? Pick him up, Billy.'

"Billy picked me up by my overcoat and held me against the office door again, managing to give me another short jab under the heart as he did so. Frank then approached to finish off.

"'As I said, you are an educated man, Dr Brinsley,' he said quietly into my face. 'If you are as wise as your education has taught you to be, you will leave here and on your way home find yourself a ditch. You will then crawl into it and freeze to death overnight so that you will be found stiff and cold in the morning. If you are not that wise then you will find your way home and never, ever come here or anywhere else near my family or our establishments ever again. Do you understand me?'

"I nodded as best I could.

"'And if you are not even that wise,' he continued, 'well, you really don't want to know about that, do you?'

"It was not really a question, and I shook my head as far as it didn't hurt me to do so.

"'Now get yourself out of here,' he ended. He rammed my broached bottle of Glen Cona back into my overcoat pocket and signalled to Billy. I was pulled away from the door with another short jab to the kidneys. It was agony. The door opened. The two heavy minders were still there.

"'This is Dr Brinsley's last visit to us,' Frank instructed them mildly. 'It is always a shame when we have to say farewell to such a valued customer, so please, with our compliments, see he gets a drink on the way out.'

"I could hear George giggling in the background as Billy threw me to the heavies, then the office door closed and my interview was over. It could not have taken much more than five minutes but it was the most sinister five minutes of my life."

Chapter 50

"Mark stopped talking at that point and poured himself yet another brandy from what was left in the bottle on the table between us," Gerard sighed. "I thought that might be the end of his account, except that he didn't sound finished. I was puzzled. His interview with the Craters sounded quite dismal and absolutely terrifying but it could hardly be said to have achieved anything. He certainly didn't get his 'sorry' out of them. But he sat there with a grin on his face as if he was pleased with the outcome. He seemed to be teasing me into asking him to continue.

"'Is that it?' I asked.

"He shook his head, sloshing the brandy over his teeth. He swallowed it and smiled.

"'Not quite,' he replied. 'The heavies frogmarched me back downstairs to the bar where one held me immobile against it.

"'Pour Dr Brinsley a whisky,' he ordered the barman. 'A triple, on the house.'

"The drink was poured and put in front of me so I drank it, thinking that was it.

"'Another,' ordered the minder.

"I hesitated this time, but it was clear I was not going to be allowed to argue so I downed that one too.

"'And another.'

"'I had to object this time, but some excruciating pressure in my back pushing my liver up against the edge of the bar cut my protest short. I drank it, if only to anaesthetise the pain I was getting. Without another word I was again frogmarched, this time out the back door and into the alleyway where they keep the rubbish skips. I thought for one moment that this was the end of me for sure and that I was going to be dumped in one of them to freeze and suffocate overnight. With nine whiskies aboard, plus the three I had earlier on in the evening, I would have been helpless for hours. Instead I was pushed into the back of a car and driven around while I got more and more drunk, and finally I was thrown out on some grass not too far from where you live. I don't know how long it took me to stand up but I wandered around and was awfully grateful eventually to recognise the end of your street. I could only have been pickled to the eyeballs when you opened your door. I know I was just about on the point of collapse. But that was it, the end of my bender.'

"He lapsed into silence and gazed into his again empty brandy glass. He said nothing, but tired though I was I sensed he was still waiting for me to prompt him. It took me a while to get to it but there was one detail that niggled at me and wouldn't let go.

"'One thing that puzzles me, Mark,' I asked. 'You said that when you left the Craters they gave you back your bottle of whisky. You didn't have it on you when you collapsed through our front door. I presume it dropped out of your pocket or you lost it in your drunken meanderings around the neighbourhood.'

"'I most definitely did lose it,' he answered triumphantly. 'I couldn't leave it lying around. It was far too dangerous. As soon as I could I pulled the cork on it, poured what was left in it over the ground and smashed the bottle in a litter bin so that no destitute alcoholic could find any dregs in it. It was far too dangerous to do anything else.'

"A cold sweat came out all over me and it took me a few seconds to find enough breath to ask my next question.

"'What do you mean by dangerous, Mark?' I asked. 'What was in the whisky?'

"He looked up at me and smiled, then enunciated very slowly and clearly, 'PNA'.

"Aunt Gwendoline, I couldn't breathe, I didn't know what to say, I choked, I almost passed out.

"'What?' I shouted at him. 'You mean that horrendous, nasty, cancer causing chemical you told me about earlier on this evening?'

"'The self-same,' he replied, still nodding and smiling.

"I was almost sick.

"'Mark, that's monstrous. That's evil. It's beyond words. To spike someone's drink with something that will make them mildly sick is bad enough, but to deliberately feed them that lethal, evil, cancer generating poison, no. It's beyond all that anyone could ever think of. Mark you are talking murder and it's a particularly horrible way for someone to die. You are talking of killing someone with cancer.'

"'But Gerry,' he replied. 'That's what PNA was designed for.'

"I couldn't believe he had said that."

Aunt Gwendoline was not listening. She had almost passed out too. Rani was on her feet turning round frantically in fast little circles, jumping up and putting her paws on her mistress and barking. Aunt Gwendoline heard none of it. All she could hear was the roaring of the skyfire that was an inferno in front of her. It was exploding with the gas inside it, the heat of it so intense it was blistering her skin. Its frame was buckling and bending past the point of fracture until it folded and creased then tore itself apart in an agony of flame. And from its gondola three stars fell. Three shining, bright, five pointed stars that shrieked out in pain as they plummeted earthwards, the wind of their fall fanning their incandescence until all that they were made of was totally consumed, and then in a final shriek they blinked into blackness and continued unseen to oblivion a hundred feet below. Three men. Three brothers.

"They're rotten ones, my bairn. Rotten devils."

"But they are men," she tried to cry.

"They're rotten beggars, but they'll not come here to bother us again."

In desperation she looked upwards to the skyfire. It was still writhing in its death throes and as it did so the last two stars flew from it. Two stars, not so bright and falling more slowly, began their descent. She reached out her hand to them.

Chapter 51

"Aunt Gwendoline. Aunt Gwendoline, are you all right?"

She blinked her eyes open and looked up into Gerard's anxious face.

"Yes, quite all right, thank you," she replied gently. "My dear boy, would you get me a glass of water?"

"Yes, of course."

He shot off to the kitchen while she tried to make herself breathe more deeply and evenly. She heard the glass rattle under the tap, and then his pounding footfalls as he returned.

"Here you are."

"Thank you, dear boy."

She took the glass and breathed between sips.

"Hush, Rani. Hush. It's all right. I just had one of my little turns, that is all. I'm sorry, Gerard. Did I frighten you? It's not a problem you know. I have always had low blood pressure."

She swallowed some more of the water and quietly began to stabilise her thoughts. Three stars, three men, the three Crater brothers Frank, Billy and George. It had to be so.

"That's better," she smiled weakly to her grand-nephew. "And poor Rani, I gave you a bit of a fright too, didn't I? I can see you were anxious, weren't you? You are a good dog. Thank you very much for letting me know."

She put the glass on the table between them, forcing herself to relax and not quite controlling the shaking in her hand.

"I'm sorry, Gerard," she continued, "My little turn interrupted your story. You were saying that Dr Brinsley said he had spiked a bottle of whisky with a nasty chemical."

"Yes, I was saying that. But Aunt Gwendoline, do you think we ought to talk anymore? It is such an appalling thought, so evil, so indescribable. Cancer of all things. I still feel sick just thinking about it, and I can see it upset you."

"Not at all," she contradicted him. "You must finish telling me what happened. We cannot leave your friend's little joke unfinished, can we?"

"You think it was a joke then?" he asked.

"Of course I do," she replied. "The story is so outrageous it could not possibly be true. The poor man's mind was clearly unbalanced by the murder of his wife and by the justice system not calling her killers to account, so his imagination went wild. Impotent rage is a right of us all, but a sense of humour is a very positive sign of recovery."

She tried to sound confidant.

"I'm not so sure it was a joke," he replied with equal firmness.

"You're not? And why is that?"

"Because the story isn't finished yet," he answered flatly.

Aunt Gwendoline said nothing. She clasped her hands together so that their trembling should not be so obvious. She knew the story was not finished. There were still two stars to fall. Six stars had initially been thrown from the dying skyfire. One was for Janet Brinsley and three were for the three Crater brothers. That left two to fall. Of those one had to be for Gerard. And the other? There was only Mark Brinsley. Gerard and Mark, the two friends, with some sort of aura reaching out to engulf them both. Would she be able to catch them? She did not know.

"I was utterly shocked when Mark told me what he had done, or at least what he said he had done," Gerard resumed hesitantly. "I really don't believe that one human being could do such a thing to another. If someone has been hurt enough and is angry enough I can imagine them shooting or stabbing someone in a moment of rage, but not doing what Mark said. It was so cold-blooded, so calculated, so inhumane, and not at all like the friend I thought I knew. I wanted it very much to be a fabrication, a bizarrely imaginative story that came out of his grief, but his gaze never faltered and he didn't flinch for an instant as he spoke. I can't be convinced it was all a joke. I asked him how he got hold of the PNA chemical.

"'I made it,' he answered. 'As I said earlier, it's a simple molecule. Its synthesis offers no challenge to a chemist of my experience. The only thing you have to watch is that you don't accidentally touch it or breathe its fumes.'

"He then went on to describe how during those three weeks after the aborted trial, when we all thought he was throwing himself into his work as a distraction to his grief, he set about making it.

"'I had to work at night when nobody else was around,' he explained. 'I couldn't risk any of the students coming into contact with it. It would have killed them on piece. So, after they had gone home, which was usually by about eleven o'clock, I set to work. I scrubbed a work area thoroughly to make sure it was chemically clean, set my reactions going, and then had everything put away and the whole place cleaned up again by the time they arrived for work next morning. That way the only person at risk from it was me.'

"He had all the details, and from his reputation I can't doubt that he has the ability make it.

"'But the whole proposal is so monstrous, so hideous,' I told him. 'I cannot imagine that the Mark I know could ever even think of doing such a thing. If what you told me is correct then we are talking about the most murderous, cancer inducing chemical ever to come out of a weapons research laboratory. That's how you described it. A cancer causing chemical, for God's sake. I don't know how anybody, even in the Ministry of Defence, could even think about using such a thing.'

"'Don't you believe me, Gerry?' he asked.

"'No, I don't,' I shouted at him. 'Tell me it's a joke. Tell me it's your warped sense of humour affected by half a bottle of brandy and the fact that we have talked all night and it is nearly dawn. Tell me this is all a sick, sick story, Mark.'

"My horror must have shown clearly on my face as I pleaded with him across the table, but he didn't tell me he was joking. He went very quiet for a few seconds, the stood up and looked straight at me.

"'I thought you of all the people would have understood,' he answered.

"He spoke haltingly as if trying to realign his thinking to a new set of circumstances.

"'You of all people, Gerry,' he continued, looking so puzzled at me. 'My friend, my best friend, the one who stood by me and helped me through it all. Why did you do that if you didn't believe me? Why didn't you just drop me like all the others? But you didn't do that. You stayed with me, because you were my friend. You believed in me. I thought you would understand.'

"He took a couple of unsteady steps away from the table then turned angrily back towards me.

"'I didn't do it for me,' he cried. 'I did it for Janet and our baby. No one else was going to do a damned thing for them. They were there and then they were murdered. You knew her, Gerry. You knew what Janet was like, all laughter and life and sunshine and love. Somebody had to acknowledge she was all of that. But nobody was going to. The Crater brothers did it. They raped and killed her. I saw what they did to her and nobody in this whole sodding society of ours was going to do anything about it. The Crater brothers had no case to answer. That was the verdict of our great and glorious criminal justice system. I couldn't let that happen, Gerry, not to my Janet. She mattered, Gerry, she existed. She should not have been killed like that, not without at least someone saying it was wrong. I thought you of all people, Gerry, my friend, my best friend, you would understand that.'

"I had no response for him. I was exhausted, it was dawn, and I didn't think there wasn't anything left to say.

"'Thanks for the dinner,' he mumbled as he turned away.

"I heard him shuffle a bit in the hallway as he put on his coat and then he let himself out. I remained sitting amongst the ruins of my dinner party not knowing what to think and wondering whether or not I was ever going to be fit for work ever again, much less in a couple of hours' time."

Chapter 52

Aunt Gwendoline saw the exhaustion recreate itself in Gerard and he fell into a tired silence.

"It does seem a strange set of contradictions," she summarised after a few minutes. "And I can see why it has you puzzled. If what Dr Brinsley says is true, he has extracted a terrible revenge on the men who murdered his wife. And if true, it really would be terrible and a crime beyond description. But I am encouraged that in his story he seems to have gone to extraordinary lengths to ensure that no innocent individual would be damaged by his actions. He took great care to protect his students when making his chemical, working only at night and alone so they should not come in contact with it. He was equally careful to dispose of any that was left in his bottle of whisky after he had completed his plan. He emptied the bottle and then smashed it so that not even an alcoholic tramp could inadvertently sample it. It would seem that, even after everything that had happened to him, there remained a considerable amount of humanity still left in him. That leads me to doubt his story is true."

She flinched as what felt like a hand grabbed her left shoulder. She turned to look but there was nothing there. She moved her arm to release the pressure.

"Gerard, dear boy, you knew your friend Mark Brinsley as a kind and caring man," she continued. "If it is any guidance to you, I can say that in my experience a leopard does not change his spots. If your friend was kind and caring when you first met him then that is what he will always be. There is no doubt his wife's murder affected him badly and I don't think you could expect it to do otherwise. But fundamentally, he will not have changed."

"Maybe not," muttered Gerard. "But I still haven't finished my story."

"You haven't?"

"No," he confirmed shortly.

The hand did not let go its grip on her shoulder, and somewhere in the distance Aunt Gwendoline heard what sounded like a lorry passing in the street outside. Or maybe it was the engine of a biplane revving somewhere out of sight, readying itself to come up unexpectedly behind them and frighten them with its power.

"Aunt Gwendoline I am not sure that I ought to say any more," he resumed.

The engine noise was louder and she did not need Rani to confirm it for her.

"So, I will preface what I am going to say by saying that I have no reason whatsoever to believe it is anything more than vivid imagination on my part," he added quickly.

She looked at her grand-nephew reprovingly while trying not to wince at the pain she felt.

"But I want to say it anyway, just to get it out into the open. Then I can dismiss it as nonsense and forget it. Does that make sense?"

"I think I follow you," she replied.

He hesitated, having difficulty knowing how to start. Aunt Gwendoline's smile was encouraging, although he noticed there was some tension in her face. He saw too that Rani was standing beside her but looking at some point far in the distance, sniffing the wind as if sensing something. It struck him as odd.

Chapter 53

"After Mark left, I made some effort at clearing up the remains of the dinner party although I didn't get very far," he resumed. "It was past dawn and I was very tired, so I went to bed for a couple of hours and ended up going late into work. I came home mid-afternoon because I couldn't concentrate on anything, and had an early meal and was in bed by eight o'clock. That was last night. I was absolutely bushed. I slept the clock round and didn't wake up until after seven thirty when I made the final effort to clear up the remains of the dinner party mess. As a result, it was approaching ten o'clock by the time I was showered and ready to face a day amongst the students.

"I wondered whether I should call Mark to see if he was all right, but then I didn't know how I would deal with him if he answered. As I pulled open my front door to leave, a small package with a card attached to it fell inwards on to the doormat. The card read: 'Dear Gerry, Thanks so much for the superb dinner and thanks for listening to my ramblings. Don't take them too seriously. Cheers, Mark'. Inside the wrapping was a small box of rather expensive chocolates."

"It sounds like a nice gift," observed Aunt Gwendoline.

"Maybe so," Gerard continued. "But I was immediately puzzled by it for several reasons. Firstly, Mark and Janet had never given Sue and I a thankyou gift after a shared dinner, any more than we had ever given them one. Certainly, I usually took a bottle of wine and Sue took a small gift, often chocolates, for Janet when we dined with them, and they reciprocated when they came to our house. But these were gestures given at the start of an evening, not afterwards.

"Secondly, I was puzzled that Mark had simply dropped off the gift at the front door and had not knocked and waited for me to answer as I would have expected him to. It may be that I didn't hear him. I have no idea what time he called so I could have been fast asleep or else clattering around in the kitchen making too much noise. But it did seem strange that he, as a close friend, should just leave a parcel at the front door and walk away."

"It shouldn't surprise you over much," commented Aunt Gwendoline. "Dr Brinsley had come through an extraordinary storm in his life and, by his own account, he did so with your help. A small gift is not unreasonable under the circumstances."

"I've thought about that," Gerard countered. "But then I was puzzled by the gift itself. It was a small box of chocolates, containing no more than a dozen, expensive, individual sweets. It's not the sort of gift one man gives to another, not in our culture. A man might give it to a woman or a woman might give it to a man, but a man does not give a box of chocolates like that to another man. In our culture men don't work like that."

Aunt Gwendoline sat still in her chair. She felt icy. The large knuckled hand upon her left shoulder gripped her with all the strength won from a lifetime of scrubbing floors and kneading bread. She watched Gerard stand up and walk over to the aspidistra. Perhaps he was not so insensitive after all. Something had warned him to be wary of Mark Brinsley's gesture. The strange gift that Mother had bequeathed her could have passed down her sister Lizzie's line to him.

"And that is what started me thinking," she heard him say. "I'm Mark's friend. If he had done what he claimed and he felt the very human need to tell someone about it, then I can only believe it would be me he would tell. So, what if the story he told me on Sunday night was true? Perhaps he had met the Craters and spiked a bottle of their favourite scotch with that god-awful PNA chemical and got them to drink it. On the back of our friendship, he extracted no promise from me not to tell anyone else about it. But if you had done such a thing, would you want anybody else to know? And after he had told me he probably expected me to be more sympathetic and

213

understanding. But in the end, I wasn't and I couldn't be. He was talking murder, no matter how he rationalised it, and by a method too horrible to think about. So when I didn't react in the way he expected, he began to doubt his own wisdom in telling me about it. He gave me a box of chocolates, Aunt Gwendoline, and blokes don't give other blokes boxes of chocolates."

His distress was sweating out of him. She watched him closely as he turned and stroked one of the aspidistra leaves between his thumb and forefinger while the sound of the biplane got louder in her ears.

"I hear you," she sent out to the distant flying machine. "I know you are coming and I know you are coming in the colours of a friend. But you are unable to be a friend, are you? Too much has been done to you. But we, Gerard and I, know you are coming. We can hear you."

"I suppose that what I am coming to terms with is the possibility that Janet's murder might have changed Mark far beyond what I could ever have imagined," Gerard continued. "Janet's killing was bloody and violent and she was immeasurably his world and his life. The failure of our legal system to call her killers to account could have turned him into someone that none of us, even Janet herself, would recognise. I don't want to think of that, Aunt Gwendoline. I want to hold on to the idea that, as you said, a leopard doesn't change his spots. But I keep coming back to the questions of why a gift at all, why leave it on the doorstep when he knew I was home, and why chocolates? He could have bought me a beer next time we were in the staff club at the university. But he didn't, he gave me a box of chocolates. He knows I'm a chocoholic, Aunt Gwendoline. My enthusiasm for the stuff was often the subject of jokes when the four of us were together. He knows that if he gives me chocolates I will eat them. And if he does regret telling me about that obscene chemical and how he gave it to the Craters, then what better way of ensuring my silence than to deal with me in the same way, by spiking a box of chocolates with PNA?"

He swallowed hard and gave a massive sigh of relief. He had said the words giving his doubt sound and shape.

"I don't know what to do, Aunt Gwendoline," he cried, returning to his chair. "Mark is a friend and he is still in an awful mess. My friendship might be all he has to hold on to while he sorts himself out and if I doubt that friendship then he could well be lost. I may be doing him a huge injustice but, either way, I need to find out whether or not he has doctored those bloody chocolates he gave me. I thought about leaving them out accidentally on purpose for the neighbour's dog and then waiting to see what happened. But I could not in all conscience do that to a dog if my suspicions are correct."

"I would hope not," agreed Aunt Gwendoline, looking down anxiously at Rani.

"I thought about accepting Mark's gift in complete faith and eating them," he continued.

"No!" Aunt Gwendoline interrupted sharply. "No. You must not do that. You haven't done that, have you?"

"No, I haven't," he assured her, thrown back by her vehemence. "I thought that if I did eat them and nothing happened then all would be well. But then again, if after a few months I began to feel a bit off colour then what would I do? If I went to the police and told them what Mark had said there would be no evidence to support my story. According to Mark, PNA is untraceable in the body eight hours after swallowing it. His laboratory would be scrupulously clean. I cannot imagine the Craters admitting to anything, and any tainted scotch that was left over after his last meeting with them was poured out over the grass in the park and the bottle smashed. My story would more than likely take me straight to a psychiatrist's couch. And if the chocolates are poisoned and I don't eat them, and nothing happens to me as a result, then Mark will know I'm suspicious and our friendship will be destroyed anyway. I haven't got a way out, Aunt Gwendoline. I don't know what to do."

Aunt Gwendoline leaned back in her chair. The image of the burning Zeppelin formed in front of her, twisting as it did in the sky above Low Felderby and shedding its fiery stars.

215

She counted down Janet Brinsley's star until it fell to oblivion behind the backlit silhouette of the buildings of Felderby Iron Works on the opposite side of the valley. She counted down the three flailing stars of Frank, Billy and George Crater and watched them as they flared prematurely to extinction against the blackness of the sky. And she looked up at the last two stars just beginning their fall. At that moment, the grinning image of the scarred young pilot with the emotionless eyes flashed in front of her and the roar of his biplane's engine accelerated painfully to a crescendo and cracked in her ears.

"And I know all of this because Miss Susan smashed our Alice's vase," she murmured.

Instantly, the hand let go of her shoulder and she could hear clearly again.

"What was that, Aunt Gwendoline?" asked Gerard.

"You must go home and do nothing," she answered firmly. "You must take your box of chocolates and put it away in a cupboard where you cannot find it. Do not even unwrap it, and under no circumstance whatsoever must you eat the chocolates inside. Do you understand me? This is very important. Under no circumstances eat those chocolates."

He nodded his agreement although completely puzzled by her tone.

"I'll do that, Aunt Gwendoline," he agreed.

"Good," she replied. "Now off you go. I have things to do and I am sure you have as well. Off you go and remember, do not eat those chocolates. At least not until I have had time to think about them."

She gave him only the briefest of waves as she pushed him unceremoniously out of her front door, then she leaned heavily against its solid timbers and forced herself to try and take some deeper breaths.

"Mother," she appealed into the empty air of her hallway.

She looked up into the face of her oak-cased grandfather clock and shook her head as tears welled in her eyes and trickled down her cheeks.

"Help me, our dad. Help me bring our Gerard home. Help me catch his star and bring him home."

Chapter 54

"Quick, our Gwen, wake up. Come and see the skyfire."
Alice was calling her.
*"It's a great big vase and it's all on fire. It's getting all
broken up. You must come and see it or it will all be gone."*

That was not right. She made the dream restart itself.

*"Quick, our Gwen. Quick, wake up. Come and see the fire
in the sky."*

That was better.

"Come on, look sharp now. We're nearly there."
*Granddad's tall figure was up ahead leading the way,
lantern in hand, shepherding them all in the direction of the
dugouts.*
"Everyone here?"
"Ay, Mr Penderrick. All here."
*Alice was ahead in the dark and she could hear the
creaking in Mother's chest as she laboured to keep her feet
from slipping on the uneven path.*
"Come back, our Alice. And keep hold or you'll fall."
*Over Mother's shoulder she could see the anxious shapes
of the other village women and children as they stumbled in a
gaggle past the three black ponds near the allotments at the
top of the village, and onwards up the hillside path above Low
Felderby. Above her the skyfire filled every black corner of
the sky, and it crackled and roared and rose and broached
and broke as it burned.*
*"Here we are," Granddad called. "Away now, in you
go."*

He paused at the entrance and held up his lantern to light the way in.

Sparks flew across the blackness of the sky and explosions ripped through the fabric of the skyfire while the guns popped from the hills all around them. And from the tail end gondola came the stars, two of them, faint and falling. Two five-pointed stars were waving to her and calling out to her as they fell. In an instant she reached out her hand from under her blanket and stretched it out over Mother's shoulder towards them.

The ceiling edge of the dugout suddenly cut off her view as Mother carried her in to safety. She twisted and stretched out even more.

"Easy, my bairn. No need to fret."

Just in time she saw them, both stars falling towards her hand. The first one touched her fingers and she closed her fist around it, holding it hard so it should not escape, but the other star slipped past her dimpled knuckles and continued down towards the horizon made broken by the ragged shapes of the Works' buildings. She gave out a cry. She wanted to catch that one too but she dared not open her hand in case the one she held slipped from her grasp. Then the lantern light splashed on the walls and ceiling of the dugout and she was set down on a wet sandbag.

Even as she felt the hard coldness against her back she held her fist closed, never opening it until Mother picked her up again and began jigging to comfort her. Then, and only then, safely back in the warmth of her blanket in Mother's arms, she looked down and released her grip. Her hand was empty. There was no star, yet she was sure she had caught one. She started to cry.

"Hush, my bairn. It was only a wet sandbag. Hush, they'll not come and get you. Our boys will see to that."

She turned and looked back out of the dugout entrance again. She stared at the black outline of the Works' buildings on the horizon where one star was finishing its descent. But she was sure she had caught the other one.

218

Rani pricked her ears and stared into the darkness to where a faint murmuring sound came from her mistress' bed. There were no commands she could recognise, so she waited watchfully while her sleeping mistress tried to get the child Gwen to rewind the dream and play it again, but it would not restart.

Instead, she found herself on the hillside above Low Felderby with the village behind her and the sparkling sea stretching out in the distance to a calm horizon. She could feel the morning sun warm her as she walked. She was older now and was on her way to school. The War was over and her dad was home again and the dugouts had started to fall in under the scampering feet of the village children who now used them for play.

For the moment, she was alone high up on the hillside overlooking the valley and the sea. There was a hospital in the valley where soldiers, men from the War, lived. Some sat around in wheelchairs while others stumbled with a nurse's help to one of the seats scattered around the lawns. Yet others remained in their beds as they were pushed out into the gardens to enjoy the warmth and freshness of the day. She knew the hospital well. She and the other children from school sometimes went there with their teacher to sing songs to the soldiers in their blue pyjamas. Their teacher played on the piano. It upset her to see the soldiers crying while they sang to them and she wondered why they cried so much and so quietly, and she hoped their singing made them better.

The wind off the sea caught the folds of her pinafore and flapped them gently as she shaded her eyes against the low morning sun, and in the shade of her hand she suddenly saw it, a huge, long, silver cigar floating gently out over the valley. On its nose were the red, white and blue circles of the Royal Air Force and painted on its side were the numbers R35. It was a beautiful thing with the sun shining on it, sending bright flashes from its entire length into her eyes as it eased its way round to head out over the sea.

She watched it transfixed as it floated past her, high above the valley but seemingly at eye level with her where she was standing on the hillside. She spread wide her arms in imitation of a bird, and suddenly she was not standing on the hillside any more but soaring up into the sky level with the great and beautiful beast, closing in upon it and sailing with it in the free air above the valley.

It was even more magnificent up close and she wanted to reach out and touch it and feel the softness of it and cuddle into the huge size of it. Inside the gondola she could see men working, steering and guiding the shining ship, turning pressure valves while keeping their eyes fixed on large dials and swinging a big ship's wheel to adjust its trim. Each man worked at his own task, accommodating easily the rocking movements of their airborne deck as they altered their course directly into the centre of the sun's disc.

A young officer was in command and he was the busiest of them all. Her child's interest concentrated on him. He was slightly built and quite boyish, not nearly as tall as Granddad, and he looked very smart in his uniform. The shine on his buttons showed his commission to be new but the confidence in his gestures as he gave his orders implied an age of experience. He was not wearing his officer's cap. That was sitting on a side table along with charts and pencils and rulers and a few other things, and she watched him as he directed the ship so surely in the direction he determined.

Suddenly, he looked up and saw her staring at him. He showed no surprise, although she gave a momentary start as if caught doing something mildly naughty. He smiled at her as if glad to see her and lifted his hand in a brief, friendly wave. She did not respond, pushing her hands firmly behind the folds of her pinafore and turning half away from him with a child's wariness while still watching him. He turned more openly to her and she could see clearly his wide and generous smile, and his trim moustache and the deep, indelible scar that slashed its way across his forehead from a point where his left eyebrow almost met the bridge of his nose to disappear backwards into his hairline. She decided he could still be considered handsome.

He looked at her quizzically, still smiling but with a hesitancy that was inconsistent with the sureness of his command. She looked into his eyes. They were a soft grey blue and she could see right into them. Nothing was hidden from her and in them were many messages, of appeal, of encouragement, of a wish to say something to her. She watched him, trying to understand him.

His face brightened. Through the glass of the foredeck he indicated that she should stay exactly where she was, then he rushed over to the side table where his officer's cap sat amongst the charts and pencils. He picked up a ragged fistful of notepapers and dashed back to the window and looked out at her again. He held up his notes and she could see that the sheets of paper were covered with drawings and calculations. He held them up in his left hand and waved them insistently at her. She still did not reply so he waved them again, this time with a measure of desperation in his eyes.

"I've got it," he mouthed to her. "I've got it all worked out."

And then she understood. He was on course, heading exactly where he wanted to go, and all was well.

The great airship rocked briefly and he looked quickly over his shoulder to the control dials. He looked back to her but his smile told her he had to go. She could not help herself but lift her hand from behind the folds of her frock and give him a tentative wave. His response was immediate. His grin broke across his face and reached every corner of it, stretching his moustache and burying his forehead scar in laughter lines that spoke of joy and hope and the certainty of a future. He waved his sheaf of notepaper all the more vigorously and his right hand wiped the air furiously in recognition and farewell. She waved back with equal joy.

He touched his forehead in a final salute and she was back standing on the hillside above Low Felderby, looking out over the sea and waving, waving, waving at the great silver airship that was being steered unerringly into the centre of the disc

of the morning sun, and she continued waving until she could
see it no more.

Rani lifted her head and heard the even breathing of her mistress. There was nothing to watch over and nothing to point. She turned around on her blanket and settled to sleep the rest of the night without a stir, and neither she nor her mistress felt in any hurry to rise next morning. The sun was allowed to travel well up before either truly stirred, and breakfast was easy and chatty. She listened politely as she was told about all manner of inconsequential things about which she had no idea except they were in her mistress' voice. They went for a walk in the park mid-morning, and when they got back she held up her muddy paws for her mistress to wipe them. Her mistress gave her a biscuit for being such a good dog and talked to her on and on all over again. In the afternoon, they went into town on the bus and did some shopping, and the evening was spent in polishing the aspidistra and there was more buzzing of general chatter while her mistress perused catalogues and magazines.

Two more days passed in the same way and Rani was very happy that her mistress no longer seemed disturbed. Indeed, she seemed very relaxed and her equanimity and general breeziness was not even shaken when the telephone rang early on Saturday morning.

"Hello, Wych Green four five oh four?"

"Hello, Aunt Gwendoline? It's Gerard. I'm sorry to bother you so early in the day but I was wondering if I could come and see you. I thought I ought to let you know that something terrible has happened."

"What is it, my dear boy?"

"Mark Brinsley has committed suicide."

Chapter 55

Gerard was still upset four weeks later as he strode hurriedly through the park.

"I'm sorry I'm late, Aunt Gwendoline," he panted. "It dragged on for a lot longer than I expected. I suppose I should have learned by now that the law does not move at any sort of civilised pace."

While the inquest proceedings had delivered him the sense of closure that was the main reason for his attending them, the discussion of the matters peripheral to Mark's death had irritated him.

"It was the university that was the problem," he explained. "Their huffing and puffing about how they had already reviewed their laboratory safety procedures in case any more of their chemistry department staff took it into their heads to raid the chemicals store and swallow a handful of cyanide, was quite nauseating. I was quite disgusted. Mark was not even mentioned in their presentation to the coroner. All they were concerned about was whether or not the university would get any blame for such an event either in Mark's case or in the future. You would never have thought that they were there because of a tragedy that happened to one of their most respected senior lecturers."

"Still, you are here now," Aunt Gwendoline soothed him. "And Rani is thoroughly enjoying an extra bounce in the fresh air. Off you go, Rani, and enjoy yourself but don't go too far, there's a good dog."

She had surprised him with her request that they should meet after the coroner's hearing so he could tell her about it, but he was pleased to see her.

"You were telling me on the electric telephone that Dr Brinsley's funeral went off well?" she prompted.

"Yes," he confirmed, settling into his stride beside her. "It was a sombre affair as you might expect. Mark's parents flew over from Canada and Janet's parents were there as well. It was all very tearful. The coroner released Mark's body early for them seeing that there was no real doubt about the cause of his death. 'Took his own life while the balance of his mind was disturbed' was the predictable verdict, and everyone accepted it. He went to his laboratory very late Saturday evening four weeks ago, took a bottle of potassium cyanide from the poisons cupboard and swallowed about a desert spoon full. Death was predictably quick. His body was found slumped across his desk in his office next morning by the security staff."

"Could anybody be sure of his state of mind at the time?" she asked.

"There was a note," he replied. "But it only expressed his wish to have his ashes scattered on a particular hillside. Apparently, he and Janet used to go there to watch the sunrise together, and he had scattered her ashes there earlier. There's a small rehabilitation hospital amongst the trees about halfway down the valley and the whole slope looks out eastwards over the sea. It is a beautiful spot. I went there at sunrise one morning last week with his and Janet's parents and we had a small ceremony for both of them."

"So, there is no doubt he intended to take his own life," summarised Aunt Gwendoline.

"No doubt whatsoever. Cyanide doesn't give you a second chance. Once it is in the mouth, there are a few painful seconds but the end is certain. It's too quick for an antidote. Mark knew exactly what he was doing. Aunt Gwendoline, do you mind if we sit down for a moment? There is something that is bothering me. It may take me a while to explain it but I think it might be important."

"Of course, dear boy. Rani seems to have found some leaves to snuffle around in and she won't go far. Is this seat here acceptable?"

They sat on the park bench and Aunt Gwendoline called Rani so the dog knew her whereabouts.

"So, what is it you want to tell me?" she asked.

Chapter 56

"Apparently, I was the last person to see Mark alive," he began. "I only found that out when Sergeant Chak came to see me as part of his enquiries. He guessed that on the day Mark killed himself he might have called round to see me, and he did, quite unexpectedly, and spent about an hour with me. I told Sergeant Chak that Mark had seemed all right, certainly not depressed. If anything, he was the reverse. He was quite jolly and gave no inkling that he was going to take his own life. After a few more questions Sergeant Chak was satisfied. I don't think he was looking for any complicated explanation, just an understandable scenario to present to the coroner and to Mark's family."

"I take it that you didn't mention Mark's conversation with you the night of your dinner party," asked Aunt Gwendoline.

"No, I did not," he replied after a pause. "There seemed little point in it. As we agreed when I told you about it, I was not sure that the story Mark spun me about spiking a bottle of whisky for the Craters was anything more than a fantastic fiction. The thought that anyone, particularly Mark, could do such a thing, even if the balance of his mind was disturbed, was so outrageous as to be unbelievable. So, no, I didn't mention it. Mark was a decent, gentle man who loved his wife and his work and who had everything to look forward to. He was well respected by all who knew him, nobody ever said anything against him, and it would not be right to smear his name with such an unimaginable allegation after his death, particularly as there was no evidence to support it."

Aunt Gwendoline listened to how definite he sounded on the matter.

"There were your chocolates," she reminded him. "The one's he gave you after your dinner party and the ones about which you had so many doubts. They would be evidence."

"No, they wouldn't," he answered instantly.

He paused and looked away over the park, struggling to find the words to express what he had to say.

"No, they couldn't be evidence Aunt Gwendoline," he repeated more calmly. "Because they were gone by the time Sergeant Chak came to see me."

She looked at him quizzically while he continued gazing out over the playing fields.

"May I ask what you did with them?" she asked.

"I didn't do anything with them," he replied. "When Mark called to see me on that Saturday he died, it was totally unexpected and to the time he left there didn't seem to be any point or purpose in his visit. He arrived very cheerily, greeted me warmly, apologised and said he hoped he wasn't interrupting anything, and then proceeded to bat on about everything and nothing and wasn't it warm for the time of year. He was exceptionally good company, as he always used to be, and we were soon enjoying relaxed banter about how the university was going to the dogs and what needed to be done to save it. It was all very easy and relaxed.

"After a short while, I asked him if he would like a cup of coffee. He accepted so I went off to the kitchen put on the kettle. No sooner had I gone than he then called out to me.

"'Any chance of a biscuit, Gerry? A chocolate one preferably, of which I am sure you of all people would have a good supply.'

"I heard him laugh as he said this, and then before I could answer him he added 'Oh don't bother, there are some chocolates here. Aren't they the ones I gave you the other day? They'll do. Do you mind if I open them?'

"I was thrown by the question. I know that when I came round to tell you about Mark's gift you told me to go straight home and put them away in a cupboard, not even to unwrap them and under no circumstances to eat them. Well, I did go straight home but when I got there I was in such a knot about them that I just left them on the coffee table in the lounge and closed the door. I couldn't face them. They were still unopened and still in their wrapper as you said. And there they sat until Mark spotted them. I didn't know what to say when he asked me if he could have one, so I called back, 'Go ahead, help yourself.'

"I have to admit a great load lifted from my mind. Mark obviously knew what he was doing and clearly the chocolates were harmless. I was overjoyed, and I suppose I might have taken a couple of minutes longer making the coffee. Nonetheless, I was quite surprised when I took it into the lounge to see that he had already polished off two thirds of the whole box full. It was only a small box I know, but as we drank our coffee Mark kept it very close to his elbow and continued chatting and stuffing himself with the remaining chocolates until there were none left.

"'Goodness me,' he said. 'Have I finished them all off? That's terrible. You must think me an awful friend, buying you a box of chocolates and then scoffing the whole lot like that. Isn't that miserable? Terribly sorry, Gerry, I'll have to get you some more, knowing how much you like them'.

"I didn't think anything more about them and treated the whole episode with great amusement."

"So, there were no chocolates left by the time your detective sergeant friend came round to interview you," nodded Aunt Gwendoline. "That is interesting."

"It's more than that, Aunt Gwendoline," Gerard replied.

He fought to find his words.

"It took me a while to put all the information together, but if you remember when Mark described to me how that awful chemical PNA did its ghastly work, he said that it disappeared from the bloodstream in twenty minutes and after eight hours it was undetectable in the body because by that time it had combined with whatever tissues it was going to work on and was on its irreversible path to doing the damage it was designed for."

"Yes, I remember that," she agreed cautiously.

"Well, it was exactly eight hours after Mark ate my chocolates that he went to his laboratory and committed suicide."

"Gerard," answered Aunt Gwendoline sharply. "I know what you are thinking. Now stop it. You have been thinking far too much of late."

But in her own mind she saw the flaming Zeppelin and the last two stars that fell from it, the one she had caught and the one she had not. She looked with deep affection into her grand-nephew's eyes.

"I wouldn't be too distracted by coincidences," she continued more quietly. "As you say, you have no evidence except the memory of a late night conversation which was by your own account fuelled by the best part of a bottle of brandy."

"Perhaps," he persisted. "But I am also sure that you would have seen, as I did, a short report, two column inches on page three of the local newspaper. It went under the by-line of a journalist named Amanda something-or-other, and it reported that Billy Crater of the Crater gangland family had been rushed to hospital after suffering an acute bout of illness while out at dinner. The article went on to tell how he is undergoing further tests at the Julia Hope Centre."

"I did see the item," she confirmed.

"And you would also know, as I do, that the Julia Hope Centre is the major cancer diagnosis and treatment centre for this region."

"Gerard, my dear boy, you can go mad looking for patterns in random events," she insisted in return. "Most likely on the evening of your dinner, your friend Mark was just letting loose some thoughts that had come to him in the darkest moments of his grief. It doesn't mean he would ever act upon them and it says a lot for how much he valued your friendship that he felt he could let loose such thoughts in your company without fear of condemnation. It takes a very close friend to hear such thoughts and recognise them for what they are, and not to judge the person for them. You were a very good friend to him."

"And I believe he was a very good friend to me in return," he replied. "The best. He did suffer a most horrendous event in his life and he was let down by the instruments of our society whose job it is to bring accountability on behalf of its citizens. He did go over the edge, and no wonder, and his mind did become unhinged. And while he was in that state he did a terrible thing. He committed murder. But as you said, 'a leopard doesn't change his spots'. He did not change his spots, Aunt Gwendoline. He remained the caring man he always was, and when his sanity returned he recognised what he had done. And he saw what damage he had set in train for me, his friend, and he took the only path open to him to prevent it. That's what I believe, Aunt Gwendoline. That is what I truly believe."

The image of the young pilot with the scar on his forehead pressed itself into her mind, a young man with dead eyes coming in the colours of a friend. But almost instantly it was replaced by the picture of the same young man with clear eyes, so confidently steering his airship eastwards across a valley in which there was a hospital and out across the sea into the morning sun, knowing exactly where he was going.

"You mean that you do not believe he committed suicide while the balance of his mind was disturbed?" she asked.

"Precisely," Gerard insisted. "When he took his own life, he knew exactly what he was doing."

Aunt Gwendoline looked hard at her grand-nephew, and his eyes did not flicker.

"'Greater love hath no man than this, that a man should lay down his life for his friends'," she quoted. "If that is what you want to believe, then so be it."

"I do believe it," he affirmed. "Mark was a good friend, the best that anyone could have."

They both looked out over the park, lost in their own thoughts.

"By the way," Aunt Gwendoline continued. "In all this talking about Dr Brinsley you have never told me what he looked like."

"Mark," he grinned. "He was nothing special. He was not tall, a touch shorter than me, youthful in general appearance, slim, slight frame. Unfashionably, he had a moustache, not a big one but just a trim, neat one, and he had a scar on his forehead, the result of an accident in the chemistry lab when he was a student. It was rather a deep scar and stretched a long way back over his left eyebrow. I gather the explosion that caused it would have taken out his eye if he hadn't been wearing safety spectacles. But appearances aside, the thing everyone remembers most about him was his enthusiasm. Whenever I brought him something to analyse from four thousand years ago, he would never believe the job impossible. He had a pile of old notepaper on his desk and he used to grab a handful of it and start scribbling on it, drawing out chemical structures, jotting down odd thoughts and performing calculations, and he would keep them all together until he had solved the problem. And then he would call me and I would go over to see him, and he would be standing on the steps of the school of chemistry with his sheaf of notes in his hand. And he would wave them at me and call out 'I've got it. I've got it all worked out'. And he would spread out the sheets on his desk and go through all his calculations and show me how he had done it. He was a marvellous teacher, Aunt Gwendoline, and I shall miss him very much."

He stopped abruptly on the edge of tears.

"I am sure that is how you will remember him," she ended.

Rani sensed her mistress' change of attention and trotted back to her without a call, wagging her tail stump vigorously in the pleasure of the afternoon.

"I really must get you home," Aunt Gwendoline smiled at the dog. "You have been out for quite long enough and my goodness, Rani, look what dirty paws you have."

"I'll run you home, Aunt Gwendoline," smiled Gerard. "I have the car handy and it will be no trouble."

"That's very kind of you but we cannot have those dirty paws on the upholstery, can we, Rani? By the way, have you heard anything of Susan?"

"Yes, as a matter of fact I have," he replied. "She was at Mark's funeral, which pleased me. I hadn't expected to see her there after all the reservations she had about him. She's a lovely girl but it seems that we are unlikely to see each other again, at least not for a long time. She's got a job in Spain and will be moving there at the end of the month."

Chapter 57

The tea was Assam and the sandwiches were smoked salmon and cucumber, and Aunt Gwendoline had been out especially that morning to buy some fresh cream chocolate éclairs as something of a celebration for them. A faint perfume of lavender permeated the air from the pure beeswax polish applied to the gloriously nut brown and gold antique furniture that filled the room, and fine Beswick, Meissen, Wedgwood and Staffordshire porcelain pieces, all washed gently using only the purest soap, gleamed at them from their appointed positions. All clocks were showing the correct time taken from the ever-constant Victorian oak-cased clock in the hallway, and the aspidistra had been sponged and wiped until its leaves were sparkling and glossy and the moisture in its root soil checked to be correct by fingertips humidically trained over a lifetime. Rani had been brushed and assured that fresh cream chocolate éclairs were not for dogs, and she rested watchfully content with a plain biscuit at her mistress' feet. Gerard could only look about him and imagine the gloved butler and the capped and pinafored parlour maid presenting him with his tea and éclair.

"So, you're off to Australia," Aunt Gwendoline began. "It sounds exciting for you."

She was rather relieved if she cared to admit it. Although Australia was in the same part of the world as many of those other more jungly countries she was constantly reading about in the newspapers, it did sound a lot more civilized.

"Yes," he replied. "It was something of a surprise. Some colleagues at the Australian National University heard about my efforts to get my dig up and running in Vietnam, so they have organised a six month sabbatical for me. They've even convinced the Australian Government to chip in some money from their overseas development fund to help with the work. I leave for Canberra in a couple of weeks and I'm looking forward to it. I've been brushing up my French to communicate with the local officials in Ban Long. Hanoi University is providing most of the field support, and hopefully I will also be able to pick up enough Vietnamese to get by."

There was no doubting his excitement.

"Australia," she mused. "That's where your Chatterwood vase came from if I remember correctly, wasn't it?"

"Great-aunt Alice's vase that Sue broke? Yes, so you told me." He became thoughtful. "It's very strange, but it now seems such a long time ago. So much has happened, and it all seemed to start with Sue driving my golf club through Aunt Alice's vase."

"Yes, it was strange," Aunt Gwendoline agreed.

"I still find myself thinking about Mark and Janet and what wonderful people they were. They had so much to give and so many dreams to pursue. It does seem unjust that a single, violent act can cause so much loss well beyond itself. To be completely honest, that is part of the reason I am going to Australia. I feel I need to get away for a while. I shall be back, of course, if for no other reason than I will miss our Wednesday afternoon teas."

He gazed around the room with all its treasures. It was comfortable and sheltering and he knew he would always be at home within it.

Aunt Gwendoline looked at him pensively.

"Come," she instructed.

She stirred herself and walked towards one of her glass fronted cabinets.

"Help me with this, will you? My fingers don't go in the directions they should any more."

He opened the cabinet with the key she handed him, and from its far corner she pulled out a blue and white Chatterwood vase, a sister to the one that had been smashed by his golf club. She ignored his stunned expression.

"Your vase was one of a pair that came from my parent's house," she explained. "They were given to my father by one of the river pilots who used to bring the cargo ships into port so the iron and steel from Felderby Iron Works could be loaded. Presumably the pilot in his turn got them from one of the crew of such a ship."

She up-ended the familiar blue and white porcelain and scrutinised the maker's mark on its base.

"When our father died, Alice took one of them," she continued. "They had not much value as a pair, and since Alice insisted on living in one of those fashionably modern houses that date so quickly and don't appreciate fine porcelain in pairs, I took the other. You will notice that this one is in far better condition than the one she gave you. Perhaps you would like to find a place for it in your luggage when you go to Australia. It is, after all, where it came from. Don't be too concerned about it, though. It has little monetary value, and in spite of what your mother might think it is not Ming."

She placed the vase in his hands, closed her cupboard door and returned to her chair, chortling to herself as she went.

"I don't know what to say," he gasped.

"Just keep it with you to remind you of home," she replied. "Who knows, you may find more Chatterwood on your travels around Australia. I should imagine there might be quite a bit of it knocking around odd corners in somewhere like Tasmania."

"I'll do that," he laughed. "Aunt Gwendoline, you are a surprise. I wondered how you knew my vase so well, and all the time you had the other one of the pair. I would have to say that is taking unfair advantage. I will keep it with me, if only to remind me of you."

She beamed at him and rather enjoyed the moment, a feeling obviously shared by Rani who stood happily beside her vigorously wagging her tail stump.

"But now I must leave," ended Gerard, "I still have lots to do back at the university if I am going to catch my plane to Sydney. Thank you, Aunt Gwendoline. Thank you so much, for everything. In the meantime, I will miss our Wednesday afternoon chats, so look out for the postcards."

She saw him out of the door, waved to him as he closed the garden gate, and watched him as he strode firmly and happily up the road clutching his Chatterwood vase under his arm.

"He's a good 'un, our dad," she shrugged to her Victorian oak-cased clock. "One of the best, but then you knew that didn't you?"

"And you needn't look so pleased with yourself," she scowled at the aspidistra as she returned to her sitting room.

She looked down into its dark green centre and noticed a new leaf uncurling from the base.

"You can't claim all the credit," she snorted at it. "I agree it was not an unreasonable idea of yours to use our Alice's vase as the means of bringing the whole business to my attention, but you were lucky that our Gerard's young lady friend was not more badly hurt. If that had happened then I don't know that I would ever have forgiven you. But you got away with it, so we'll say no more."

She stood back and softened her tone.

"We managed it, didn't we, Mother? You, me and our dad. We did bring him home safely and that is all that matters. And now he is off once more to the other side of the world. Hopefully, he will keep our other vase with him, but don't be in too much of a hurry to break that one like you did the other. I would like something left in my china cupboard when I finally come to leave this earth, and Australia is a very long way to go should I have to get there in a hurry. I'm not sure my old bones could manage it."

She looked down at her companion and smiled.

"Yes, I know, Rani. I am just a silly old woman who talks to an aspidistra. Everything just happens as it does without any interference from me and I would be foolish to think otherwise. Now, what I could do with is a really good cup of tea. Something with some real stiffening in it, some Chai I think, and I am absolutely certain we will be able to find a nice piece of fruit cake for a very good and patient dog. How does that sound? Come along and we will see what we can find."

The aspidistra settled back in its decorated pot on its table in the corner, and Aunt Gwendoline considered the wisdom of attempting a little skip of triumph as she walked out to her kitchen. Had she been a few years younger she would not have hesitated.